Shades of Honor

WENDY LINDSTROM

Winner of the Romance Writers of America's
prestigious RITA Award

Shades of Honor
The Longing
Lips That Touch Mine
Kissing in the Dark
Sleigh of Hope

rustic studio
PUBLISHING

This novel is a work of fiction. Names, characters, places, and incidents are either products of the author's imagination or are used fictitiously. Any resemblance to actual events, locales, business establishments, or persons, living or dead, is entirely coincidental.

Originally published by St. Martin's Press
Copyright © 2002 Wendy Lindstrom
Digital edition published by Wendy Lindstrom
Copyright © 2012 Wendy Lindstrom
Second edition published by Rustic Studio Publishing
Copyright © 2013 Wendy Lindstrom

ISBN: 1939263077
ISBN 13: 9781939263070

Cover design by Kim Killion of Hot DAMN! Designs

Publishers interested in foreign-language translation or other subsidiary rights should contact the author at www.wendylindstrom.com.

Chapter One

Fredonia, New York
August 1870

He always knew he'd come back. Everything he'd ever wanted was here.

Radford Grayson inhaled pine-scented air deep into his lungs and listened to the whine of a saw blade chewing through dense wood. It echoed along Canadaway Creek, which cut a deep, winding path behind the sawmill and emptied into Lake Erie a few miles north of Fredonia. The sound made Radford's legs tingle from the memory of standing on the vibrating sawmill table as a boy, feeding the huge whirring blade for his father.

He missed the rhythmic sound of saws and the gasp and belch of the old boiler. He missed the spongy feel of sawdust-littered earth beneath his feet and the constant squabbling of his three younger brothers.

He needed to stay this time. Even if it meant living a lie.

Rebecca was depending on him. Radford had let her down so often, his four-year-old daughter feared everything. Even now, he could feel her tremble as she clutched her blanket and cowered against his thigh.

"Let's move over there," Radford said then led her to the far end of the building where it was quieter. Kneeling, he cupped her face in his palms, vowing to himself that it would be the last time he uprooted her, that they would make a real home in this small village of Fredonia that held so many of his cherished memories. "I'll tell Uncle Kyle to stop the noise then come get you," he said, hoping it was Kyle running the saw.

Rebecca caught his hand. "You said you wouldn't leave me."

"I'm just going inside this building. I'll only be gone a few seconds."

As though she had expected his answer, Rebecca's hand slipped from his. Eyes full of resignation, she sat on the mill steps, slowly drawing her knees up until her toes pointed and her heels rested against the back of the stair tread. She bunched her blanket on her knees and laid her head on it, staring silently at the swaying maple trees beside the barn.

Her dejection pierced Radford, but he knew the noise inside the building would panic her more than his momentary absence. "I'll hurry, sprite." He stroked her brown curls then started up the stairs.

"You promised, Daddy..."

Those three little words, spoken so softly to his back, stopped Radford mid-stride.

He had promised not to leave her again.

Rebecca's fear of being without him was real. Radford's last job with the railroad had taken him away too many times when she'd begged him not to leave her. In infancy, she'd been abandoned by her own mother. Olivia Jordon had refused to sacrifice her life as a ballerina for marriage and motherhood. Later, Rebecca's nanny, the only woman Rebecca had grown to love, began her own family and moved away. The last nanny had abused Rebecca so badly that his daughter hadn't spoken for a month after Radford dismissed the wretched woman. No wonder Rebecca was afraid to be left alone.

Though it would have only taken a moment to hail his brother, Radford turned back, unwilling to subject Rebecca to any more unnecessary doubt. He knelt down and offered his hand, melting at the sudden joy reflected in her eyes. "We'll see if we can get Uncle Kyle's attention another way."

Radford carried his daughter around a stack of hewn trees, marveling at the size of his father's once-small operation. Thrilled with the chance to work the sawmill again, he surveyed the new two-hundred-foot plank structure that had replaced his father's old building. It boasted a slab-wood sign that read Grayson's Lumber and Timber Works hanging proudly over a door made from several unmatched slats. Radford chuckled at the irony of a lumber mill displaying its scrap in such an obvious manner.

He knew immediately it had to be Kyle's idea. Though only a year younger than Radford, Kyle had established himself as a businessman by the age of ten. Radford smiled, remembering how Kyle had started selling the sawdust from the mill as insulation around the foundation of homes and businesses, and how he'd wanted Radford to become his partner. But Radford had been busy learning to run the family sawmill for their father, who had grown too crippled to endure the long days. Radford expected to spend his life building their family sawmill, but the war came and he enlisted in the Union Army. After his first bloody battle, Radford was so ashamed of his actions, he'd lost the ability to come home and look his father in the eyes, or endure his brother's misplaced admiration.

The thought of Kyle, and his two younger brothers, Duke and Boyd, filled Radford with an urgent need to see them. Tightening his arms around Rebecca, he turned a slow circle, drinking in the glorious feel and scent of home.

He lowered her to the ground then scooped up a handful of earth and wood fragments. "Smell that, sprite? That's white pine and rich farming soil. Home, sweetheart." He opened her hand and placed the sawdust-speckled soil in her palm then smiled when she sniffed it.

"It smells like..." Her brow furrowed and she sniffed again. "Like... Christmas."

"It is, sweetheart." He pressed her hand to his heart. "In here, it is."

Rebecca's gaze shifted and she pointed behind him. "Who's that?"

Radford looked over his shoulder then stood. The yard was deserted except for a skinny boy in a wrinkled shirt and baggy brown britches who was dragging a thick iron chain from the barn. He watched with admiration as the determined lad struggled to pull the heavy iron rope toward his feed wagon. After a moment the boy paused, drew his shirtsleeve across his forehead, and glanced at the mill with an audible sigh.

That's when Radford's curiosity turned to true amazement. It wasn't a lad at all. It was a girl.

Gads! It was Evie Tucker!

The sight of Kyle's fiancée in boots and britches caught Radford off guard. He thought Evelyn would have outgrown her boyish ways at age twenty-one. The last time he'd seen her was four years earlier at his father's funeral. Though she had worn a dress on that occasion, Radford had been too blinded by grief to notice more than Evelyn's blossoming figure. Now she seemed taller and thinner, though far from feminine in her men's clothing, especially with her long, black hair twisted in an unflattering braid. Why, he wondered, did females insist on hiding what men found most sensual in a woman?

Well, Evelyn's figure, or lack of one, was Kyle's concern. Not Radford's. He took Rebecca's hand. "Let's go meet your future Aunt Evelyn," he said, crossing the yard slowly to accommodate Rebecca's short legs. Despite Evelyn's disheveled appearance, Radford smiled to himself as they approached his old neighbor. To a man who had lived with constant change most of his twenty-five years, there was something welcoming in the familiar sight of Evelyn in boy's clothing. It reminded him of his youth when he and his brothers had played with Evelyn, when his conscience was clear and he could sleep without malignant nightmares that ate his soul.

Radford ran his thumb over Rebecca's small hand, the feel of her soft skin drawing his mind away from the past. He halted behind Evelyn. "Need some help, Tomboy?"

Evelyn froze with the chain clenched in her tired, callused hands. There was only one person who had ever called her Tomboy. The last time she'd heard that nickname was the day Radford left for Syracuse with her father to join the 149th NY Volunteers.

Slowly, Evelyn turned to view a man she hadn't seen since she was seventeen. Tall, lean, and proud, Radford still stood like a soldier. Power radiated from him, but there was a compelling warmth in his smile that drew her eyes to his. A breeze played with the dark hair tangled in his collar while Evelyn's wandering gaze reacquainted her with Radford Grayson.

"Have I changed so much that you don't recognize me?"

She flinched. What a hen-witted female she was to be gawking at Radford as if he was a prince from one of her girlhood stories. All the Grayson men were handsome. She shouldn't have expected Radford to be anything less, but merciful heaven, she hadn't expected him to be so... changed.

Drawing a deep breath, she strove for a calm she couldn't quite manage. "Kyle and I thought you were coming in tomorrow or we would have picked you up at the train station."

He waved aside her concern. "I hailed an omnibus in Dunkirk that brought us to Fredonia." He shook his head, his dark eyebrows raised. "I didn't realize the town had changed so much. The only thing familiar was the Common. The maple trees and twin fountains are looking older, but the parks are the way I remember them."

"You walked clear out Liberty Street with Rebecca?" Evelyn asked, telling herself to stop staring, but unable to obey her own command.

"It's only a mile. I enjoyed the walk."

"Did you stop to see Papa or your mother when you passed?"

Radford's expression grew wistful as he surveyed the empty yard. "I wanted to come here first." After seconds of silence, he turned back and frowned at the chain in her shaking hands. "Why isn't Kyle helping you with this?"

"I can manage alone," Evelyn said, though her hands ached from gripping the thick iron links.

"That doesn't mean you should." Radford took the burden from her and coiled it over his forearm with slow, measured movements that seemed to require little effort compared to her mighty struggle.

She flexed her stiff fingers. With the decline of her father's health, she had, by necessity, found ways to manage their livery on her own. Though she realized she didn't have the strength to lift a chain that size, she knew she could feed it into the wagon a few feet at a time. It wasn't Kyle's lack of consideration that had left her struggling on her own. He would have helped her had she only thought to ask him.

Still, Radford's unsolicited assistance made Evelyn feel uncomfortable, as though he'd rescued some fair damsel from distress. The ridiculous image nearly made her laugh. She was far from being a fair damsel, and the source of her distress was standing right in front of her. She couldn't drag her gaze away from Radford's handsome face. Something in his voice seemed warmer, hopeful, not so brittle and angry anymore. His smile reached his eyes now. Maybe that's why she couldn't look away when he caught her staring.

With a small grunt, Radford heaved the chain onto the bed of the wagon then stepped back and dusted his hands against his trousers. "Who's running the saw?"

"Kyle," Evelyn answered. "Duke and Boyd left at six-thirty, but Kyle had a job he wanted to finish tonight. He'll be a while, yet."

Evelyn glanced down at the little girl, who stood like a miniature statue beside Radford. "I assume this is Rebecca?"

A proud smile lifted Radford's lips and he captured his daughter's hand. "Can you say hello to your aunt?" he asked, but Rebecca hid her face behind the long length of his thigh. Radford gave Rebecca a comforting pat, his fingers spanning the breadth of her tiny shoulders. "I guess the trip wore her out."

Noting gentleness in the hands that Radford once wore as fists, Evelyn trailed her gaze up his forearm. It was tanned and corded with muscle that shifted each time he stroked his daughter's small back. Intrigued by the contradiction of strength and gentleness, Evelyn wondered if he'd finally escaped the demons that drove him away years earlier.

He met her eyes and smiled. A rush of warmth slammed into Evelyn's chest and she glanced away. How unfair that Radford should be clean and handsome while she was covered with hay-dust and smelled like her livery. He probably thought Kyle was out of his mind to be marrying her.

To hide her unease, and to soothe Rebecca's, Evelyn squatted to the child's level. "I used to have a yellow blanket just like yours," she said, giving it a friendly tug, "but your uncle Kyle tossed it in our well. I cried until your daddy brought his fishing pole over and tried to fish it out for me." Evelyn left the story unfinished, thinking Rebecca would be curious enough to ask what happened; instead she tugged at her daddy's hand until Radford picked her up.

Evelyn stood. "I take it Rebecca doesn't like stories?"

"She's just shy."

"Well, we'll get her over that, won't we?" she said, giving Rebecca a soft pat on the leg.

Both Radford and Rebecca stiffened.

"Please don't do that."

The warning in Radford's voice jerked Evelyn's gaze to his face. "Do what?" she asked, confused by their odd response to a natural act of affection.

"Touch her. It frightens her."

Though Evelyn knew firsthand a father's protective instinct toward his daughter, Radford's overreaction was unusual. So was Rebecca's cowering.

"A friendly pat shouldn't frighten any child."

"I agree," he said. "But Rebecca is too young to understand that you won't hurt her. She's afraid. That's all that matters to me."

"Then you should explain... that is, maybe I could help her if..." Evelyn's sentence trailed off as she stepped away from them. "Never mind."

Radford felt Rebecca relaxing as he rubbed her back. She was like this with everyone. Trouble was, she would eventually warm up to Evelyn and that would cause bigger problems.

He studied Evelyn with renewed curiosity and she met his gaze unflinchingly. Her quiet display of strength reminded Radford of her father, of the fierce pride that had sparked William's eyes during the war.

Now Radford could understand what Kyle saw in Evelyn Tucker. A backbone of steel.

What sort of woman had she become? Though Radford had rarely thought of her over the years, the sparkle of an emerald ring or necklace had always conjured the vision of a wild girl with flashing green eyes. They were still the emeralds he remembered, but shadowed now. Yet, as Evelyn stood before him, dirty and disheveled, there was a restless energy that intrigued him, that made him want to know what she was thinking.

He gave himself a mental shake. He couldn't afford to be interested in Evelyn. All he wanted was peace. To work an honest job that he could be proud of. To build a comfortable home where Rebecca could learn to laugh again. And to share an occasional mug with his brothers after a day of working beside them in the mill.

That was enough.

"I'd better go see Kyle then get over to Ma's," he said, aware of their growing mutual discomfort.

"Would you tell him I'll be up in a minute?"

With a relieved nod, Radford went to find his brother.

At one end of the building a set of wide double doors was thrown open to the August evening. Steam spat from a huge, gasping boiler housed deep in the interior then another scream from the mighty saw blades split the air.

Rebecca clapped her hands to her ears and cowered against Radford's neck.

When the saw finished its pass, Radford yelled inside and waved Rebecca's blanket overhead. "Kyle! Stop that noise and come meet your niece!"

Kyle's head came up and he faced in Radford's direction for several seconds before straightening his stance. "Radford?" His voice boomed from the other end of the building. "What are you doing here?"

Radford laughed at Kyle's lack of preamble. "Looking for a job. You hiring?"

There was no response at Kyle's end except the quieting of equipment and whistling sound of steam escaping in an endless, drawn-out sigh. Finally, Kyle walked toward them from the shadowed depths of the building. Joyful anticipation expanded Radford's chest. It had been so long. So many wasted years.

When Kyle stepped into the waning sunlight, Radford eyed him with pride. His brother had become a giant of a man. Wider in build than Radford, though an inch or two shorter, Kyle still easily topped six feet. Radford couldn't begin to imagine the changes he would find in Duke and Boyd.

Kyle extended his hand. "You're early."

Radford experienced a moment of confusion before it dawned on him that Kyle wasn't going to welcome him home with the backslapping hug he'd expected. Mile after mile of the trip from Boston, Radford had staved off anxiety with visions of a joyful, rollicking reunion with his brothers.

Kyle was offering a handshake.

Hope began slipping away like steam from the cooling boiler, but Radford took Kyle's broad hand in his and gave it a hard shake. What could he expect after being absent since the war? Though he'd come home occasionally during the last five years, he'd never stayed more than a few weeks before his shame drove him away again. It wouldn't this time, he vowed silently.

Radford glanced at the mill building. "You've made changes while I've been away."

"We expanded the building and bought a new mill so we could keep up with Tom Drake. You remember Tom?"

"Of course. Our toughest competitor with the pretty daughter."

Kyle nodded, but turned his attention to Rebecca who was peeking at him. A grin climbed his cheek as he studied her. "She resembles her uncle Boyd, but you'd better hope she doesn't grow up to be as wild as he is."

Radford glanced at Rebecca and knew that wildness would be a welcome change from her frightening withdrawal.

"Come on," Kyle said, gesturing for Radford to follow him. "I'll show you the mill." They entered the building and stopped by the saw where Kyle proudly laid his hand on the heavy iron husk. "This girl has doubled our output. These dual saws chew through twenty thousand feet of timber a day. The smaller saw speeds up our cutting time and allows us to use thinner blades, which means less kerf and sawdust waste."

Radford remembered his father's crude mill. The thought of running the new, powerful machine made his hands itch. A wide leather drive belt wove through a series of pulley wheels and up over a mandrel shaft that was powered by a stationary engine and boiler. A sawdust elevator had also been attached to the mandrel shaft to carry the waste outside where three huge piles spilled across the ground.

"Are you still selling the sawdust?"

"Of course," Kyle said as if it was a dumb question.

Radford laughed then scanned the interior of the building. "Why are those logs wet?" he asked, balancing Rebecca on one arm to point at a nearby stack of logs.

"We rinsed them. It saves the blades from eating dirt so we spend less time sharpening them."

No wonder they had grown so much, Radford thought with pride. Fighting the sudden urge to fire up the saws, wrap his hands around the metal levers, and finish slabbing the white pine waiting on the carriage table, Radford throttled back his excitement. Tomorrow, he would do it. He'd stand beside the huge blades and feel the vibrations shimmy his legs. He'd look over and see his brothers and pretend he heard his father's voice shouting orders in the yard. Then he could silence the other voices and everything would be all right again.

"Let's go out through the office so I can lock up," Kyle said, waving Radford and Rebecca into a room with a thick maple table in the center. The walls were buried behind metal hand files, saw blades, log hooks, and shaving knives. "It's not pretty," Kyle said, stepping outside and pulling the door closed behind them, "but we're doing a good business. Since I was left in charge, I did what I thought best."

The meaning behind Kyle's words didn't elude Radford. He knew he hadn't been there for his younger brothers when they needed him to run the mill after their father died. The best he'd been able to do was send money home to keep them going. More than anything, Radford had wanted to resume his normal life after the war, but he couldn't suppress the nightmares or his violent physical reactions caused by them. His lack of control had shamed him so deeply that he moved to Boston to escape the sympathy in his brothers' eyes. Unfortunately, his leaving had forced Kyle to run the mill instead of pursuing the law degree he'd wanted, and though Kyle had never said anything, Radford could still sense his brother's resentment.

"You've done a great job, Kyle. I wouldn't have changed a thing," Radford said with sincerity. He glanced at Rebecca, who had suddenly perked up at the sound of Evelyn's wagon rattling across the yard.

When she pulled up, Kyle propped his elbow on the side rail. "I guess your father wasn't up to the ride tonight. I thought he was feeling better."

Evelyn shook her head. "He thinks he is, but he was too tired to even climb the stairs. He's napping on the sofa."

Radford's chest constricted with fear. "What's wrong with William?" he asked, praying it was only a cold or sore back, but knowing from their shared experience in battle that it would take more than that to keep William Tucker down.

"He's had seizures," Kyle said.

Radford met Evelyn's worried gaze as she filled him in. "He had his first one six months ago. The second one happened three months later. He got his strength back after his first attack of apoplexy, but the last time drained him. He can talk now, but he still needs a cane to walk."

Radford's gut tightened with the instinctive need to protect William, the man who'd been like a father, his friend, his mentor since he was a boy. They had survived a war and too many years of hell together for William to be laid low by some inexplicable seizure.

"Has he seen a doctor? A good one?"

"Both times," Kyle said. "And he's been told he won't be able to work the livery anymore. Evelyn has been running it for him for the last six months, but it's not doing so well." He glanced at Evelyn. "It's not her fault. She manages fine and works hard, but it's too much for her." Evelyn straightened on her seat and opened her mouth, but Kyle held up his hand. "It is, Ev. You're killing yourself." Ignoring her scowl, he turned to Radford. "Naturally William will be passing the livery to Evelyn and me when we marry, and I'd like you to run it for me— if you're staying, of course."

"What?" Radford and Evelyn asked in shocked unison, their glances clashing before flying back to Kyle.

"I have all the men I need at the mill. William can't work, and despite what Evelyn says, she can't run the livery alone," he said, glancing at Evelyn but directing his statement to Radford.

Radford couldn't have been more shocked or offended had Kyle struck Rebecca. Radford owned a fourth of their mill. Was Kyle worried that Radford had come home to reclaim his position as eldest? Was that why he was trying to keep him out of the mill? All Radford wanted was to work with his brothers. He just wanted to be a part of their life and to have them in his.

"I had planned to have one of my men help in the livery, but I'd feel better knowing you're there. I need someone I can trust, Radford. I'm too busy building Evelyn a house and running the mill to supervise the livery."

Radford's heart contracted so hard, he felt the brutal wrench clear to the pit of his stomach. His arms weakened and he lowered Rebecca to the ground, standing her at his side before he dropped her. Kyle didn't want him here. It was in his eyes. He was welcoming Radford home, but not back to the mill.

"William needs help," Kyle continued, pecking away at Radford's conscience, seemingly oblivious to the dreams that were shattering within him. Panic welled up inside Radford, but he forced it down. Maybe he had expected too much. Maybe Kyle needed time to adjust, to realize that he only wanted to be a part of the family again.

Evelyn shot a panicked look at Radford then turned to Kyle. "I can manage alone for a while longer if you can't spare one of your crew right now."

"No you can't, Ev. I'd rather you didn't work at all, but until we're married, I can't change that or make any decisions about the livery without your father's consent. It'll be a relief knowing Radford is there taking care of things," Kyle said, as if the issue had been decided. He held up his hand to stop her argument. "We can talk about this later. Your father is set on having Radford run the livery. He's even extended an invitation for Radford and Rebecca to stay with you, which should make it more convenient for everyone."

Evelyn's face blanched and Radford thought his knees were going to fail him. Everything he believed he'd come home to had turned to ashes. Kyle had made it clear that he wasn't welcome at the mill. And if Evelyn's offended expression was any indication, he wasn't welcome in her livery, either.

In the midst of this realization, Radford reached down and captured his daughter's hand, reminding himself of the single most important reason he'd come home. Rebecca. He would sacrifice or endure anything for his daughter.

"Why hasn't Papa said anything to me about this?" Evelyn asked.

"The subject came up last night during our euchre game while you were asleep. Your father and my mother got into a heck of a row over where Radford and Rebecca would be staying. They both wanted them. Ma said her son belonged at home. William claimed he'll be lost in an empty house when you marry me and move out." Kyle grinned. "If you hadn't gone up to bed you could have watched the show. It was the first time I saw my mother lose an argument." Kyle turned back to Radford. "William needs your help, Radford. He's hoping you'll lend a hand."

Radford glanced at Evelyn who kept her eyes downcast, and he knew she didn't like the situation any better than he did.

"Will you do it?" Kyle clapped a hand on Radford's shoulder in the first truly warm gesture he'd shown him since arriving. But it had come too late.

Several uncomfortable seconds passed while Radford struggled to mask his painful disappointment and inexplicable sadness. Consumed by a fierce longing to restore himself to his family, he knew he couldn't force Kyle to accept him. This time he'd have to earn his place. And it was time he repaid William for saving his life at Gettysburg. Tightening his hold on Rebecca's hand, Radford unclenched his aching jaw. "I'll do it," he said hoarsely.

<hr />

Evelyn couldn't stifle her gasp. She didn't want Radford in her livery! She needed a place where she could be herself. Her horses didn't care that she wore britches and couldn't dance. They didn't know she couldn't dress her hair or flirt or stitch a straight seam. She could talk to the horses about remedies for colic, the price of oats and linseed oil, and how to repair a harness. Outside the livery, Evelyn was a misfit. She was unable to connect with anyone, male or female. Even with Kyle, it was difficult to communicate. She couldn't imagine how awkward she would feel in Radford's presence.

"What's wrong, Ev?" Kyle asked.

She only shrugged. Kyle had changed so much in the past few years that she wouldn't know how to share her concerns with him even if she dared to. It was Radford's fault. If he had stayed after the war and done his duty as eldest son, Kyle wouldn't have been forced to become the ambitious businessman she barely knew anymore. During the past five years, he'd grown so focused on the mill it seemed he no longer even noticed her. She sighed and picked at her chipped fingernail. Maybe their marriage would resurrect the closeness and friendship they had once shared. Maybe then Kyle would notice that she'd become a woman, albeit a lonely one uncomfortable in her own skin, but still a woman.

The old Kyle would have noticed the difference. He'd always understood her. Even when they were children, Kyle was the only person she could depend on, who could comfort her. It was Kyle's shoulder she had cried on when her mother died laboring to have a son who didn't survive the grueling birth. All her life, Kyle had been a steadfast, dependable friend.

But she wanted more than friendship. She wanted love.

Kyle wiped his neck with a handkerchief then blew out a tired breath. "This is the only way I can help with the livery right now, Ev."

"I understand," she said. When he wasn't working at the mill, he was working on their house. He didn't have time to help her shovel horse dung. She accepted the fact that she needed a man in her livery to appease society's narrow-minded sense of propriety, and to help her with the daily labor that physically drained her. She'd expected a man from Kyle's crew, but it looked as if it would be Radford.

She laced her fingers and squeezed her hands between her knees, wondering how she would ever keep her eyes on her work with Radford in her livery.

Chapter Two

"I thought you were a railroad man for life," Kyle said to Radford as he hopped onto the back of Evelyn's wagon.

Radford lifted Rebecca onto his lap to make room for Kyle then braced an arm against the plank rail as Evelyn drove out of the sawmill. There was nothing to like about railroad life except the money. "Rebecca needs a more settled life than I could give her working for the railroad."

"Well, this is about as settled as you can get," Kyle said, his gesture encompassing the sawmill, the tannery, and the grist mill as they traveled down Liberty Street toward Fredonia.

The dip and sway of the wagon set their feet swinging and Radford was struck by the memory of four grubby little boys sitting shoulder to shoulder on the back of their father's lumber wagon, sharing a jar of cold water and seeing who could spit the farthest after a long, dry day at the mill. A breeze rustled through the surrounding trees, carrying the fresh, green scent of summer. Radford closed his eyes, listening to the occasional burble of Canadaway Creek, the jingle and clop of Evelyn's sturdy Morgan as it pulled her wagon toward home. There was an essence of peace here that he longed to feel within himself.

"Keep your eyes closed," Kyle said, "and tell me exactly where we are."

Despite his melancholy, Radford smiled as he recalled the game they used to play each night on their way home from the mill. When he felt the slight leftward shift of his body, his grin widened. "We're passing the fat oak tree that sits on the inside curve of the road next to Tom and Martha Fisk's place. The one Boyd fell out of the night he spied their daughter Catherine undressing for bed."

Kyle's chuckle told Radford he'd guessed correctly. Radford opened his eyes. The tree was still there, minus the branch Boyd had broken in his fall. The Fisks' house was freshly whitewashed, yet appeared smaller than Radford remembered. Maybe it was Tom and Martha's eight kids that had made it seem so large, but Radford had always thought it dwarfed their own small home a short distance down the street. Now it didn't look any larger than William Tucker's two-story house that sat beyond his mother's home on the far side of a vast apple orchard.

The wagon slowed, turned, and rolled to a halt in his mother's driveway. The magnolia trees his father had planted in the side yard were bigger, the bushes thicker, the house older, but it was still home. Had he been alone, he would have sat quietly, reacquainting himself with the sound of evening crickets, the smell of cut grass, the sharp rap of someone's hammer echoing across the orchard. He would have walked out back in search of that blackened spot of grass where he and his brothers had built their summer fires. He would have slipped inside the barn to see if his father's old stallion still remembered him.

Instead, he dragged his gaze away from the barn and carried Rebecca to the house. Why dredge up memories from a life he could never recapture? All that mattered now was Rebecca's happiness.

Kyle waved them inside and Radford glanced at Evelyn as he stepped around her in the foyer. Though she hadn't spoken another word about the livery, her expression told him there was plenty she was holding back.

"Someone's here to see you, Ma," Kyle hollered then grinned at Radford.

Drying her hands on her apron, his mother hurried into the foyer. Her auburn hair was pulled back in a bun just the way Radford remembered and he smiled when he saw her. All his life his mother was rushing through chores and it was comforting to see she hadn't lost that vitality.

When she spotted Radford, she gasped, "You're home!" Tears filled her eyes and she ran forward to hug him. "You're really home."

Radford pulled her against him with his free arm and she wept as though he'd returned from the dead, which in Radford's opinion wasn't far from the truth. He hadn't seen his mother since his father's funeral. Rebecca had never seen her.

His mother sniffed and lifted her head, gazing at Rebecca with eyes full of love and wonder. "What a sweet, sweet baby." She smoothed her hand down Rebecca's arm and across her back as if she needed to touch her granddaughter to believe she was real.

Rebecca whimpered and burrowed in her blanket.

Radford caught Evelyn's worried frown. It was obvious she thought he would step away from his mother's loving inspection, but Radford didn't move or warn her away. This was the one person he wanted Rebecca to trust, the one who would always love her, who would give Rebecca the maternal love he was incapable of providing.

His mother would never abandon Rebecca like Olivia had. Or abuse her like that merciless bitch, Gertrude.

The sound of heavy feet in a distant room drew their attention. "Duke! Boyd! Come see who's here," his mother called, her face bright with excitement.

Duke's warrior-like frame rounded the corner first, and it was apparent that he'd been roused from his evening nap. His hair was pushed up on one side and his flannel shirt gaped open, exposing a thick-muscled chest full of hair, and a silver deputy's badge that dangled from his shirt pocket.

Radford grinned at his brother. "Close your shirt, Deputy Grayson, and come meet your niece."

Duke's eyes opened in surprise. With a laugh, he clasped Radford's hand. "It's good to see you!" He glanced at Rebecca. "Now there's a fine-looking lass."

"Must take after her uncle Boyd," said their youngest brother as he emerged from the living room, tucking his shirt into his narrow waistband. Boyd's hair was freshly combed and as dark brown as Radford's. Though the youngest and much leaner in build than Duke or Kyle, he equaled them in height.

Radford grinned and his spirits lifted. "What makes you think I'd have a daughter and allow her to resemble you?"

Boyd charmed them with a matching set of dimples. "Because everyone claims I look like you, dear brother, so you'd have no choice in the matter." He peeked at Rebecca, but she pulled her blanket over her head.

Radford laughed with the others and slapped Boyd's shoulder, casually moving him back a step. "Better luck next time."

Boyd shrugged. "I usually don't get that response from the ladies unless they're pulling the blanket over both of us."

"Boyd Grayson!"

He flinched at his mother's sharp reprimand then grinned and caught her in a hug, swinging her in a circle before planting a loud kiss on her cheek. "Don't worry, Mother, you'll always be my favorite girl."

Radford took Boyd's hand, giving silent thanks for the blessing of his youngest brother. Boyd's reckless charm lightened Radford's heart and he needed that now more than ever. Even Kyle was smiling, leaning casually against the wall beside Evelyn. Maybe Radford had misjudged him. Maybe Kyle had asked him to run the livery because he really did need help.

Rebecca yawned and laid her head on Radford's shoulder. "I'd better get her settled," he said, rubbing her back.

His mother touched his arm. "I know William wants you and Rebecca to stay with him, but I'd rather have you here."

Radford was sorry to disappoint her, but at the moment, he didn't want to share a house with Kyle. He leaned down and kissed the top of her head, hoping to ease her disappointment with a little "Southern sugar" as the Rebs used to call it. "It'll be more convenient to stay there."

"Why?" Boyd asked, his expression perplexed.

"I'm going to run the livery for William."

Boyd turned to Kyle. "The livery is going to be your business, not Radford's. Why not let him run the mill?"

Kyle scowled. "Because that position is taken. Would you prefer to work the livery in Radford's place?"

"A pretty lady and a hayloft does have its appeal," Boyd said, giving Evelyn a lusty wink that made her laugh and afforded Radford a glimpse of white teeth and a surprisingly nice smile. Boyd's expression sobered and he turned to Radford. "Was this Kyle's idea?"

By the scowl on Boyd's face, the truth would only start a war that Radford was trying to avoid. "I'm repaying a debt to an old friend," he said, answering as truthfully as possible. He would work the livery for William and let Kyle adjust to his being home. He owed him that much.

⸻◦⊱◦⸻

"You could have said no," Evelyn told Radford on the ride home with him and his sleepy daughter. "You're the eldest. Kyle would have had to respect that."

Radford turned toward her, his eyes dark and unfathomable in the twilight as they met hers.

"It would have been wrong to say no to Kyle after he's worked so hard to build the business," he said.

It unnerved her to see him study her as though trying to remember an old acquaintance. They didn't know each other. They may have been neighbors once, but too many years had passed for her to feel any neighborly connection with him. It didn't matter that they would become related upon her marriage to Kyle. Radford didn't feel like a brother-in-law, either. He was a stranger. The fact that his smile now reached his eyes didn't lessen the sense of mystery surrounding him or the panicky feeling in her body when he looked at her.

Ashamed of her disheveled appearance, she ducked her head. Heat crawled up her neck and burned her cheeks. Why couldn't he have arrived on a Sunday morning when she'd be wearing a dress for church instead of her father's old work clothes?

Radford shifted beside her and settled Rebecca on his lap. "Why am I sensing that you don't want me in your livery?"

His astute question added to her discomfort and she clenched her fingers around the reins, wishing he would quit talking to her in that private voice that caressed her ears. "I'd rather work alone, that's all. You might have made some sort of compromise with Kyle if you'd been more insistent," she said, striving to calm her erratic heartbeat as she maneuvered her wagon down the dark road.

"Do you really believe that?" he asked softly.

She didn't. Not after seeing the fire in Kyle's eyes when Boyd had challenged him. But brothers could forgive each other anything, couldn't they?

"I don't blame him for being protective of the mill," Radford said.

"You shouldn't. Kyle has worked hard to build up the business and support your family."

"I know that. I guess I just didn't expect him to change so much these past few years."

Neither had she, but Evelyn had seen for herself what responsibility and obligation had done to a boy who'd once embraced life with passion. Kyle had been crushed by his burdens until pieces of his laughter broke away and he became weathered and hardened by the weight.

Rebecca lifted her arms and Radford moved her to his shoulder. She snuggled against him and hooked her small fingers in his hair. "I can't believe Kyle has had time to court you," he said, turning back to Evelyn. "When are you planning to marry?"

She shied from Radford's gaze. Kyle hadn't needed to court her. She'd committed herself to him four years ago when his father died. At the time, she'd been Kyle's friend for years, but it was the only occasion she'd ever seen him cry. Knowing he needed someone to lean on, she had promised she'd always be there for him. Their recent engagement was simply a natural extension of their joint promise to never leave each other.

"Was I prying?" he asked, breaking into her memories.

She glanced at him then turned her face to the breeze. "Of course not. Kyle and I plan to marry in November if he can finish the house that soon. I thought your mother would have written you about the wedding."

"I told her not to reply to my last letter because I'd be coming home shortly." He gave Evelyn a sheepish grin. "That was almost four weeks ago."

"What took you so long to get here?"

His eyes darkened and he turned away. "Rebecca wasn't ready for the trip."

Chapter Three

Wondering if Radford sensed her father's love, Evelyn observed them as they talked. Radford's eyes reflected her father's joy and he appeared as happy with their reunion as her father seemed to be. She didn't know what had happened during the war to bond Radford and her father so closely, but there was no denying the special connection between them.

While he talked, Radford stroked Rebecca's back. She lay on his shoulder with her finger tucked in her mouth and her eyes drifting closed. Evelyn recalled the numerous times in her childhood she'd fallen asleep on her own father's shoulder. He'd been everything to her, especially after her mother died. He'd kept her close while he worked the livery and ultimately taught her their business. Until today, she would have never believed her father would overlook her feelings because of his respect for Kyle and his love for Radford, but he had.

As though Radford felt her assessing stare, he shifted his attention to her, his eyes questioning her reason for studying him.

She nodded at his daughter. "Rebecca's asleep. You can put her in the nursery. It connects to your room, which is at the top of the stairs, first door on the left," she said, wishing the nursery didn't also connect with her room on the other side.

He pushed his chair back and stood. "Thank you, Evelyn." He turned to her father. "Thank you both for the hospitality."

Her father waved away Radford's appreciation. "It's your home as long as you want to stay. Now go on up." He watched Radford carry

Rebecca upstairs then he turned to Evelyn, perusing her with that same loving, but probing, expression he'd used on Radford.

Thinking he'd seen her studying Radford, she dropped her gaze and fiddled with her cup. She wet a corner of her shirt cuff in her water mug and rubbed at an old coffee stain.

"You're gonna scrub a hole right through that mug if you keep at it," he said, clapping a hand over hers. Her braid had fallen forward onto her lap and her father lifted the tail, brushing the curled end across her cheek as if to tickle a smile into existence. The playful gesture was one he'd performed a million times since she was old enough to remember, but for the first time in her life it made Evelyn's eyes mist.

Why hadn't he told her about his plans to have Radford run the livery?

"I didn't do this to hurt you," he said quietly.

From years of confiding in him, Evelyn spoke from her heart, without reservation, trying not to place blame, but feeling too upset to keep it to herself. "I know, Papa, but it does hurt. You've never kept things from me before. Don't you trust me anymore?"

"This ain't about trust, pixie. It's not about you or me at all. It's about keeping Radford at home this time."

She raised her eyes, noting how tired and frail her father had become, how thin his white hair had grown in the last year. She didn't want to upset him, but after working the livery with him for so many years, and managing it alone for months, she deserved to be included in his discussion with Kyle. "I know you own the livery, Papa, but it's home to me. It's all I've got."

He shook his head. "You've got Kyle. He's honest, dependable, and proud, all the qualities a woman would want in a husband. Radford has nothin'. Without that sawmill or his brothers, he don't have a reason to stay. That's why I'm askin' him to run the livery."

"What if he doesn't want to do it?"

"There'll be trouble if Radford goes back to the mill right now. Kyle's a good man, but he's young and blinded by ambition. Without the livery, Radford has no choice but to force his way back into the mill." He met her eyes with tired certainty in his own. "We both know Kyle won't stand for that."

She didn't want to admit it, but her father was right. That mill was Kyle's life. "Maybe you could talk to Kyle. He would listen to you."

Her father shook his head and leaned back in the chair with a long sigh. "Kyle's his own man now. He don't need my advice anymore and wouldn't appreciate it if I gave it. He has fought hard to drag that mill out of the muck. Radford will have to earn his way back, too. This is their fight. I'm just offerin' those boys a little breathin' space and a chance to work things out."

Breathing space? What about her? Evelyn hadn't drawn a full breath from the moment she laid eyes on Radford. After enduring his probing gaze and inquisitive questions on the ride home, she was certain she didn't want Radford in her livery.

"Why doesn't Radford just find other work if he thinks he can't settle things with Kyle?" she asked, fishing for a way to suggest bringing in a different man to help in the livery.

"He's got his pride. Radford won't stay where he's not welcome. That boy's still strung with tension. It's like a volcano stirring inside him that ain't gonna die until it spews its poisons. He's gonna keep runnin' and fightin', carrying all that baggage until he finds a way to make peace in his life. Challengin' Kyle for the mill won't give anybody peace. It's just gonna drive Radford away again." Her father reached out and patted her cheek. "Trust me on this, pixie."

Knowing she had no other choice, Evelyn swallowed her apprehension. "How long do you think this will take?"

"I don't know. Maybe a week. Maybe a year."

She groaned under her breath and hoped he would leave in the morning.

After helping her father to his bedroom, she went to her own room. The creak of floorboards and deep murmur of a man's voice in the adjoining nursery captured her attention as she changed into her nightrail and crawled into bed.

The slow, methodical rumble of wood rolling over wood told her Radford was sitting in the rocking chair with Rebecca, perhaps reading her a story or trying to calm her fears. Evelyn lay in the dark listening... imagining... envisioning Radford sprawled in the rocker, shirt unbuttoned, feet bare, his tanned hands resting on Rebecca's back, or brushing the curls away from her sleepy eyes. He was too tall to rest his head against the back of the chair. Instead, he would close his eyes and press his lips to his daughter's dark head as the motion of the chair lulled her to sleep.

The image came so vividly, Evelyn was embarrassed at how intimately she had studied him that evening. She tossed off the sheet and rolled over, trying to chase thoughts of Radford and Rebecca from her mind. She didn't want to think about them, didn't want to know about the poison-filled volcano inside Radford, and didn't want to know his secret pain. She didn't want to know why Rebecca shied away from everyone except her father's tender touch. She wanted sleep. Not this powerful curiosity that was consuming her.

⊷⊶

In the predawn hours, Radford finally surrendered to sleep, his mind slipping from his rigid control as it unfurled toward the world he tried to keep at bay. He dreamed he was in Georgia in the middle of a slow-moving river, swimming through the darkness toward the enemy.

At the sight of Thorndyke McCutcheon, Radford's heart lightened and he met him a few rods from shore. Lowering his feet, he searched with his toes until they touched the muddy bottom of Peach Tree Creek. He removed the packet clenched between his teeth and held it above the brown Georgia water that slapped against his neck. "This better be worth the bloodsuckers attached to my ass."

Thorn laughed quietly. "Well, if it ain't Rad the Radical. I thought that was the 149th making camp over yonder. Haven't seen you New York boys since last winter in Alabama. I'm glad you're well."

"And you, my friend. Anything worthwhile in that bag?"

"Y'all know us Southern boys got the best tobacco ever grown."

"Then hand it over so I can get my feet out of this muck."

Thorn glanced at the water. "Disgustin' shit, ain't it?"

Radford grinned at his Confederate friend. "My smoke better be worth it or I'll swim back over here and plant you in it."

Thorn chuckled. "Y'all keep makin' me laugh and we'll get our asses blown outta this river. Now tell me you got coffee in that sack."

He swapped bags with Thorn, who immediately opened it and stuck his nose inside. "That smells better than a Southern girl's bloomers."

Radford smiled, but it faded fast. "How many men did you lose today?"

"Too many," Thorn said. "I cain't do this much longer." Water splashed his face and he wiped it with the back of his hand. "Sometimes I'm not even sure I can make myself do it again tomorrow."

"I know, Thorn, but the fact is, we will. I hope you're nowhere near my brigade when it starts." Their regiments had fought each other on the same battlefield before Radford and Thorn had become friends. Now they dreaded the possibility that it could happen again.

They hated the fighting, but if not for the war they wouldn't have met at Gettysburg and become friends. They'd met again at Stevenson,

Alabama, when Thorn was posted as picket on the opposite bank of the river from where Radford's brigade was camped. Thorn had spent his days hollering across to Radford's regiment, sharing jokes, news, and his sweet tobacco then meeting Radford after dark to play cards and share their homesickness.

"I have to get back before I'm missed," Radford said, gripping Thorn's wet palm. "God be with you."

"Same to you, Radical. Stay well, my friend." Thorn stuck the coffee packet in his mouth, gave a two-finger salute and shoved off.

Radford swam through the dark, feeling the pull of the Georgia waters swirling around his weary body, dragging him deeper into the darkness. Disjointed images swirled in his head then ignited into bright flashes of men killing each other. His heart pounded and he was running across a cornfield at Collier's Mill, the smoke eating holes in his sinuses and stinging his eyes. Through the haze he saw Thorn running toward him, blond hair flying, rifle raised, his bayonet glinting in the fierce July sun as the Confederate line charged the Union ranks.

Thorn! Radford lowered his rifle. Nooooo...

⚬⟞⟝⚬

Evelyn called Radford's name for the second time, but he thrashed in oblivion. It was indecent and intrusive of her to be in his bedroom, but she had been unable to ignore the tormented moans drifting through the nursery into her own room. And now that she'd seen the agony etched in Radford's moon-shadowed face, she could not leave him writhing in the throes of such misery.

Biting her lip, she bent close to his handsome face. Touching his stubbled jaw, she called his name. Like a bolt of lightning, his arms streaked out and knocked her to the mattress. He rolled atop her and covered her legs with his knee, his thumb pressed hard on her throat. "Don't move!" he hissed by her ear.

She froze obediently and stared into his deadly glittering eyes, knowing with blossoming certainty there was something terribly wrong with this man. "Ra-Radford," she croaked, growing frantic for air.

Radford shot to his elbows, his eyes wide with disbelief that quickly turned to horror. He jerked his hand away and vaulted from the bed, his naked backside cast in golden moonlight before he cursed and dropped back on the bed. He yanked a blanket across his lap and ran trembling fingers through his hair. "What are you doing in here, Evelyn?"

Shocked by his attack and her first glimpse of a nude male body, Evelyn tried to scramble from the bed, intending to race from the room.

He caught her arm. "Are you hurt?"

She whimpered and recoiled from his touch. Her throat burned and she wasn't about to trust him after his crazed response. And he was unclothed beneath those blankets! With caution, she inched toward the end of the bed.

"I asked if you're all right."

"I—" She clutched her throat and coughed. "I'm sorry," she squawked, her voice ragged.

"You're sorry?" He raked his hair back with an exasperated sigh. "Don't ever put yourself in danger like that again!"

Her glance flew to his face. "Danger?"

Their gazes locked and he gave a solemn nod.

"What is wrong with you?" she asked.

He shook his head then with a miserable groan, he buried his face in his hands. "Things you don't want to know."

That low, agonized confession pierced her heart. No one deserved the mental torment she had witnessed as he thrashed upon his mattress.

"You... you won't attack me if I stay, will you?" She perched indecisively on the edge of the bed, ready to bolt if he didn't answer immediately.

Radford sighed and lifted his head, his eyes dark, hurting. "No, Evelyn." Slowly, he reached out and cupped her jaw, drawing his thumb across her cheek. "I would never intentionally hurt you. I'm sorry that I did."

Her skin came alive beneath his touch. His gentle caress and remorseful, searching gaze brought her compassion soaring to life. "Would it help to talk about it?"

He shook his head and lowered his hand to the mattress.

"I'm a good listener."

A melancholy smile touched his lips. "I'm sure you are."

"Do you have nightmares often?" she asked, though she wasn't sure she wanted him to confide in her. Something told her the less she knew about Radford Grayson, the safer she'd be. And he certainly wasn't dressed for conversation.

"Not every night." He held her gaze. "I shouldn't disturb your sleep often."

"I wasn't worried about my sleep. I... I'm worried about you." Embarrassed by her bold words, she ducked her head, shielding her eyes behind the curtain of her hair.

The mattress shifted and Radford leaned forward to brush her hair back.

Surprised by his touch, she glanced up, her gaze tangling with his. "I didn't mean that the way it sounded," she said. "I don't think you're unsafe."

"You probably think I'm insane and I wouldn't blame you." He gave her a self-effacing smile. "Maybe I am." He drew her hair behind her ear. With infinite tenderness, he touched the abused area of her throat, searching her eyes until her heart pounded and the air crackled with tense silence. "I'm sorry I hurt you," he said.

"You didn't."

"I did," he insisted softly. He drew her hair over her shoulder, letting it slip through his fingers and fall back to the inky pool at her hips. "You have nice hair." His gaze floated over her and his expression grew troubled, as though a complete stranger suddenly appeared before him. "I hadn't imagined you like this," he said, his voice quiet, his eyes intense. "Not like this."

Embarrassed by the way his gaze lingered, she gathered her nightrail and pulled it away from her body, hoping to shield her nakedness beneath the thin calico fabric. "I... I'm not dressed."

"I'm aware of that," he said quietly while his thumb glided slowly across her parted lips. Tilting her chin with a single finger, Radford's dark eyes inspected her. "You'd better leave, Tomboy. I'm feeling dangerous after all."

Chapter Four

As the first rays of dawn crept through the apple trees, Radford lifted his face to the warm caress of morning air and took a good look around his new home.

The stone fence girding the front yard had surrendered to a thick tangle of morning glory vines. In several areas the rocks had given way and would need to be rebuilt. He eyed the house. A few new boards and a fresh coat of paint on the porch and balcony would save William's house from appearing rundown. Though the barn was also losing paint and the livery sign dangled from one nail above crooked double doors, it was a solid structure needing minor repairs. The horse shelter in the paddock behind the barn was rotted beyond saving and would have to be replaced.

It would be enough work to keep Radford busy, to keep his mind off his nightmares and the sweet sound of his father's sawmill beckoning in the distance. For a while, the fecund smell of hay and horses would have to replace the scent of fresh-cut pine. He could live with that for now.

With new resolve, he pushed open the livery door and came up short when he saw Evelyn wrestling with the oversized chain she had borrowed from Kyle. Radford intended to apologize to her for his behavior last night, but had no idea how to explain his appalling actions. It wasn't only the nightmare that had unnerved him, he was used to waking up in that state of panic. It had been Evelyn's presence. He couldn't believe that the woman perched on the side of his bed in a thin nightrail with waves of gorgeous hair tumbling around her slim hips was really Evelyn.

To think he'd be spending each day working beside her was distressing, but he comforted himself with the knowledge that he would be kept busy with customers. They would come from morning to late evening to stable their horses or have them shod, others would want to rent rigs and mounts. Inevitably, he would cross paths with Evelyn while doing their daily chores of grooming animals, cleaning stalls, oiling harnesses, and making repairs, but when their day ended, Radford would go help Kyle build his house. He might have to share the burden of livery work with Evelyn, but that's all they would share.

He would forget about last night and the feel of her hair slipping through his fingers and the heat of her body beneath his own when he'd pressed her into his mattress.

"If you're looking for something to do, I could use some help with this," Evelyn said, whacking her hands against her britches. She sat on a stump of wood beside the iron-encased wooden wheel and stared at it with a defeated sigh. "I need to take this to the blacksmith, but I can't get it off without lifting the axle."

Glad that she had provided an easy way to begin a conversation, Radford looked at the beam twelve feet over his head. "How did you get that chain over the rafter? You could barely get it to the wagon yesterday."

"I tied it to a rope and pulled it over. Unfortunately, I don't have enough strength to pull the carriage off the ground, and I've already loosened the hub," she said with disgust, giving the wheel a whack with her hand.

The carriage shifted and the iron links grated as they slipped against the axle. "Look out!" he yelled, lunging forward to reach around Evelyn and steady the carriage. His chest brushed her back and he smelled soap and hay on her hair. "Put your stool under the axle," Radford instructed, nodding toward an old hickory stump that she was sitting on.

Reacting quickly, she rose up and wrestled the thick stump from beneath her, brushing her elbows, back, and bottom against Radford in all the wrong places. Torn between bolting from the livery or tightening his arms around her, he forced himself to concentrate on the chain, afraid it might slip further and cause the carriage to fall on the unsecured wheel.

Evelyn pushed the thick block of wood beneath the axle then turned to him, her face only inches away. "I'll hold the block steady while you tighten the chain."

"No. You'll get hurt if that axle pulls from the hub." He gripped the chain and wondered if it was his hand or the metal beneath it that trembled. A long silky strand of hair had escaped Evelyn's braid and dangled down her back reminding him of how it had cloaked her slender body last night. "What time do the customers usually start coming?" he asked to distract himself while he adjusted the chain.

"We haven't had many lately."

The thought that Evelyn and William might be experiencing financial troubles because of William's illness brought Radford back to his senses. He would turn this livery around then go back to the mill.

"That should do it," he said, securing the chain then backing up a step to let Evelyn squeeze from between him and the carriage wheel. "Business will pick up when I get the forge going. I'll be able to shoe horses and maybe even fix this wheel band by tomorrow."

"You can fix that?" Evelyn asked, her eyes lighting up.

To his distress, he found himself staring again. Evelyn was refreshingly transparent, unlike Olivia who'd been an emotional chameleon. The first time he'd seen Rebecca's mother was at a theater in Boston where he had gone to escape the pain of his memories.

Olivia's ballet performance had swept him away so completely that it was the first time in years his mind had been quiet. After the show, he'd gone backstage to introduce himself to Olivia, and that began a fiery ten-month affair that ended when she walked away from him and their infant daughter. Olivia Jordon wanted the stage, not a husband and child.

"It's all right if you can't fix the wheel," Evelyn said, as though his lack of response was meant to be a negative answer.

"It won't be a problem," he said then stood up and grabbed the chain. "You'd better stand back." Iron links rumbled over the beam as he pulled on the chain, gouging fragments of wood that floated down upon them. He pulled again and the carriage inched upward until the wheel was suspended four inches off the livery floor.

"It must be nice to be so strong," she said. "I could do three times as much work in a day if I had a pulley and half your strength."

Or three times as much destruction, Radford thought. Though his strength had kept him alive during the war, knowing how he'd used that power to survive was not something he wanted to remember.

"Kyle lifts logs by hand just to prove he can," she continued, oblivious to Radford's unease. "He says it keeps him in shape."

Radford squatted beside the wheel and pulled the pin from the hub. "Kyle's been strong since he was born. He doesn't need to work at it."

"I know, but don't tell him that. His head is fat enough."

Radford grinned despite himself. Maybe working with Evelyn wouldn't be so bad after all. She was easy to read and she spoke her mind honestly. As long as she kept her fanny away from his groin, he might be able to keep his thoughts where they belonged.

"You won't tell Kyle what I said, will you?"

Radford didn't respond right away, just studied Evelyn with curiosity that deepened to appreciation. Slowly he stood. "You have my word." He reached out and picked a wood fragment off her shoulder. "I'm sorry about last night," he said. "I didn't know what I was doing."

Her eyes widened then she dropped her chin and took a step back. "I've already forgotten about it."

"Good," he said. "I want to help you, not scare you to death, or make you think you're working with a crazy man."

Her head jerked up and she looked at him with the same confused, frightened expression that had been on her face last night after he'd choked her.

Radford's gut cinched with regret knowing he'd hurt her. With one finger, he reached out and pushed open her collar. The light bruises on her neck sickened him as much as the distrust he saw in her eyes. "I'm sorry, Evelyn. Sometimes I forget where I am," he said quietly. "I forget that the war is over and that I can't fight the battles again—that I can't save my friends." Tenderly, he drew his thumb over the marks on her neck as if to soothe them away. "My memories make me angry, and sometimes, violent. Don't risk yourself trying to rescue me from them. No one can."

Throughout the morning, Evelyn did her best to forget about the incident in Radford's bedroom, but her mind kept drifting back to it. What had happened to make him so violent? Who was Thorn? Had the war ruined Radford's mind? She wiped the grime off her hands, her thoughts racing.

She stretched her back then straightened and whacked her grease rag against the stall, remembering how she'd started blathering like a fool the minute Radford had entered the livery that morning. She'd been so nervous she had nearly knocked the carriage onto its axle. What a halfwit. She'd lost every shred of her common sense the second Radford was within ten feet of her. Her brain had stopped working altogether when he touched her throat. Thank goodness he'd left the livery before she could decide if she was frightened or excited by his touch.

When he'd returned to the livery later that morning with Rebecca, he'd acted as if nothing had transpired between them. For two hours, Evelyn had watched Rebecca sit on her blanket, as she was doing now, observing the horses and fat bumblebees that zipped in and out of the livery. Despite Rebecca's curiosity, she'd kept her father in sight. When Radford moved, she would pick up her blanket and settle herself where he stopped. She sat on the steps while he scraped the porch floor. She sat on the paddock fence while he measured the rotting shelter. She sat on the dusty floor of the livery while Radford inspected the forge.

Several times Evelyn started to approach Rebecca, to take her by the hand and show her all the things the child seemed so curious about, but she held back, sensing that Radford didn't want her to interfere with his daughter. But watching Rebecca was heartbreaking. Little girls should be running through the yard, shrieking and giggling and wearing the grass thin. That's how Evelyn had been before her mother died. That's how Rebecca should be. Not this unnatural, quiet watchfulness.

Evelyn was actually relieved when Radford took Rebecca and went to his mother's house for supper. Though Kyle ate with his family, he came to see Evelyn afterward.

"What did Radford do all day?" Kyle asked, taking a chair opposite her on the porch.

"I'm not sure. We didn't see each other much."

"Wasn't he in the livery?" Kyle asked.

"Occasionally."

"Well, he must have talked to you."

He did more than talk, Evelyn thought, remembering the feel of Radford's thumb gliding across her throat. "He measured the shelter." She shrugged. "I was too busy to notice more than that."

Kyle leaned forward and propped his elbows on his knees, his fingers interlaced between them. "Sounds like he is going to be making some repairs."

"Didn't you talk to him at supper?"

"Not about the livery. He was too interested in what we're doing at the mill."

Evelyn detected a note of unease in Kyle's voice. "Does that bother you?"

Kyle quirked a brow. "Why should it?"

"I thought you might not like Radford being involved in the sawmill after you've done so much to make it successful," she hinted, hoping Kyle would give her some insight that would help her find a way to get Radford back to work at the sawmill and out of her livery. Any man from Kyle's crew would be a safer choice.

"I've worked too hard to turn it over to anyone. Besides, my gut tells me that Radford won't stay long enough for me to be concerned."

"Why?"

"Because he hasn't stayed in one place for more than a couple months since the war. Why do you think he did so well with the railroad?"

Evelyn shrugged. "I thought the railroad made him travel."

"They did, but—" Kyle shook his head. "Never mind. It's unimportant." He gazed off toward the dark orchard, a wounded look in his eyes. "I learned long ago not to worry about Radford. Or depend on him." He released a long sigh. "What happened to your throat?"

Evelyn's stomach flipped. He would be enraged if he knew she'd been in Radford's bedroom. If he knew she'd been in Radford's bed, seen him unclothed, Kyle would kill his brother—then her.

"I... I stumbled over a bucket and hit my throat."

"On what?" he asked, studying her neck with concern.

"The wheelbarrow." She hated lying, but knew the truth would elicit unnecessary concern at the least, and a war at most.

Kyle shook his head. "It's a good thing Radford's helping you now. I won't have to worry so much about you being alone out there."

She covered the bruises with her fingertips, but Kyle reached out and caught her hand. He pulled her onto his lap and looped his arms around her waist. "I think it's time I taught you about monkeyshines."

"Monkeyshines?" she asked in surprise. "You want to teach me about pranks?"

Kyle laughed and shook his head. "No. Monkeyshine is just another word for an exciting kiss. You're going to be my wife and we've never really kissed each other, have we?"

"We haven't had time," she said, though the idea of being romanced by Kyle pleased her. "And we have too kissed. Remember New Year's Eve?"

"That was not a kiss, Ev. That was a peck. Nothing at all like a monkeyshine. This is a kiss." He lifted her chin and pressed his mouth to hers.

It was the first time Evelyn had received a passionate kiss. Kyle's lips were softer than she expected and the stubble on his chin was rough against hers, but not unpleasant. He smelled of fresh-cut wood and soap. To her immense relief, kissing wasn't unpleasant at all.

Until Kyle licked her lips.

Before she could react, he tightened his embrace and swept his tongue across her lips with slow, bold strokes.

Shocked, she broke the kiss. "What are you doing?"

He loosened his hold. "I was just about to ask you the same. You're supposed to open your mouth when I kiss you." He grinned at her shocked expression. "That's how it's done when you're engaged."

Evelyn ducked her face, ashamed that she knew nothing about kissing. It had been so much easier during the days when Kyle wanted her to climb trees or skip rocks in the creek. Those were things she could do, but it was awful to be such a failure at the simple duties of womanhood. It didn't matter that she grew up without a mother for she was sure that she lacked within her the necessary substance of femininity. That was something nature provided. Not a thing to be learned.

Kyle squeezed her shoulder. "Was it that bad, Ev?"

She glanced up to see a teasing glint in his eyes, but she saw no humor in her lack of knowledge or womanly attributes. She wanted love. How was she supposed to share that special bond with Kyle when she didn't even know how to kiss?

His expression turned sympathetic. "We're not used to each other yet. That takes time."

"I don't know a thing about men or monkeyshines. I don't blame you if you're disappointed."

"I'm not. I'm just getting to know my future wife." He tipped her chin, forcing her to meet his eyes. "We'll be having children together, Ev. There's no need to be shy with me."

Her discomfort with Kyle wasn't shyness. She wanted the sort of relationship married people should have and was more than willing to form that physical bond. She just didn't know how. Seeing the sincerity in his eyes eased her worry. She'd always been able to depend on Kyle to make things better. He could teach her how to kiss. He would give her a secure future and the family she desperately wanted. He was devilishly handsome, intelligent, and steadfast, the kind of man any girl would want. She would learn to love him.

She would.

And she'd learn to kiss him, she thought, lifting her mouth to his waiting lips. His attentions were far from repulsive, but it felt decidedly odd kissing her best friend, despite his handsome face and obvious talent.

It made her think of an illicit kiss between cousins.

Chapter Five

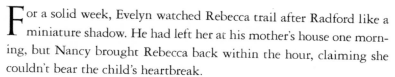

For a solid week, Evelyn watched Rebecca trail after Radford like a miniature shadow. He had left her at his mother's house one morning, but Nancy brought Rebecca back within the hour, claiming she couldn't bear the child's heartbreak.

Though Rebecca was quiet, Evelyn could see a spark in her eyes when she studied the horses. Many times Evelyn felt the little girl's curious gaze on her. Whether she filled the oat bin, fed the horses, or mucked the stalls, Rebecca would be raised up on her knees, watching her with avid interest.

This morning Rebecca sat on her blanket with her shoes off, talking to herself and picking her toes. She seemed so lost, so small and alone, that Evelyn decided she just had to approach her.

"Rebecca," Evelyn called softly.

Rebecca's head lifted.

"Would you like to give the horses their oats today?"

Rebecca stared at the oat scoop in Evelyn's hand, her expression momentarily confused before her eyes suddenly came to life. She glanced at Evelyn's Thoroughbred then gave a shy nod.

"I don't want her near the horses," Radford said from the stall beside Evelyn.

Rebecca immediately sank back upon the blanket, the excitement ebbing from her eyes.

Evelyn cursed under her breath. "I'll be right beside her."

"They'll frighten her."

Having watched Rebecca all week, Evelyn didn't believe that for a moment. Though Rebecca was unnaturally quiet and withdrawn, she was curious about the world around her. The horses fascinated her, and in some small way, so did Evelyn.

"How will she learn about horses if she never gets close enough to touch one?" Evelyn asked, resting her elbows on the half wall between the stalls. Radford had his back to her, allowing Evelyn to observe the way his shirt tightened across his shoulders as he swept the hayfork across the floor to spread fresh straw. His denim trousers were dusty and loose from bending and squatting, but Evelyn knew the fabric covered a hard-molded backside and long, sinewy legs. Moving her gaze up to the dark hair tangled in his collar, she wondered how it would feel then chastised herself for the thought.

"Rebecca's never been on a horse," Radford said, shaking the last of the straw from his fork.

"Papa claims I sat my first horse as soon as I could sit up on my own."

"I'll teach her how to ride when I think she's ready."

"All right," Evelyn said, but she needed to make Radford understand what was happening to his daughter. "I think Rebecca needs a playmate her own age. I know she's warming up to Papa because he's so silly, but being surrounded by adults all the time can't be good for her."

Radford planted the tines of the fork in the straw and hooked his palm over the handle. "I know you mean well, Evelyn, but Rebecca wouldn't play with a child her age."

The certainty in his voice piqued her curiosity. "Why not? I think Tom and Martha Fisk's little girl would be a wonderful playmate for Rebecca. You've never met Helen because she was born while you were away, but she's a darling."

"I'm sure she is," Radford said, "but Rebecca still wouldn't take to her. She didn't take to Janie in Boston or Emily in Saratoga Springs.

Both girls were her age and Rebecca refused to have anything to do with them. She's just too shy."

"What were those girls like?" Evelyn asked, sure that there was a reason Rebecca shied away.

"Like little girls." He raked his hair back. "I don't know."

Evelyn took a step back. "I'm sorry. I know Rebecca's your responsibility and I shouldn't intrude, but I can't stand to see her sitting on her blanket every day. She needs to play and explore."

"She will. When she feels comfortable letting me out of her sight, she'll run off and play as little girls do."

It would more likely be when Radford was comfortable letting Rebecca out of his sight, but Evelyn withheld comment. It would do her no good to antagonize Radford further for being a protective father. But she could goad him into getting out of her livery so she could keep her eyes on her work for a change. "Rebecca can't just sit here every day of her childhood, Radford. Why don't you go play with her? I can handle chores this morning."

"Rebecca knows I have to work during the day and that we'll have our time together in the evening. She can go play anytime she chooses." He opened the stall door and glanced back. "Need anything before I go outside?"

Evelyn shook her head and watched him leave, as Rebecca trailed after him with her ragged blanket tucked beneath her arm, her shoes forgotten by a bale of hay. Evelyn picked them up and took them to the tack room with her, feeling as though she had failed Rebecca. She sat at her desk and placed the tiny shoes before her, studying them with her chin propped on her fists. Why was Radford trying to keep her away from Rebecca? Couldn't he see that his daughter was brimming with curiosity? The fact that she sat quietly on her blanket each day didn't mean she wasn't utterly miserable.

"Evelyn, are you still in here?" She glanced up at the sound of Radford's voice. He stood in the doorway, his expression drawn, and Evelyn suspected he'd come back inside to tell her to mind her own business where Rebecca was concerned. "The veterinarian is outside asking for you," he said, gesturing with his chin toward the front door.

"Calvin's here?" she asked with surprise. She followed Radford out of the livery and greeted the short, balding man. Calvin Uldrich had been friends with her father since before she was born, and was one of the only people who still frequented her livery. "What a nice surprise, Calvin."

"I wish this was just a social call, Evelyn, but I need your help." He stuffed his hat back on his head. "I've got a stallion that needs some tending, if you have the time."

"What's wrong with him?" she asked, nodding toward the frightened sorrel tied to the back of Calvin's carriage.

"Take a look at his neck, but stay back. He's in pain and pretty wild right now."

Evelyn approached slowly, inching forward until she could see his neck. The horse flattened his ears and snorted, the whites of his eyes showing. The instant she saw the injury, rage consumed her. "Who did this?" she demanded, pointing to the stallion's lacerated flesh.

"My twelve-year-old grandson. He wanted to help me doctor the animals, but we needed to clean the barn first. He took the horses outside for me, but I didn't realize he'd chained my stallion until late last evening. By then the damage was done." Calvin sighed and rubbed the back of his neck. "He feels terrible about hurting Gus." He arched a bushy white brow at her. "I don't have the time or energy to try and rehabilitate him. I was hoping you might."

Evelyn glanced at the stallion in pity. To keep these beautiful creatures in gentle captivity was one thing, but to treat them without compassion, even unintentionally, was the lowest form of cruelty. "I'll try, but I can't promise anything."

"He's yours if you can rehabilitate him."

"What?"

"You and your father have always lent a hand when I've needed one. Now I can finally repay that kindness. Besides, I'm too old for spirited horses. My gentle Nellie is all I can manage now."

Evelyn admired the majestic stallion before her. If she didn't take him, who would in his present condition? Calvin couldn't sell him, and if he didn't have time to work with Gus, the horse would remain as wild and dangerous as he was now.

"All right, Calvin, but let me know if you change your mind."

He nodded and untied the rope from his buggy. "I was hoping you wouldn't be stubborn. Let me help you get him inside before I leave."

Evelyn shook her head. "No, thanks," she said, barely able to drag her gaze from the horse. "It'll go better if I do it alone."

⊷⊷ ⊶⊶

Radford watched the veterinarian drive away and wondered why Evelyn hadn't accepted his help. The flattened ears of the stallion told Radford they could have used it. He saw Rebecca standing inside the livery door and waved her outside. "Wait on the porch for me, sweetheart," he instructed, but Rebecca didn't move. Her gaze was fixed on the high-strung stallion that snorted and sidestepped Evelyn's slow advance. "Go on now," he repeated. After Rebecca was out of harm's way, Radford stepped forward to assist Evelyn. The stallion's nostrils flared and his head reared up.

Evelyn held up a hand to stop Radford. "Don't move. Don't say anything. And don't block the door," she said quietly.

Intrigued, Radford waited. Evelyn began talking softly to the horse, varying the tone of her voice until the sorrel's ears flicked. With small steps, she moved toward him, arms outstretched, crooning in a singsong voice. The stallion kept his eyes on her, snorting and prancing, and backing away. When she inched to the right, the stallion adjusted his body to keep her directly in front of him. They continued their face-off for several minutes while she slowly backed the horse through the open barn doors.

Radford followed along in awed silence, listening as Evelyn urged the stallion on with soothing, seductive tones that conjured visions of her in her nightrail, her soft slender body tempting him to draw her down beside him. After long minutes of her soft murmurs that lured both him and the horse inside, Radford sighed with relief when she finally closed the stall door in front of the stallion.

Radford had never seen an injured animal handled with such mastery. The stallion had fallen under Evelyn's spell, just as Radford had that night in his bedroom.

She turned toward Radford with a triumphant gleam in her eyes. "We did it."

Radford shook his head, truly amazed at her abilities. "I don't believe it. I suppose you'll have him rehabilitated by tomorrow?"

Evelyn smiled and Radford was drawn by the genuine warmth in it. "Not tomorrow, but give me a month and Gus will be eating out of my hand."

He didn't doubt it. She'd had the same effect on him the other night. "It must be wonderful to feel that kind of conviction."

Evelyn glanced at the horse, her eyes lit with purpose. "Papa says you can't give up and expect success. Gus will be my biggest challenge yet."

Radford had heard William's words of wisdom, but they had been different during the war. He'd told Radford that he couldn't give up and expect to survive.

"Radford? Are you all right?"

Evelyn's voice startled him. He hadn't realized that he'd slipped into the quagmire of memories. He drew his watch from his pocket, hoping to distract her. "I was just wondering how I'm going to beat you at cards tonight if you're able to manipulate your opponent as easily as you did Gus."

Evelyn's lips quirked. "It's not me you'll have to worry about. Kyle's my partner and he refuses to lose."

"Then don't expect me to be merciful while I'm planning my attack."

⊷⊶

Radford's eyes were wonderful when he teased, and Evelyn secretly admired the golden sparkle beneath his dark lashes. His hair was damp at the temples and he had a sunburn across the bridge of his nose. She almost asked if it hurt, but changed her mind for fear of exposing her preoccupation with his face.

"Did you learn how to conquer the enemy in the war?" she asked.

He sighed and leaned against Gus's stall. "I learned a lot about surviving. Mostly things I don't want to remember."

"Maybe you could talk with your brothers about it. It might help you get rid of your nightmares." It also might help Radford and Kyle grow close again, she thought.

"It's better if I just lock the memories away and leave them alone."

"What happens if they won't leave you alone?"

Radford shrugged. "I don't know."

But Evelyn did. He would leave, just as Kyle and her father said he would. Rebecca would sink farther into her silent world, and Radford deeper into his private hell, wherever that was.

"May I ask you a question, Radford? About your daughter?"

"You can ask," he said, indicating that he might not answer.

Since she'd already stuck her neck out, Evelyn figured she may as well lay it on the chopping block. "Why won't you let me befriend her? Why do you keep Rebecca away from me?"

"That's two questions."

"I'm not a very good example for her, am I?" Evelyn watched his eyes while he struggled for an answer. "It's all right, Radford. You won't say anything I haven't already heard from the ladies in town."

He captured her hand, his thumb bumping over her knuckles as he inspected her. "Why don't I remember you better? I keep expecting you to be that little girl with skinned knees who ran around with Kyle, but you've changed. Regardless of your boots and britches, you're not a tomboy anymore, are you, Evelyn?"

She ducked her head, her lashes lowered in embarrassment. "I couldn't tell you what I am." All her life, she hadn't known where she fit. She felt uncomfortable in her Sunday dress, as though she had no business wearing one after trudging around in britches all week, yet she felt just as awkward wearing her father's altered wardrobe.

Suddenly, Evelyn saw herself as Radford must see her, a pitiful girl uncomfortable in her own skin. Desperate to escape his scrutiny, she tried to pull away.

"I'm not going to hurt you," he said, keeping her hand in his. "Nor am I going to let you go on thinking it's a shortcoming on your part that's determining my actions with Rebecca, because it isn't. The truth is, I think Rebecca would become too attached to you."

Evelyn's gaze snapped to Radford's.

"I've seen her watching you."

"Is that bad?" Evelyn asked, wishing Radford would release her hand. She didn't want his pity.

He shook his head. "No. But Rebecca is sensitive right now and I'm trying to keep her from getting hurt."

"I have no intention of hurting your daughter."

"Neither did her first nanny." Radford finally released Evelyn's hand. "Rebecca adored Dorothy, and it crushed her when Dorothy married and moved away. I thought Gert, her second nanny, would love my daughter and mother her like Dorothy had. She abused Rebecca. By the time I came home from a trip to Virginia, Rebecca had quit speaking. It took her almost a month to start talking again." Radford swallowed then released a calming breath. "I've never come so close to hitting a woman as I did the afternoon I came home and found Gert asleep on the sofa, and Rebecca tied to the sofa leg with an abrasive string around her ankle."

Blood surged to Evelyn's face. "I hope you shot the woman."

"I wanted to, especially when I saw bruises on Rebecca's arms where Gert had pinched her, but I restrained myself and threw Gert out of my apartment before I forgot she was a woman."

"You should have shot her," Evelyn said, knowing she wouldn't have been able to keep her hands off the woman.

"As I said, my actions with Rebecca have nothing to do with your influencing her. It's just that being motherless makes Rebecca more susceptible to forming attachments that might fall apart later on. I don't want her to lose another person she grows to love."

"Isn't she suffering as much without any feminine attachments? Without any friends she can play with?"

"She'll have that when she warms up to my mother."

Knowing Radford's mind was closed on the subject, Evelyn shook her head. "I know you're a loving father who's trying to protect your daughter from the heartaches involved in growing up. There's nothing wrong in that, but you're keeping Rebecca from learning to depend on herself. Someday she's going to want to leave the safe little square of her blanket. What if you're not there when she does?"

"I'll be there," he said, his expression absolute.

Evelyn nodded in resignation. "I hope so, Radford. But I think Rebecca needs more than your protective love."

His face blanched and he stood with his hands at his sides, eyes dark, his expression so concerned, Evelyn pitied him.

"She needs to laugh, Radford. Teach your daughter how to laugh."

Chapter Six

E velyn had been unusually quiet throughout the evening, her gaze escaping Radford's each time he glanced in her direction. Had their earlier conversation about Rebecca upset her? Did she think she had offended him by showing concern for his daughter? The truth was, Radford found it touching and quite typical of the Evelyn he was coming to know. She was a caretaker to everybody: her father, her horses, and one motherless little girl.

Unfortunately, Rebecca was too young to understand the difference between a woman's temporary kindness and a mother's lifetime love. Radford wasn't going to watch his daughter learn that heartbreaking lesson again.

Thrusting away memories that reminded him of his poor parenting, Radford retrieved the jug of chokecherry wine from the corner of the table and refilled his glass as Kyle dealt the cards.

"Pass that over," Boyd said. He took the jug and filled the other glasses before topping off his own.

"Careful, Papa," Evelyn warned. "That's your third glass."

"Well, I'm thirsty."

Radford listened to the chuckles around the table. It had been like this years ago when his father was alive. William and Mary would come over and play cards with his parents, drinking wine and laughing late into the evening while he stood by his father's knee as Rebecca was doing with him. To his surprise, the memory felt warm and welcome instead of burying him in melancholy because his father and Evelyn's mother weren't with them tonight.

Boyd filled William's glass and ignored Evelyn's frown. "My partner is just building his strength," he said, with a wink at William.

"More like drowning his sorrows over your poor card playing," Evelyn said then grinned at Boyd.

Laughter filled the kitchen and Boyd glanced at Kyle. "It's not too late to change your mind about marrying her."

"Boyd Benjamin!" Radford's mother covered her eyes and shook her head.

"If you don't want Evelyn, I'll take her," Radford said, not realizing how his statement sounded until it was out of his mouth. When Kyle raised his eyebrows, Radford scrambled to cover his blunder. "Ah... the way Duke is playing, I could use a new partner."

Flustered by the sudden attention, and Kyle's scrutinizing gaze, Evelyn took a drink from her wine glass. She wasn't foolish enough to think Radford meant that as a compliment. Not after their earlier conversation about Rebecca. He didn't like Evelyn reaching out to his daughter, but she couldn't help herself. Rebecca was clinging to the safety of her father and a three-foot piece of cotton the same way Evelyn had clung to her livery. She had felt safe inside those four walls and gave her love to her horses, who wouldn't hurt her. Now she was a misfit, uncomfortable anywhere else. Evelyn didn't want Rebecca's need for security to imprison her—as it had Evelyn.

"Your turn," Kyle said, startling Evelyn so abruptly from her thoughts that she nearly overturned her wine glass.

In her scramble to keep her glass upright, she dropped her cards. They fluttered to the floor at her feet. She leaned over to retrieve them, but saw a pair of tiny, slippered feet step forward and two small hands reach down for the cards she had dropped. Rebecca gazed up at her, her brown eyes dark and nervous as though she was afraid to touch the cards.

Evelyn nodded for her to go ahead, and Rebecca's inept fingers reached for the cards, fumbling at the edges until she managed to curl her fingers beneath them. With both fists, she gathered them to her chest, clasping the bent cards for dear life as she stood. Slowly, she moved to Evelyn's side then leaned forward. "Here," she said shyly, releasing the cards into Evelyn's lap.

A riot of dark curls spilled across Rebecca's back and rolled over her shoulders. Of its own volition, Evelyn's hand lifted and stroked Rebecca's head. "Thank you, sweetheart," she said, her voice sounding emotional to her own ears.

Rebecca looked up at Evelyn with a shy smile then stuck her finger in her mouth and took a step back, leaning against her daddy's knee.

Radford lifted his daughter onto his lap, drawing Evelyn's gaze to his. A deep sadness registered in his eyes and Evelyn experienced a sudden urge to put her arms around both of them.

<hr />

Evelyn stopped beneath the oak tree with its giant limbs spreading several feet across the yard, one of them still holding her childhood swing that Rebecca now used. "It's late," she said to Kyle, who had walked her home after their card game. "I'd better go in."

He braced his hand against the tree trunk. "Radford's capable of helping your father up to bed. Let's enjoy the breeze and talk for a few minutes."

She slipped between the ropes of the swing and sat on the wide wooden seat. "All right, but it seems all we talk about lately is our wedding and building a house."

Kyle gave a short, disbelieving laugh. "That's what most women want to talk about."

"I'd rather talk about horse races, or the cities we might visit someday. Those are the things we used to share." She stood up and playfully pinched his hard stomach. "Why don't we do that anymore?"

He shrugged. "I guess right now there are things more pertinent. Maybe after the wedding we'll have time for that."

"I hope so. I really miss our talks." She grasped his hands, needing to connect with her old friend. "I want us to be happy."

"So do I."

"I mean really happy." Evelyn met his eyes. "Like we were when we used to race our horses to the gorge. Remember the feeling of being eight years old and not afraid of anything?"

"You weren't afraid. That's why you always won the race."

Evelyn laughed and her mind traveled back to the afternoon Kyle nearly broke his neck jumping a tree stump to cut in front of her and cross their imaginary finish line. The horse had stumbled and unseated Kyle, who was lucky enough to land in a freshly plowed field. Evelyn wanted to choke him for breaking the rules, instead she offered to wash out the dirt ground into his shirt and pants. After he'd disrobed behind a bush and tossed his clothes to her, Evelyn clutched them under her arm and rode off, yelling to Kyle that it served him right for cheating.

"What are you smirking about?" he asked.

"I was remembering the day I stole your clothes and made you ride home in your undergarments."

His grin widened. "I still owe you for the beating I got that day."

"You deserved it for cheating." She laughed and swung their arms from side to side. "Remember this little ritual we used to share when celebrating something grand?"

He squinted in momentary confusion then slowly nodded. "Kinda foolish, wasn't it?"

"I didn't think so," she said, but released his hands. "We were full of enthusiasm then. Remember, Kyle? You once told me that you wanted to go out West where the trees are so tall you couldn't even see the tops of them. A tree like that would keep the mill busy forever."

He leaned a shoulder against the wide trunk of the tree and propped a foot on a thick upraised root. "Our mill couldn't handle a tree that size."

"Oh."

"Have you considered what size stove you'll need for our kitchen?" he asked.

"What?"

"I need to order the stove so it's here when I get the kitchen ready. What do you want?"

She shook her head, jarred by his abrupt change of topic. She should be used to his penchant for keeping their conversation to business, but every time he did it, she felt her hopes for an intimate union with him plummet.

"Our wedding is in less than twelve weeks, Ev. You need to make a decision."

"I know that, Kyle, I just thought we could do this another time. I thought you wanted to talk to me tonight."

"We're talking, aren't we?" When she didn't respond, Kyle shoved away from the tree. "What's bothering you? You've been acting odd ever since Radford came home. Are you still upset that he's running the livery?"

"No," she said, and though it was true she'd been acting skittish around Radford, being unable to communicate with Kyle had nothing to do with his brother. Kyle honestly didn't understand her, and she had no idea how to reach him. Sometime after his father died, Kyle had ceased to dream, and now he was incapable of going back.

"Ev." He slipped his arms around her and kissed the top of her head. "Daydreaming doesn't run the mill or the livery for us so it's best to keep our minds on what needs to be done."

He was right of course, but she missed the boy she could play with.

"Let's forget about talking," he said quietly. "I'd rather do this." He lowered his head and kissed her.

It felt as awkward as the first time, but as he deepened the kiss, Evelyn remembered to part her lips and allow Kyle's tongue access to hers. When he groaned and pulled her hard against him, she thought maybe she shouldn't have done it. When his hand started to move up her waist, she knew it for certain.

She pulled back. "That's more than a kiss, Kyle."

Heat remained in his eyes, but he dutifully distanced himself from her. "Sorry," he said. The sincerity in his expression pleased her, and she wondered if perhaps he did care more than he let on.

He cupped her chin. "That was much better, Ev."

Those simple words shattered her hopes like a stone hitting glass. Did "better" mean "good enough"?

<hr/>

The following morning after Radford and Evelyn had serviced three customers and rented out a rig, Evelyn waited on the porch with her father while Radford brought the wagon around. As he pulled up, Rebecca sat at his side, gazing at the world around her as if seeing it all for the first time.

Radford vaulted to the ground, caught Evelyn's waist, and lifted her onto the back of the wagon before she knew what was happening. The feel of his strong hands around her ribs sent a queer thrill up her sides and she grasped his arms, looking down into his eyes.

He smiled up at her. "You can let go now," he said, nodding at her fingers gripping his biceps.

"Oh!" She yanked her hands away and moved to the side of the wagon. "I wasn't ready to board yet. I need to help Papa first."

With a casual step to the side, Radford blocked her descent. "I'll give him a hand." Radford turned away and placed the toolbox on the ground beside her father to use as a step. "Can you manage with that, William?"

Her father eyed the box. "I can sure as heck try."

Evelyn stared at Radford, wondering what he was up to. He had deliberately put her out of the way then cut her off. Didn't he realize that her father was too frail to board alone? "Wait, Papa," she said. "You'll hurt yourself."

"If I can't hike these old bones aboard, Radford can give me a push."

Worried, but unwilling to argue with her father, Evelyn held her breath as she watched him struggle to climb aboard. He braced his weak left leg and stepped with the right, gripping his cane as he slowly made the step, and the next. When he finally collapsed onto the seat, his face was red, but his eyes held a look of victory.

"Keep that... toolbox handy, son," he said, winded but glowing.

Radford laughed as he chucked the box onto the wagon bed and climbed aboard. With a wink at Evelyn that heated her blood as much as the feel of his hands on her waist had, Radford urged the Morgans forward and drove them to town.

"Why don't you leave Rebecca with Evelyn?" her father suggested to Radford when they stopped at Brown and Shepherd's store. "She ain't interested in horse feed and flooring nails. There's all kinds of gewgaws for her to look at in Aggie's store."

"We'll only be at the feed depot a few minutes, William."

"That's right, so let Rebecca go snoop around here for a bit."

Evelyn saw the indecision in Radford's expression, but he turned to his daughter and asked reluctantly, "Do you want to stay here?"

Rebecca glanced at Evelyn, who encouraged her with a smile then shifted her gaze back to her daddy. "Will you come back?"

"Of course, sweetheart." Radford's expression softened and his shoulders dropped. "You don't have to stay if you don't want to."

"I will," she said hesitantly.

Radford's expression said he didn't want to leave Rebecca with anyone, but to Evelyn's surprise, he climbed down and stood Rebecca on the boardwalk.

Thank you, Papa! Evelyn vaulted from the wagon before Radford could touch her again. Her ribs were still tingling from the feel of his hands on her waist.

"I'll keep her right beside me," Evelyn said then opened the door to Brown and Shepherd's before Radford could change his mind.

Rebecca followed Evelyn inside, her tiny nose pointed upward as she sniffed the air.

Evelyn gestured to a table across the store. "The scented soaps and spices make it smell pretty in here. Look around if you like."

At first, Rebecca lingered near Evelyn then grew bolder and began to wander the store.

Evelyn selected a can of Eureka harness oil, a can of lard, a bag of flour, and a jar of molasses. Her hand lingered on a small cake of jasmine-scented soap, a fragrance her mother used to wear. She lifted it to her nose, basking in the lovely scent, immersing herself in the nostalgia of old memories.

She could buy it this time if she wanted to. Business was already picking up now that folks knew Radford was at the livery.

It pricked her pride, but Evelyn understood it wasn't her lack of skill that caused her livery to fail. It was mostly because she was a woman doing a man's job. Maybe her father saw that and thought

Radford's presence would give her a chance to bring the business back to life. Then again, maybe he had just lost faith in her because business had gotten so bad.

Evelyn laid the soap back in the basket and wiped her hand on the front of her shirt, hoping to keep some of the scent with her. The feel of her coarse cambric blouse returned her sanity and she turned away from temptation. How foolish of her to bother with frivolities. She spent her time with horses and hay and work that made her hands as rough as a man's. What use would someone like her have for scented soap?

A quick in-drawn breath drew her attention to the front corner of the store. Rebecca was pressing both hands to her cheeks and staring at a cradle that held a small doll with a painted porcelain head. The sleeping baby doll was wrapped in a soft white blanket with a pink bonnet on her head.

Slowly, Rebecca squatted beside the cradle and peered inside. Her eyes took in every inch of the sleeping infant until she appeared breathless with wanting to touch it.

Evelyn laid her items on a stack of boys' clothing then went to Rebecca. "She's a pretty little thing, isn't she?"

"She's beau-tee-ful...." Rebecca fairly breathed the words, she was in such awe over the rosy-cheeked baby. Her small fingers closed over the side of the cradle, but she did not touch the doll.

Evelyn wanted to tell her she could take her home, but a doll like that would cost far more than a simple cake of soap. Regretfully, she knelt beside Rebecca and unthinkingly stroked the tiny, rounded back, her own heart full of misery. She had no idea how Radford managed his finances and wouldn't risk embarrassing him by showing him something that he might not be able to afford to buy for his daughter. But she would find out the price and talk to him about it later.

"I'm sorry, honey, but I don't have enough money to buy your baby doll today."

Rebecca's expression fell and she cast a long, sad look at the doll.

"Maybe we can come see her another time, sweetheart."

Rebecca touched the white blanket that covered the infant, letting her fingertips trail across the cotton softness. "Bye, baby," she whispered. She gathered her worn blanket and turned away, following Evelyn without a single word of complaint.

Evelyn felt awful, especially since Rebecca accepted the loss as though she were used to going without the things she loved. Other than her blanket, Rebecca had no toys that Evelyn had seen. Where was her doll? Didn't Radford know that little girls needed things like baby dolls?

Evelyn searched for the items she had left on a pile of ready-made clothing. A small pair of britches caught her eye and she picked them up, thinking how much easier it would be for Rebecca to play in them instead of her dresses.

"Oh, Evelyn, surely you're not thinking of purchasing those for this precious child?" Agatha Brown asked, stopping beside her and peering down at Rebecca.

Evelyn smiled at the store owner. No, she wasn't considering it. She would never make Rebecca into a misfit like herself. "I was looking for my jar of molasses."

"Well, thank goodness," Agatha said, retrieving Evelyn's missing jar from between two piles of trousers. "You know how children like to imitate."

Before Evelyn could reply, the bell over the door rang. Both women glanced up as Radford came in, scanned the store with anxious eyes then headed directly toward them.

"There you are," he said, scooping Rebecca into his arms as though he'd been away from her for a year rather than fifteen minutes. "Have you introduced yourself to Mrs. Brown?" he asked, winking at Agatha.

"We haven't had a chance, young man. Perhaps you can introduce yourself, as well."

"You don't remember?" Radford asked with mock surprise. "Well, I used to be your best customer. Remember those delicious molasses cookies you used to sell every Saturday morning?"

The barest hint of pleasure crossed Mrs. Brown's face. "Why, I haven't baked them in ten years."

"I'm disappointed to hear that. I moved back to Fredonia just for your cookies."

A small laugh escaped her. "You just gave yourself away with that Grayson charm."

Evelyn was astonished by how much younger a simple smile made Mrs. Brown look. Why, if she tried, Agatha might even be pretty.

Radford took Mrs. Brown's hand. "Radford Grayson, at your service," he said, bowing slightly, "and this is my daughter, Rebecca."

"Your mother must be thrilled to have you back home."

"She certainly is," William said, as he thumped into the store. "How are you, Aggie?"

Agatha's gaze flew to William. "Since you've finally decided to grace my store, William Tucker, I'd like to know if I'm ever going to see your daughter in anything but britches."

Though Evelyn suspected Mrs. Brown was tweaking her father, she couldn't let him be taken to task for her appearance. "I wear a dress every Sunday, Mrs. Brown."

William tapped his cane on Evelyn's toe. "I'm old, but I'm still capable of fightin' my own battles." William gave Mrs. Brown a solicitous grin. "Besides, Aggie and I are old sparring partners, aren't we?"

A flicker of amusement flashed in the woman's eyes before it was quickly disguised. "We are nothing of the sort."

He rubbed his jaw. "Hmmmm... I recall being threatened by a frying pan once."

"You hush your mouth in front of these children!"

William hawed until he swayed on his cane. "I forgot how easy it was to get you in a pucker, Aggie."

"Let me wrap these for you," Mrs. Brown said, ignoring Evelyn's father as she took Evelyn's items to the counter.

William hobbled over and joined them. "You're blushing, Aggie."

Mrs. Brown pursed her lips. Her eyes sparkled and a dimple marked her cheek. "It's stuffy in here. Maybe I just need some fresh air."

William drew himself up as if greatly honored. "Are you asking me to stroll the boardwalk with you?"

Mrs. Brown caught her laugh behind her hand. "Certainly not."

Evelyn took her package and exchanged a curious look with Radford. As if he sensed her unease, Radford pointed to a jar on the counter. "I'll take four licorice sticks, please," he said, placing the necessary coins on the counter.

"It's been too long, Aggie," her father said then gave her a bold wink before Evelyn guided him from the store.

Evelyn climbed in the back while Radford helped her father onto the wagon seat then set Rebecca between them. "You too old to enjoy a good chew, William?"

"It's been years since I had one of these," her father said, sticking it in his mouth with a happy grin.

"What's going on with you and Agatha Brown?" Evelyn asked, but he didn't answer. She scooted forward and opened her mouth to pursue the question, but Radford filled it with a licorice stick. He wagged his own piece of candy in front of her nose as though shaking a warning finger then gave Evelyn a knowing wink.

Lord, his eyes were disconcerting at such proximity. It was like coming nose to nose with a tiger. Evelyn felt her whole body flush and wasn't sure if her mouth watered from the candy or the vision in front of her.

Radford handed a licorice to his daughter, but directed his question to Evelyn. "I hope she wasn't any trouble."

The reminder of Rebecca walking away from the doll without a peep rent Evelyn's heart. Blast it all! She'd been too caught up in her father's escapade to ask the price of the doll.

"Wait! I forgot something," she said, vaulting from the wagon then rushing back to Brown and Shepherd's.

Chapter Seven

Intrigued by the throaty, enchanting voice coming from the back of the livery, Radford stealthily crept toward the sound. He peered around the edge of a stall and saw Evelyn sitting on a small stool with her back to him, singing softly and poking at something in her lap. After a moment, she lifted her head and raised an open palm toward the stall in front of her.

"Come here, Gus," she cajoled, her voice so low and alluring that Radford had the sudden, insane urge to do as she bid.

Jolted by the sensual tug of Evelyn's voice, Radford clenched his fists. It was growing incredibly difficult to perceive her as a tomboy when he witnessed moments like this. She had a private softness to her manner, a natural grace that emphasized too clearly the woman she'd become in his absence. No wonder Rebecca was drawn to the woman in Evelyn. He certainly was.

A snort from the stall regained Radford's attention and he stared in disbelief as Gus lowered his muzzle into Evelyn's palm. He had been certain the horse was ruined or would take months to rehabilitate, yet Gus was responding to Evelyn after only two weeks. What was it about Evelyn that had such allure? And why did he have to notice?

Radford watched from a distance as Evelyn slowly stood up. The horse shied when her hand neared his recent wound, but she continued the same methodical petting and crooning, running her palms along his sleek coat until he calmed.

Imagining the soothing comfort of Evelyn's hands, roughened from work, yet gentle in her ministrations, made Radford envy the horse. How long had it been since he'd been touched with any affection? Five years now? Not since his affair with Rebecca's mother, he was sure. Though it had been lust he shared with Olivia Jordon, that base emotion would be welcome right now. Her grand performances in bed had kept the loneliness from swallowing him during his dark nights. Olivia knew exactly how to use her smooth ivory hands to distract him. Too well, he thought dismally, knowing he had been one of many for the beautiful ballerina. She was an artist at making love, posturing seductively, dropping her lashes just enough to look breathless, powdering her skin to the sheen of polished pearls.

Radford had greedily devoured every night of the ten months they'd spent together. Memories of their coupling stirred an ache deep within him, but it was the need to be held by someone that hurt more than the abstinence. It had been so painfully long since he'd felt the comfort of a woman's arms.

He dragged his thoughts back to less painful ground as Evelyn sat down on her stool. Silently, he crossed the livery then knelt beside her, willing his hands not to touch the long, thick strand of hair that had come loose from her braid. He was lonely, that was all. That was why he was drawn to Evelyn. Her compassion touched everyone, and the wounded couldn't help but respond.

"What are you doing?" he asked.

Evelyn let out a small yelp of surprise. "You have a bad habit of scaring me, Radford!"

He smiled, thinking of the many times in the past four weeks he'd startled her just by being in the livery. She'd been used to working alone and still seemed surprised when he made a noise or appeared from around a corner, which was often now that they were actually getting some customers each day. Though Evelyn had been courteous, Radford could sense she was still uncomfortable with him.

"What's that for?" he asked, glancing at the material in her lap.

"I'm sewing. I need something to do that won't distract Gus, and this forces me to get my mending done."

"Does the singing help?"

Evelyn wrinkled her nose. "It's awful, but it gets Gus used to my voice. It seems to soothe him."

She had a wonderful voice, but was delightfully modest. "Gus seems to be coming around."

"Oh, he is," Evelyn said, her emerald eyes fairly dancing with excitement. "Yesterday, he took an apple right from my hand. Today he's going outside for a while."

When her smile reached her eyes, Radford was stunned by her beauty and had to struggle not to stare. "I don't think we'll get anything around Gus's neck without undoing your progress," he said, telling himself he needed to start spending his evenings helping Kyle on his house as he'd planned to do until he realized that Rebecca wouldn't let him leave the house at night.

"I'm not using anything to get Gus outside. If you want to help, open the gate when you see me leave the barn, but do it slowly so you don't frighten him."

Recognizing a perfect opportunity to put some distance between himself and Evelyn, Radford went outside to finish his chores.

It was some minutes later when Evelyn placed her stool several feet outside the door. Baffled, Radford laid down the shovel he'd been using to dig up a tree root then moved to the gate to await her signal. To his growing confusion, Evelyn sat down and went on sewing and singing as though sipping tea in a parlor. Several minutes later, Gus tentatively poked his nose out of the open doorway.

Radford watched in amazement as the horse eventually moved into the sunshine. For every couple of steps the horse took toward her, Evelyn quietly moved the stool that distance away until, after several minutes, she was sitting in the middle of the paddock and Gus had followed her in through the open gate.

Radford closed it gently behind the stallion and shook his head as he watched the horse wander over to the wheelbarrow full of hay and begin nibbling. Admiration for Evelyn's ingenuity gave way to more appreciative thoughts and he found himself studying her as she carried the stool to the edge of the paddock, striding with inherent grace despite her baggy clothing.

There was nothing rusty or halting about Evelyn, nothing overdone or exaggerated. She reminded him of the willows that grew along the pond's edge, tall, lithe, and unadorned as they swayed with the wind, so unlike the fussy wildflowers that preened and flailed in the slightest breeze.

She was the exact opposite of Olivia's bright, affected beauty. Where Rebecca's mother had been seductive and hot, Evelyn was sleek and cool. Her cheeks were rosed by fresh air and sun, rather than rouged with the powders Olivia had used. Evelyn's hair resembled midnight mink and Radford remembered how beautiful it looked unbound. Suddenly, he couldn't remember what he had found so erotically appealing in Olivia's auburn locks.

The contrasts between the women were intriguing, but it bothered Radford that he was becoming preoccupied with them. What did it matter that Evelyn exuded a natural beauty that Olivia never possessed? It wasn't for him to notice. He shouldn't be thinking about Evelyn at all.

Turning away to break the path of his thoughts, Radford sighed in relief when he spied Rebecca. "There you are," he said, watching her walk out the back door of the barn, trailing a stick in the dirt behind her. She stopped and swirled it in the soil Radford had dug up from around the stump. "What are you doing, sprite?"

She shrugged. "Making pictures."

Radford grinned as she moved away then he went back to digging the tree stump. From time to time, he would look for Rebecca, who was wandering nearby, drawing in the dirt or trailing her stick along the side of the barn. As the afternoon wore on, Radford grew hot and impatient with the stubborn stump and turned his attention to hacking it from its dogmatic grip on the earth.

⁂

Evelyn was in the livery brushing her prized Thoroughbred when she heard a loud bang and Rebecca's scream.

She flew out the back door, her heart bursting with fear as she saw Radford leap the paddock fence.

"Dear God," she whispered, spying Rebecca lying on the ground beside the overturned wheelbarrow. Gus pranced at the other side of the paddock, snorting and pawing the worn grass.

Evelyn ducked between the rails and ran to Radford, falling to her knees beside Rebecca. "What happened?" she asked, her chest pounding with fear.

Radford didn't spare her a glance as he reached for his daughter. He cupped Rebecca's face in his palms then gasped in relief when her eyes opened. "Thank God," he whispered.

Rebecca blinked again then scrambled to her knees, clawing at Radford until she was held tightly in his arms. "That horse k-kicked me," she said, bursting into tears.

The breath rushed from Evelyn's lungs as she glanced at Gus, who was certainly agitated enough to kick anyone. "What happened?"

"I don't know," Radford answered, his voice trembling. He eased Rebecca away and checked her face and body for injuries. "Where did he kick you?"

Rebecca pointed to the overturned wheelbarrow and mound of hay beside it. "He kicked that and it fell on me," she wailed.

Seeing that Rebecca was only frightened and not seriously injured, Evelyn sagged back on her knees, her eyes meeting Radford's. "What was she doing in the paddock?"

"I said, I don't know!" Radford snapped. With shaking hands, he set Rebecca away from him. "What were you doing out here, Rebecca?"

She hiccupped and pointed to her stick lying a few feet away. "I was gonna t-train him."

"What?" Radford asked, his expression baffled.

Evelyn glanced at the stick in sudden understanding. For the last several days, Rebecca had watched with avid curiosity as Evelyn trained her yearling. Apparently, she was trying to imitate Evelyn's actions, just as Agatha Brown had warned she would do. "I think Rebecca was using her stick as a riding crop. She must have spooked Gus."

Radford's gaze shot from Evelyn to Rebecca, whose tears were still rolling down her cheeks. "Did you touch that horse?" he asked, pointing to Gus who had backed to the far side of the paddock, his eyes still white with fear.

Rebecca nodded. "I was gonna train him."

Radford's nostrils flared and his voice came out hard. "I thought I told you to stay away from the horses."

"I wanted to train—"

"I don't care what you wanted to do! Do you realize that horse could have killed you?" he scolded.

Rebecca's eyes widened and she shrank back.

He gave her a gentle shake to get her attention. "Do you understand that?"

Rebecca's chin quivered and her eyes flooded, tears flowing down her cheeks like a river. She nodded in jerky movements.

"Don't you ever do that again, young lady!"

Evelyn clenched her fists. "You're scaring her, Radford."

Radford's angry gaze swung to Evelyn. "I sure hope so. It might save her life."

"Being afraid won't save her from anything. She needs to be taught what can hurt her."

"That's what I'm doing."

"No you're not. You're making her fear your actions if she disobeys you. That doesn't satisfy her curiosity about Gus."

"Look where curiosity got her today." He turned Rebecca toward Evelyn.

Rebecca's cheek was brush-burned and her clothes were covered with hay fragments, her tiny interlocked fingers were stained with dirt and tears. Her pathetic sobbing wrenched Evelyn's heart and fired an anger deep within her.

Burning with indignation for Rebecca, Evelyn glared at Radford. "You have only yourself to blame for being blind. Even I could see the curiosity brimming in Rebecca's face every time she looked at the horses. You can't keep her wrapped in cotton, Radford. She's a healthy little girl, who's curious about the world she lives in."

His lip curled. "She's a little girl who needs her father to protect her."

Radford's voice was cold, condescending. Pride kept Evelyn's gaze pinned to his. They stared at each other in frigid silence. Rebecca's soft crying and Gus's agitated pawing mingled with the distant sounds of the lumber mill.

Was he so wrong to want to protect his daughter? Radford wondered. Isn't that what a father was supposed to do?

Evelyn stood and brushed the dirt off her knees. "You protect her then, Radford, but don't ask me to ignore Rebecca when I know

I can help her. She deserves to be a carefree little girl. And she needs a doll!"

"She had one. She gave it to her nanny's baby when they moved away."

Radford saw the momentary flicker of surprise in Evelyn's eyes before they became cool again. "Do you think that maybe she regrets giving away her baby doll?"

"I bought her one to replace it, but she pushed it under her bed and never played with it." Radford sighed and shoved his hair back with a shaky hand. "I think it's best if you leave this alone, Evelyn. You don't understand what Rebecca's been through."

Her shoulders stiffened. "Maybe not, but I understand little girls who are frightened and alone and just want someone to love."

"Rebecca doesn't want a doll!"

"Fine!" Evelyn shouted. "But she needs to feel safe in the world around her, not just on her blanket or with her hand tucked in yours. She was trying to venture out on her own today and got hurt because she isn't prepared. Until you recognize that, you're imprisoning her and cheating her out of her childhood."

Radford was not going to feel guilty for caring enough to protect his child. He'd failed to do that once and Rebecca had suffered because of it. "I'm trying to see that she survives her childhood, Evelyn."

Her head jerked up, eyes snapping. "Animals survive, Radford. People live. Little girls laugh and explore!"

Radford's teeth clenched as he caught Rebecca in his arms and stood up. "What makes you an authority?"

Evelyn's face drained of color and her lips thinned. "Experience," she said quietly. "Being motherless."

Radford didn't have the breath to stop Evelyn when she strode away. Instead, he cupped the back of Rebecca's head and pulled her to his shoulder. She buried her face and shuddered. "I'm sorry, sweetheart." He stroked her back. "Daddy's sorry."

"I was gonna train that h-horse," Rebecca cried into Radford's neck.

"I know, sprite."

"I was gonna give him an apple, too."

Radford's gaze swept the paddock. Beside the wheelbarrow lay Rebecca's withered, half-eaten apple. She must have carried it in her pocket since lunch, saving it for Gus. She'd seen Evelyn feed them to the horses. She'd seen Evelyn guide the yearling with her riding crop. God only knows what other potentially dangerous things she'd seen Evelyn do.

Rebecca lifted her head and scrubbed her eyes with grubby fists. She blinked and looked at him. "Don't be mad no more, Daddy."

"I'm not. I was just scared."

"Is that how come you yelled at me?"

"Yeah," he said, his throat thick with regret. Guilt swept through him. He had never yelled at Rebecca. Never.

Rebecca was all he had, the only good thing left in his life, his only reason for facing each day. Maybe Evelyn was right. Maybe he was blind. Or maybe he was just selfish.

Without Rebecca, he had nothing. But what did she have? What was Rebecca getting from him?

Chapter Eight

When her father stumped into the kitchen the next morning, Evelyn stood up and poured his coffee. "Do you think Radford will be going back to the mill soon?"

He kissed her cheek and took the thick mug she offered. "He'll go back when he feels he can."

"It's been four weeks already."

He paused, lips on the rim of his cup, eyebrow lifted. Slowly, he lowered the mug. "It may be four more."

"Why?" Her outburst made him grimace, but he settled himself at the kitchen table without comment. Evelyn knelt beside his chair and took his hand. "Papa, I don't want him here. Kyle can help me. Or he can hire another man."

"What difference does it make who's helpin' us out?"

The difference was that Radford was turning her life upside down. One minute she wanted to hit him for being blind to Rebecca's needs, the next, Evelyn was melting over his obvious love and tender affection for his daughter. Though they had spoken little since their argument yesterday, Evelyn had forgiven Radford's comments, knowing he'd been upset. Still, his presence in her livery scattered her senses and drew her attention to things she didn't want to notice. He directed her eyes like the wind turning a sail. Before she knew it, she'd be examining his handsome face and wondering if he kissed like Kyle. She had to get him out of her house!

"I think Radford is unhappy running the livery," she said, trying one last selfish attempt to sway her father.

"'Course he is. He wants to be at that mill with his brothers where he belongs."

"Then why doesn't he go? Why doesn't he just challenge Kyle and get it over with?"

"Because now ain't the time and he knows it." He reached out and patted Evelyn's cheek. "You're worrying about nothing."

"Nothing?" Evelyn's heart sank along with her hopes. "Papa, I love walking into that livery in the morning, feeling I belong there, pouring my heart into each job I do because you taught me to. Those horses are special to me. I love the musty smell of that old barn and the way the sun makes the hay gold in the morning and bronze in the evening. When I'm out there, I feel you working beside me. Sometimes when Radford uses the forge, I hear his hammers ringing and it's like you're right there, but it's not the same anymore." Evelyn swallowed to clear the emotional thickness in her throat. "That's my world, Papa. Our world. And it means a great deal more than nothing."

He ran his palm over her hair and sighed. "I asked you to trust me, but maybe I asked too much. That livery belongs to you and Kyle just as surely as the sawmill belongs to Radford. Ain't nothing gonna change that, pixie."

"I wasn't worried about Radford taking over," she said, grasping her father's trembling fingers. "It's just that the livery feels different with him there. I don't feel comfortable like I used to with you working beside me, and I don't want to lose that."

"Maybe you need to. You haven't let yourself care about anything else in years. You need to go out and visit friends once in a while. Have Kyle take you to a dance some Saturday night."

She didn't dance. She didn't have any friends other than Amelia and Agatha. She had the livery and her father. And feelings for Radford she didn't understand.

"I don't care about those things, Papa. I'm happy here." She kissed her father's frail hand. "If Radford isn't back at the mill by the end of summer, will you ask him to leave?"

The life seemed to drain from her father's eyes and he pushed his coffee cup away with a sigh. "You may as well cut out my heart. I love that boy. He's been through hell most people couldn't even imagine. If the livery is that important to you then I wish to God I'd never owned it. Because now it owns you."

—————

Evelyn plunked the saddle and bridle on the fence wishing she'd never approached her father about getting Radford out of the livery. It had crushed him to think he may have to choose between herself and Radford. She'd been unfair to her father, and to Radford. She shouldn't have condemned him for wanting to protect Rebecca. He was a good father, shortsighted maybe, but Evelyn should have realized it was his fear that made him so harsh with Rebecca, and held her temper in check.

Sighing, Evelyn climbed between the rails and gave a short, shrill whistle for the bay-colored, snip-nosed yearling. He trotted to her on spindly legs and she lifted her palm to give him a lump of sugar. It was then that Evelyn saw Rebecca near the fence, clutching her yellow blanket, watching.

"Daddy's in the barn with a man," Rebecca said shyly.

Knowing he was with a customer, Evelyn crossed the paddock, wondering if Radford knew his daughter was outside. Rebecca's gaze followed the colt as he picked at tufts of grass along the fence, and Evelyn realized she had an opportunity to lessen Rebecca's fear of horses. "Would you like to pet Jake?"

Rebecca eyed the colt, but she didn't move.

Evelyn squatted beside Jake and waited for Rebecca to decide, hoping the incident with Gus wouldn't give her a lasting fear of horses. The child's steps were hesitant, but to Evelyn's delight, she came. Rebecca took her finger from her mouth and tentatively touched Jake's forelock. He lifted his head and knocked her hand away, causing her to step back.

"That's his way of playing." Evelyn held her hand flat with palm facing upward. "Hold your hand like this and let him smell you so he knows who you are. Then you can give him a treat."

When Rebecca raised her hand, the yearling sniffed it then snorted in her palm. She gasped and jumped back, clasping her hand to her stomach.

Evelyn chuckled and held out a lump of sugar. "Want to feed him a treat this time?"

Rebecca's nod was hesitant, but she accepted the treat and held it out like Evelyn had shown her. Jake sniffed it, wiggled his whiskered lips over the lump then pulled it into his mouth. Rebecca squeaked and scrubbed her hand against her belly as a breathless giggle escaped her.

It was the first time Evelyn had ever heard Rebecca laugh. The sound was so innocent, so beautiful, it made her eyes sting. Oh, Radford, why aren't you here to see this?

Evelyn tugged Rebecca's blanket. "Since your daddy is busy, why don't you sit on the railing and watch me train Jake?"

Rebecca's eyes lit up, but she hung back as Evelyn went to work. Minutes later, Evelyn saw her creep a short distance into the paddock where she squatted, finger in mouth, to observe.

"Will he kick me?" Rebecca asked.

"No, honey. Horses are beautiful, gentle animals." Evelyn squatted beside Rebecca. "The only reason Gus kicked at you was because you frightened him."

Rebecca's brow furrowed. "He was scared?"

Evelyn nodded. "He was hurt by a boy. Now he's afraid of people. It's going to take time for him to trust us again so you need to stay away from Gus unless I'm with you."

"Daddy would be mad."

A soft laugh escaped Evelyn. "Yes, he would. But only because he's afraid Gus will hurt you."

"Do I have to go inside now?" Rebecca asked, her eyes lingering on Jake as she squatted in the middle of the paddock, her small bottom touching the ground.

"I like having you here," Evelyn said, unable to send her away. She held Jake's reins out to Rebecca. "Want to help me?"

Excitement illuminated Rebecca's eyes and she stood up, clenching her hands in front of her belly. "How?" she asked, entranced by the colt.

"Just hold on to these for me." Evelyn slipped the reins into Rebecca's small hands and showed her how to grip them then watched from the corner of her eye while setting up step blocks.

The sound of wood clunking drew Jake forward and Rebecca's eyes flew open. She clutched the reins to her chest and gritted her teeth, her gaze flying to Evelyn with frightened uncertainty.

Evelyn nearly laughed at Rebecca's surprised expression, but was too touched by the child's determination and her obvious desire to succeed at the job she was given.

"Whoa, Jake," Evelyn commanded from her squatted position and, thankfully, the colt obeyed.

Jake picked at tufts of grass, wandering from patch to patch while Rebecca followed with the reins clenched in her tiny fists. When Evelyn finished laying out the course, she stood and dusted off her hands. "Walk toward me and he'll follow you."

Uncertainty flared in Rebecca's eyes, but she took two halting steps, checking over her shoulder with each one to see if Jake followed. When the colt lifted his head and trailed along, Rebecca's face beamed with such confidence it warmed Evelyn clear to her bootlaces. She too felt as though she had accomplished something special.

Evelyn placed her hands over Rebecca's and showed her how to walk Jake through the course. After the first pass, she let Rebecca do it on her own. After three mostly successful trips, Evelyn knelt beside the smiling little girl who was stealing her heart. "You were wonderful, sweetheart."

Rebecca pulled at the front of her dress and rocked onto the outside edge of her shoes. "I like Jake."

"He likes you, too. That's why he's sniffing your pocket. He wants a treat."

Rebecca's expression fell. "I don't got one."

"I do." She reached in her worn shirt pocket and pulled out a small apple. "Do you remember how I showed you to feed him?"

Rebecca's nod was full of enthusiasm. "Like this," she said, making her hand flat.

"That's right." The apple dwarfed Rebecca's hand. "Don't let him nibble your fingers. It hurts."

Rebecca giggled and turned eagerly to Jake.

When Evelyn stood to remove Jake's halter, she saw Radford leaning against the fence watching them with an odd, lonely expression on his face. Dread pulsed through her and her stomach flipped. Please don't let him spoil Rebecca's happiness, she thought. Don't let him crush the first rays of confidence that light her eyes.

Not wanting Rebecca to overhear in case Radford was upset, Evelyn slipped the bridle off Jake and pointed to the railing near the barn. "Would you hang this on that fence rail for me?"

Rebecca proudly grasped it with both hands, held it to her chest, and walked away, her hair bouncing softly against her back.

Evelyn lifted the saddle free and walked to the opposite side of the paddock where Radford stood, silent and watchful. She parked the saddle over the railing, resting her hand on soft leather. "I thought you'd rather have her with me than wandering off alone. I noticed you weren't outside with her."

"I was watching, like you suggested." A light shadow of whiskers dusted his jaw and lent a rugged edge to his handsome face. His gaze held Evelyn's, probing, searching, seeming to look right into her soul. "It's not Rebecca who's afraid, is it?" he asked quietly. "I knew that's what you were trying to tell me yesterday, but I didn't want to hear it. You were right, Evelyn. It's my own fear I can't get past."

Evelyn had never heard the despair and regret that filled Radford's voice, and it fed her guilt for being the cause of his heartache. "I shouldn't have said those things."

He turned toward the mid-September breeze and raked his hair off his damp forehead. "I was the one who said things I shouldn't have. I'm sorry about that. When I saw Rebecca on the ground, my heart stopped. I've never felt that kind of fear." His eyes met hers. "Not even in the war." He sighed and shook his head. "I was angry, too. Only I realized I wasn't angry with you or Rebecca. It was my own shortcomings I was fighting. It's hard to admit that I've been a lousy father, but I have."

Evelyn's gaze shot to his. "You're a wonderful father."

"No I'm not." His eyes sought Rebecca who was busy wrapping the reins around the railing. "But I want to be." He placed his hand over Evelyn's, trapping it between his callused palm and the saddle horn. "Will you help me?"

His hard, warm palm felt good and Evelyn wondered if Radford sensed her reaction to him.

"I don't know how to make Rebecca laugh," he said, as though giving his final confession, his eyes sad. "I'm failing her."

Ashamed, Evelyn realized how deeply she'd hurt him with her angry words. "I'm sorry I made you feel this way. I had no idea I would cause so much harm."

His lips tilted in a sad smile and he ran his thumb across her knuckles. "You know, it's been months since I've heard Rebecca laugh. I can't buy her the happiness you've given her today. I wouldn't have understood that if you hadn't challenged me to notice. Thank you for giving me some much-needed advice." His expression softened. "You're the only one Rebecca has had anything to do with since I've been home. Ma is crushed that her own granddaughter won't let her cuddle her. Your father is just aching to get her on his knee." Radford released Evelyn's hand and leaned his elbows on the fence. "Rebecca seems to trust you. Even more than... " He cut himself off and glanced away.

"I won't hurt her, Radford."

His gaze returned to Evelyn's and she saw him studying her, searching her eyes for something, lingering on her face until she felt the heat move up her neck. "I'm glad Rebecca has found someone to look up to."

The absurdity of the statement made Evelyn smile. "I'm hardly what you'd call a role model for a young girl. Believe me, I've been told as much by the ladies in Fredonia."

"Then they're fools." His eyes held hers, communicating his sincerity.

Warmth surged through Evelyn. That Radford would bother to look beyond her choice of clothing, past her feminine ineptness, deeper than the self-sufficient manner she wore like armor, was something no one else had ever done. Somehow, he saw beneath all that to the shy, vulnerable woman no one really knew. Not even Kyle.

"When can we meet Tom and Martha's little girl?" he asked.

Evelyn's chest expanded with hope. "You'll let me bring Helen home to play with Rebecca?" At Radford's nod, Evelyn smiled. "I'll go get her as soon as they return from visiting their relatives in Ohio."

"I hope it's soon," Radford said, watching Rebecca walk toward them. "I've got some making up to do."

Chapter Nine

Since the day in the paddock, Radford had accepted Evelyn's help with his daughter, and Rebecca had trailed Evelyn like a puppy ever since. She was full of questions and quick to imitate. Rebecca was opening up to Radford's mother, as well, and despite being unrelated to Evelyn's father, she'd given him the honorary title of "Grandpa," which pleased him immensely. Rebecca had even let him read her a story and was now sleeping beside Evelyn's father on the sofa.

Seeing the spark return to her father's eyes and the wariness disappearing from Rebecca's filled Evelyn with a new sense of contentment as she knelt on the porch to help Kyle and Radford finish painting.

Other than a brief greeting, they had remained silent while they worked. Typical men, Evelyn thought, dipping her brush then finishing the railing spindles, which by some pact the men wouldn't touch. Though Evelyn was used to working without conversation, she had hoped that Radford and Kyle would talk to each other, if only to share old memories or discuss business at the mill. They grunted, sweated, and slugged down liquids by the gallon, but neither of them spoke two words throughout the evening. Evelyn shook her head, wondering how brothers could work shoulder to shoulder and be miles apart.

"Your sleeve is marking the paint," Kyle said, drawing her attention to him. He laid down his brush and rolled her cuff to her elbow with paint-speckled, efficient hands, his eyes focused on his task as if he were sharpening a saw or honing an axe, not touching the arm of the woman he was going to marry.

Unconsciously, she gazed over his shoulder at Radford, whose muscled arms were bared to the shoulder. Crisp black hair lightly sprinkled his forearms and the backs of his hands. As he swirled his brush inside the pail, gathering the last of the paint onto the bristles, he glanced up and gave Evelyn a tired smile that made her stomach cinch.

She ducked her face. Gads, she'd been having a time trying not to react to Radford. Just the weight of his hand on her back as he stepped around her or the brush of his shoulder against hers while working beside her brought her senses bursting to life. Why hadn't she experienced those reactions with Kyle? Perplexed, she found herself comparing Kyle's muscular build to Radford's lean body as they stroked their brushes across the last few slats of the floor.

"I'll be back in a minute to clean up," Kyle said, balancing his paintbrush across the top of the pail.

With a relieved sigh, Evelyn sat back on her heels and watched him walk to the outhouse they used during the day when they were too dirty from work to use the water closet inside. Rubbing the back of her neck, she released a long, slow breath. She couldn't keep letting her eyes and mind wander to Radford. Yet, spending so much time together made it nearly impossible not to do so, especially after the argument they'd had over Rebecca that day in the paddock. Somehow they had revealed themselves to each other during those tense moments. Their angry words had stripped away their pretenses and left them vulnerable to each another. There was a depth to Radford she hadn't known existed, deep wounds that still pained him. And he was afraid. He'd said he was failing as a father, but she sensed a deeper despair, a level of desperation buried beneath his heartbreaking confession.

She closed her eyes and rolled her neck to release the tension. Radford's secrets were none of her business.

"You have paint on your chin, Evelyn."

She opened her eyes to find Radford watching her, wearing a tender smile. She lowered her face and wiped her chin across her lifted shoulder to avoid his eyes.

"You've made it worse."

She used the bottom of her shirt to scrub her chin then displayed her face for his inspection. "Gone?"

His smile widened and Evelyn forgot about everything outside the realm of Radford's face. There was something warm in his smile, something personal in the lazy way it developed, something in his eyes that said it was just for her. But his smile faded and Radford gave her a curious, probing look that made her tighten up inside.

"You know, I wouldn't have paired you and Kyle," he said, surprising her with the unexpected comment. "I don't think I know two people who are more opposite than you."

It hadn't always been that way, but Evelyn had no wish to discuss feelings better left unexplored. "We've been friends for years."

"So have you and Boyd."

Evelyn laughed. "Yes, but I couldn't handle all that wildness and oozing charm."

"Then why not Duke?" he asked with a grin.

She shook her head. "I could never marry a lawman. I'd always be afraid he'd go to work and never come home. Duke is steady, but too high a risk. Besides," she added with a grin to lighten the conversation, "neither one asked me to marry him."

Radford smiled. "Well, it's a good thing one of us did. Ma's sure happy about getting you for a daughter-in-law. She's always bragged about her little angel."

Evelyn didn't feel like an angel. She had noticed far more than was modest about her future brother-in-law since he'd been home.

"Your mother's biased because she helped raise me."

The reminder made Radford sorry he'd said anything. He could see how Evelyn's eyes lost a bit of their sparkle, though she tried to hide it.

Radford crossed the porch then knelt beside her. The urge to stroke her hair was strong, but he withheld the hand that started to lift of its own accord. "I'm sorry I brought up hurtful memories. Since my father passed away, I've gained a deep appreciation of the pain you've suffered. We all lost someone special when your mother died."

For the second time, he found himself searching her eyes, trying to recognize her as an old friend. But it dawned on him that she had never been his friend. She was the little neighbor girl who had played with Kyle while Radford was helping his father at the mill. During the war, she was William's daughter. Now Evelyn was Kyle's fiancée.

Then why was Radford seeing another woman in the shadows of Evelyn's eyes? And why did he feel the need to reveal that woman?

Uneasy with his thoughts, Radford sought to redirect them. "Did you know that your mother used to spit watermelon seeds with me? She usually beat me, but we had a grand time seeing who could hit the trunk of the oak tree."

Surprise erased the shadows in Evelyn's eyes. "My mother did that?"

He lifted a strand of Evelyn's hair and tucked it behind her ear. He trailed his fingers down the silky skein before releasing it. "Your father laid wagers with my dad."

A gasp of laughter escaped Evelyn. "They wagered on my mother spitting?"

Radford nodded and swiped at a maple leaf that skittered across the porch floor. He was glad he'd made her laugh. He liked her laugh. The leaf, slightly tinged by autumn color, landed on the freshly painted floor. He plucked it up. "Your mother told me that to catch a falling magnolia petal would make a wish come true. I don't know if it works with maple leaves, but we can try. Make a wish, Tomboy." He tossed the leaf and watched it flutter to the grass.

"I wish you'd tell me another story about my mother. It makes me feel like she's still alive."

Radford saw the bittersweet remembrance in her eyes and he ached for her. He knew the magnitude of that loss, understood the helplessness, the anger, the yearning. "I wish she was," he said. "She was an unforgettable lady."

"I wish I remembered her better. Papa says I resemble her, but I can't see it."

Radford smiled and cupped Evelyn's paint-speckled cheek. "She was beautiful, Evelyn. And so are you."

"Paying compliments to my fiancée?" Kyle asked, planting his foot on the bottom step with enough force to make it shudder.

Radford jerked his hand from Evelyn's startled face and glanced into Kyle's snapping eyes.

"Well?" Kyle demanded, his angry gaze swinging between Evelyn and Radford. "You seem quite taken with my fiancée, Radford."

"I think I smell our dinner scorching," Radford said to Evelyn then sighed with relief when she rushed into the house. The look on Kyle's face told him there would be unpleasant questions that Evelyn didn't deserve being subjected to.

"I asked what you were doing," Kyle said, his voice growing harder.

"I was scrubbing paint off Evelyn's chin." Radford forced a nonchalance he didn't feel. "If I were you, I wouldn't ask her to do the painting in your house."

Kyle's brow went up. "She seems capable."

Evelyn was good at everything she did, but Radford was trying to keep Kyle from misconstruing an awkward but innocent situation. "Let's just say she's better off in the livery." He knew that would please Evelyn immensely, but make his life torture. He needed some distance from her to clear his head of the dangerous thoughts that had been plaguing him the past few weeks.

Kyle crossed his arms, his scowl deepening. "Do you need the help, or do you just like the company?"

Radford sighed and stood up. "Kyle, we were talking about her mother. Evelyn misses her. That's all it was about."

Kyle eyed Radford for a long moment as if deciding whether to believe him. "That had better be all it was."

"I'm your brother! What do you think was going on?"

They stared at each other for several tense seconds before Kyle's shoulders relaxed and he gave a dismissive shrug. "Forget it. I wasn't suggesting anything."

Yes he was, Radford thought, but was too relieved that the suspicion in Kyle's voice had disappeared. "Look, just go in and spend some time with your fiancée. I'll be in after I clean these brushes."

Without a word, Kyle climbed the steps and went inside.

Radford gathered the bucket and brushes and cursed himself all the way to the livery. Where had his brain gone during those few minutes with Evelyn? Nothing had existed except the desire to remove the sadness brimming in her lovely eyes, but how could he have led them into such an awkward situation? He had no right to touch Evelyn, not even innocently. He had no business wondering what secrets she kept hidden. No matter how she stirred his curiosity, or how his heart ached for her loss, he should have kept his hands to himself. Gads! He had enough problems with Kyle over the mill. He couldn't afford to add jealousy to the mix.

Resolved to get out of the house and salve Kyle's ruffled feathers, Radford rushed through supper then tossed his napkin at his brooding brother. "Finish up and you can show what you've done on your house before it gets too dark to see."

Kyle quirked a brow. "You're finally going to get over there?"

Radford glanced at Rebecca. He'd been waiting for her to warm up to his mother so he could leave her there in the evenings, but Rebecca still wasn't ready. He would just have to take her with him. "Are you too tired to go for a walk with Daddy?"

Before Rebecca could answer, William set his glass down with a thunk. "Would you carry Grandpa's plate to the sink, sweetpea?" he said to Rebecca. She nodded, slid off the chair then gripped the plate with both hands. "Thank you, darlin'." As Rebecca went to the sink, William slanted a look at Radford. "You don't need to drag that little one everywhere you go. Let her stay here and help Evelyn with the dishes."

"I'm not sure she'll want to stay."

"Let's find out." William tapped his spoon against his glass to get Rebecca's attention. "I forgot to give you my spoon," he said, grinning when she eagerly returned for it. "Might as well take your daddy's plate, too."

Rebecca's face brightened and she hurried to Radford's side. He handed her his empty plate, but before she turned away, Kyle tapped her shoulder. "Do you want to take mine, too?" he asked.

When she nodded with enthusiasm, he stacked his plate on the one she held then laid his empty glass on top. He ruffled Rebecca's hair as she turned away, but she was too busy concentrating on the glass that rolled against her chest.

Too late, Radford realized he should have removed the glass. Rebecca had only taken two steps before it rolled over the edge and shattered against the floor. The plates flipped sideways and she clutched them to her chest, covering the front of her dress with gravy and leftover potatoes. She stared down in horror at the broken glass surrounding her scuffed shoes.

Evelyn knelt in front of Rebecca before Radford could leave his chair. She took the plates and put them on the floor. "I break glasses all the time so don't you worry about it." She wiped the front of Rebecca's soiled dress with a dish towel then gently bumped her chin with the bunched-up cloth.

Rebecca's mouth puckered and the tears she tried to hold back spilled over her lashes.

"Oh, honey." Evelyn swept her arms around Rebecca and rocked her. "Don't worry about that old glass. It doesn't matter one bit."

"It broke," Rebecca cried.

Evelyn stroked her back. "It's all right." Her gaze went to Kyle. "What were you thinking?" she asked, her voice soft, but somehow condemning.

Radford saw the regret in his brother's eyes as Kyle looked at Rebecca. "I guess I wasn't." He pushed back his chair and stood. "Looks like I'd better learn before we have our own." Kyle patted Rebecca's shoulder then reached down to pick up the pieces of glass.

William flapped a hand at him. "Leave that. She'll be over this before you boys cross the yard. Now get goin' or you won't get anything done tonight."

Radford would have rather stayed and comforted his daughter, but William's steady gaze told him Evelyn's arms could do the job. Though his conscience lingered behind in the kitchen with his little girl, Radford followed Kyle outside and across the apple orchard.

"Sorry," Kyle said, keeping pace with Radford. "I feel like an ass."

"I know the feeling. Rebecca suffers my poor judgment all the time," Radford said. "If she's survived my mistakes, she'll survive yours."

"I wasn't just talking just about Rebecca."

"I know." Radford swung an arm around Kyle's shoulder and gave him a fond shake. "Forget it." A fresh breeze lifted Radford's hair off his forehead and he suddenly welcomed the few hours of freedom. "Let's drag our little brothers out of the house."

Duke and Boyd were lounging in the parlor when Radford and Kyle hauled them from the sofa. They walked four abreast down Liberty Street, talking and bumping shoulders. Their feet struck up a rhythm on the hard-packed earth as they unwittingly matched their strides, their long legs stretching out in front of them as they walked a few hundred yards beyond the sawmill.

"We just finished framing it up last night," Kyle said, heading into the field beside the sawmill where the ribs of his house stood like a skeleton in the grass. He pointed to a spot in the northeast corner of the house. "The parlor will be there, the kitchen beside it, and the main bedroom in the back. There'll be more upstairs, but I'll finish them off after we move in."

Boyd's eyebrows shot up. "Are you trying to hurry this along for any special reason, Kyle? Could you be getting eager to get your bride in her master's bed?"

Duke grinned, but Radford felt a tug in his gut at the thought of Evelyn in Kyle's bed. Irritated by his constant preoccupation with Evelyn, Radford cursed under his breath. Maybe he should have just kissed her the night she woke him from his nightmare and just gotten it out of his system. She'd have probably slapped his face, but that might have put an end to his attraction before it had a chance to manifest itself.

"I want to get the house up so I can concentrate on expanding the mill," Kyle said, ignoring Boyd's jab. "If we add another saw, it should increase our output by another twenty thousand feet a day."

Boyd glanced at the mill with a critical eye. "I suppose we could manage if Radford ran the new saw."

"He'll be running the livery."

"Radford should be sawing timber, not shoveling horse shit."

"I'll run mill myself, Boyd!"

Kyle's sudden irascibility surprised Radford—and made him angry. He was staying away to put Kyle at ease, to give him time to accept his presence again, but it appeared nothing was changing. Kyle was still possessive and territorial. A flash of irritation prodded Radford to defend his position, to have it out with Kyle and let the pieces fall where they may, but one glance at the mill made the words die in his mouth. The vast business was created with Kyle's sweat. Not his.

"Once you're married," Boyd said, "you won't think of anything but getting back in bed with your wife."

A slow, reluctant smile appeared on Kyle's face. He took off his dusty hat and smacked Boyd on the shoulder. "You're a pain in the ass."

Boyd grinned. "It's my mission in life."

With a grudging laugh, Kyle propped his boot on a large rock. "Think we can roll this monster away from the house?"

His eyes were filled with mischievous challenge and so reminiscent of the old Kyle that Radford felt an acute pang of melancholy. There were many times during their youth when the four of them would combine their strength to achieve tasks they couldn't accomplish individually. In the deepest part of Radford's wounded soul, he missed the uncomplicated comradery they had all shared in those days.

Taking up the challenge, the four of them squatted next to the rock, digging their fingers beneath the lowest possible crag until they each signaled their readiness by a nod of the head. Radford counted off three measured beats then gave the command to lift. Heads dropped and shoulders hunched. Necks corded and muscles strained.

Radford glanced at the reddened faces of his brothers, and in that moment, the importance of moving the rock, of succeeding together became a symbol of belonging for him. The stone dug into his shoulder and he felt his forearms scrape across the gritty sides as the pressure built in his chest. Slowly, slowly, he felt the rock leave the sucking, wet earth. With a loud growl they bowled it over until it rolled like a listing ship. For good measure they gave it one more shove until the dirt-covered bottom faced the sky. Hoots of triumph abounded as they gasped for breath.

Boyd sat on top of the filthy rock and hung his head. "Why didn't we just hitch up a horse?"

Radford squeezed Boyd's shoulder. "You're missing the point. We didn't need a horse because we had each other." With their combined strength, the four of them had been able to move the boulder, but more importantly, his brothers couldn't have done it without Radford's help. In those few moments they had needed him.

Boyd slapped his hands to his thighs and stood. "It's too late to do any work tonight. Let's go to the Pemberton. Kyle's buying."

"Like hell," Kyle said. "Duke and I bought last time. You can put your money on the bar for a change."

Boyd caught Radford around the neck and pulled him along behind Kyle. "I think it's your turn, Radford."

Two loud snorts came from Duke and Kyle, making Radford laugh. Their youngest brother was a clever rascal with a manipulative side, but Radford couldn't have loved Boyd more than he did in that moment. Boyd's ability to charm anyone who crossed his path was a talent. His ability to make Radford laugh was a welcome gift.

Chapter Ten

Patrick Lyons thumped four foaming mugs on the bar in front of Radford and his brothers. Boyd caught his wrist. "Let's go a round, Pat. I win, you buy this round."

Pat grinned and planted his elbow on the bar, but Duke yanked Boyd back by the collar. He dragged him to the empty stools at the far end of the bar. "I came to drink tonight, not break up a brawl because you idiots overturned some unsuspecting patron."

Kyle smirked at Radford. "This ought to be good for a free round. Maybe you should try Patrick next. You stomped his ass a few years ago."

"No, thanks," Radford said. "I've been in enough battles without adding arm-wrestling."

"The war was a long time ago."

Radford rotated the bottom of his mug on the oak top of the bar, watching the golden liquid swirl up the sides. He gestured down the bar where Boyd was giving his victory whoop. "Every time I look at Boyd, I see Dad. He loved tipping with William and cutting up like Boyd is doing."

Kyle nodded in agreement. "One minute he's got me splitting my sides over some dumb stunt he's pulled, and in the next second I want to pound him for being such a pain in the ass." Kyle shook his head and laughed. "Actually, he's just like Dad in that way."

"Yeah. Kind of tough to see it so clearly tonight without getting dragged down." Radford turned to Kyle with a melancholy smile.

"Guess I'd just like to enjoy a beer without a head full of restless memories."

Kyle nodded as though he understood, but silence stretched between them for several uncomfortable minutes before he spoke. "Is it because you can't stand the memories? Is that why you left after Dad's funeral?"

Radford shrugged. "I left for so many reasons I'm not sure I could list them all."

"I've always wondered if it was because of me."

Radford's eyebrows went up. "You?"

Kyle nodded. "Seems like I was always giving you grief. I was jealous that you were fighting for an honorable cause, earning respect, and making Dad so proud all he could talk about was you. I was pissed that he wouldn't let me go with you."

Surprise rushed through Radford. "Why? You should be counting your blessings that you didn't. I wouldn't want to do it again."

"You were excited enough when you left for Syracuse to volunteer with William. What happened? I've always wanted to ask, but you close up when the war is mentioned."

Radford took a long drink from his mug then placed it on the counter. "You ever killed a man?" he asked quietly.

Kyle's brows shot up. "No."

"Well, it's the worst feeling you could ever experience. It doesn't sound bad saying the word, but it's sickening to hear a man scream and watch your bayonet sink into his chest while he stares at you in disbelief. It was the eyes that haunted me most. The way they'd drain of life and glaze over right there in front of me is something I'll never forget." He paused then looked at Kyle. "I did that to men."

"Jesus, Radford."

"I puked the first time I did it."

Kyle caught Radford's wrist and squeezed it. "I shouldn't have asked. I'm sorry."

But Radford barely heard him. He was seeing the bloody faces of his friends, hearing the shots and screams, smelling the acrid smoke. And he was running through the trees...

"Radford?"

He jerked, his mind crashing back to the present as he ducked Kyle's concerned stare. Radford scraped his wet palms across his trouser legs, reminding himself it was sweat and not blood he was rubbing off. "I think I'd like another ale."

"I think two would be better." Kyle flagged Patrick over with the drinks and shoved two of them in front of Radford.

Radford downed the first one, picked up the second and brought it to his lips. It hovered there a moment before he returned it, untouched, to the bar. "I could use a lighter conversation if you don't mind."

"Actually, I'd appreciate it, too."

The silence stretched until Radford found himself groping for a topic. "So is Evelyn excited about the house?" he asked, speaking the first thought to enter his head. As usual, she was foremost in his mind, but he hoped Kyle hadn't noticed.

"Hard to tell. She's worried about being away from William. We've asked him to live with us, but he's determined to stay in his own house. If he does, it'll be difficult for Evelyn to care for him after we're married, which is why I want her out of the livery. It won't be long before she's got her hands full with William and a baby."

Radford took a long drink from his mug to cool the burning sensation that started creeping up from his stomach. Of course she'd be having Kyle's baby. She'd be sleeping in his bed, making love with him, having his children.

"Are you sure you're all right?" Kyle asked.

He finished his drink and banged the mug back on the bar. "I need another ale."

"I'm ready, too." Kyle raised his mug and signaled for the bartender to bring another round. "I haven't thanked you yet for running the livery for me, but I do appreciate it, Radford. If not for you, I would have suggested that William sell it."

"Evelyn would have shot you."

Kyle laughed. "She'd have been upset, but she would have forgotten about it once she had a baby to keep her busy."

Evelyn loved the livery. She needed to be there with her horses, whether she had ten kids or none at all. Marriage had no bearing on her dedication to her father or her business, and it baffled Radford that Kyle didn't understand that. The Evelyn he knew would find a way to have a family and the livery. In fact, he'd wager his share of the mill on it.

<hr />

Hours later Radford climbed the porch steps, which was usually an easy thing to do, but tonight his feet refused to cooperate without considerable thought as to their proper function. By the time he managed the top step, he needed to brace himself against a pillar to keep from crashing through the front door.

It wasn't that he was intoxicated, really. His thinking was clear enough. It was just those feet of his that had suddenly developed a mind of their own. In fact, he was quite proud of himself. Any attraction he had felt for Evelyn had vanished into the white foam of his mug. The more he drank, the less often his mind wandered back to her, so he drank enough to chase her thoroughly from his thoughts like any good brother would do.

Kyle deserved his allegiance, especially since he was such a good drinking partner. Radford chuckled, remembering how Duke and Boyd staggered from the bar in defeat and he and Kyle had taunted them for being too young to hold their barley. But Kyle's pathetic attempts to mount his horse had Radford gasping with hilarity and stumbling along the boardwalk like an idiot. Those burly arms of Patrick's had come in handy after all. Too bad he wasn't here to open the door.

It was playing tricks on him; moving left then right then left. Radford straightened, took a fortifying breath, and eyed the screen door. He watched a moment, timing its movements then lunged for the knob. His hand hit the wood frame with a resounding crack and slid upward offering him no cushion as his side slammed into the steel handle.

He yelped and staggered back. Pain spread through his side and he saw a lovely vision of an angel in a thin white gown with gorgeous black hair flowing past her hips. The door handle must have punctured his side and killed him! Radford gripped his ribs, waiting to hit the porch floor, but before he had a chance to keel over, the angel clutched his arm.

That's when he realized it was Evelyn, and that she was standing before him in her nightclothes. Jarred from his stupor, he knew he was in no condition to resist temptation tonight.

"Are you all right?" she asked, her soft voice filled with concern.

Radford didn't want her concern. He wanted her to go back inside the house and lock the door. His thinking was too scrambled from alcohol, and his body too needy to resist temptation.

"What's wrong?" she asked.

He'd just play drunk. He *was* drunk, so if he acted despicable enough, or just plain crazy, maybe she'd go back in the house and leave him alone.

"What are you doing?" Evelyn asked, wondering why Radford was stumbling around on the porch. She had heard him when he first climbed the steps then listened for him to come inside. But after several minutes of his thumping, she decided she'd better see if he needed help, which he obviously did.

He squinted at her then blinked twice with great exaggeration. "Who are you?" he asked, listing far left then tottering back to center.

"Radford, what have your brothers done to you?"

"It wasn't their fault," he said belligerently.

Her laughter seemed to annoy him because he gave her an adorable frown. Even his lip curled a bit and Evelyn felt the urge to touch it. Oh, he was delightful like this. God forbid anyone should be traveling by at this time of night and see her on the porch in her nightrail, because she wasn't about to go inside. This was a side of Radford that her curiosity wouldn't let her leave unexplored.

He glared at her. "You can afford to laugh. You're an angel, but I... well, I'm no good."

There was something in his confession that tripped Evelyn's heart. Whether he was drunk or not, there was pain in his voice and she wondered what caused it. Maybe now that he'd dropped his guard, she could discover what he kept hidden behind those golden eyes of his. Her conscience hollered No fair, but she turned a deaf ear.

"Why would you think that, Radford?"

"You should know. You're an angel, aren't you?"

"I'm Evelyn Tucker and I have more faults than you could name."

"Evelyn wears pants." He stared purposefully at her legs. Evelyn looked down then stepped quickly out of the light.

"Don't be rude." She was thankful he was drunk and unlikely to remember.

"Well, she does," he insisted, "and she has a compaszh-nate nature," he said, slurring the words.

Evelyn giggled. "A what?"

"Her eyes are deep green... and her hair..." He leaned his head against the wall and closed his eyes. He spoke slowly and so softly that Evelyn had to move closer to hear him. "Her hair is the color of midnight in February. It's the kind of hair that makes a man want to feel it on his face." He cupped his hands as though he was holding something precious and fragile and slowly raised them to his face. He smoothed his palms across his cheeks then sighed in disappointment.

"I like her hair," he whispered, and Evelyn felt the caress as surely as if he'd touched her.

Her heart jumped and her neck tingled and she thought of touching him then, just once. Just to see what his stubbled chin felt like. But she clutched her hands behind her back instead.

Radford opened his eyes and they were accusing. "I thought angels had white hair. How come yours is black?"

"Oh, Radford, come sit down before you fall over." She took his hand and tugged gently.

"No!" He stared at her then squinted and rubbed his forehead as though trying to clear the alcohol from his brain.

"Come on," she said, directing him to a high-armed, cushioned chair that wouldn't allow him to fall from the sides.

He clenched his fists and collapsed into the chair.

"Why did you drink so much?"

He drew a deep breath and let it rush out. When his eyes met hers, they seemed clearer, more focused. "I needed to." He sank lower in the seat and rested his head against the back. "Go to bed."

"You need help getting up the stairs."

"I'm staying here. Go to bed."

She was silent a minute, studying him, wishing he'd open his eyes. "I don't want to," she said quietly.

His hand snaked out and pulled her onto his lap. She landed with a startled gasp, but he hooked an arm around her waist and drew her close, his nose an inch from hers. His face was so near her own that

Evelyn could see the shadow of his whiskers and smell the alcohol on his breath. As she lay there in his arms, all else ceased to matter, for he filled her senses so completely it left her breathless.

"Look at this." He held up his trembling hand for her inspection. "I'm not safe right now."

Without thinking, Evelyn wrapped her fingers around his. "Relax, Radford. You've just had too much to drink," she said.

He squeezed his eyes shut. "You have two seconds to get off my lap and go inside."

The intensity in his voice scared her, but the feel of his body made it impossible for her to push away.

"One..." His voice was quiet, serious, his eyes open and locked on hers.

Blood pounded through her veins and her stomach tensed, but she didn't move.

"Two..."

"I want to stay," she whispered.

He gripped her chin. "Go."

She shook her head.

"You're making a mistake." He glared at her, his eyes fierce. "Last chance," he warned, but Evelyn didn't move.

She wanted him to kiss her, and when he crushed his lips to hers, he didn't have to ask her to open her mouth. She craved one touch from him to know what he felt like. She wanted to feel his lips and his tanned face that she now held between her hands. She wanted to touch the cheeks that hollowed intermittently beneath her palms and the tongue that stroked her own. She wanted to hear the groan rolling up from his chest.

A flame of white heat rushed through her limbs and she could not get close enough to him. He smelled of alcohol and cologne and cigar and it intoxicated her as thoroughly as if she'd been matching him drink for drink, and there was not the slightest chance she could deny herself the opportunity to finally feel like a woman.

Just once, she promised, twining her arms around his neck, reveling in the exhilarating experience. Her side tingled where his hand roved and the feeling moved slowly over her hips as his palm trailed downward. Her entire body was alive and reacting. Every nuance of pleasure that rippled along her spine, from where his lips caressed hers to where his hand rested upon her leg, was now gathering in sweet agony between her thighs.

So this was a monkeyshine!

She had no idea what to do with the glorious feelings racing through her body, but she wasn't ready to let them go. She stroked his hard shoulders, wanting... wanting something outside her understanding, but in that moment Evelyn no longer needed to know. She only wanted to feel. She wanted to touch him, to feel joyously alive in her own skin. For the first time in her life, she felt conscious. Everything inside her lifted, blossomed, soared as the blood rushed through her veins beneath Radford's seeking hands.

⟞⟛ ⟛⟝

Though the alcohol had affected his speech and balance, Radford's mind had cleared enough that he knew what he was doing. He was ending his attraction to Evelyn once and for all by proving to himself that kissing her was no more thrilling or special than kissing any other woman.

But to his shock, the kiss fanned his craving to a blaze of hot need that he couldn't restrain. Whether it was the alcohol or his intense reaction to Evelyn, he felt himself spiraling out of control. He shuddered when he slipped his hand beneath her nightrail and felt the satiny skin of her thigh. Her moan inflamed him as she lay across his heated body, and her skin was so warm and smooth that he craved the feel of her unencumbered by clothes. The thought of her against him, beneath him, made his blood rush. Just one more touch. He would send her away then.

He reached for the shoulder of her gown, but Evelyn's fingers curled over his. Radford hesitated, thinking she was stopping him, but she tugged the fabric off her shoulder. The sound of buttons hitting the floor was like getting a glass of cold water tossed in his face. Radford tried to pull back, to stop himself from going any further, but Evelyn's exposed breasts fed his need. Perfect, pink-nippled breasts mesmerized him, drew him, compelled him to lower his mouth even when his conscience was begging him not to.

⟞⟨⊹ ⊹⟩⟝

The feeling of Radford's palm between her thighs jolted Evelyn back to reality. She grabbed his hand and broke their kiss, but his passion-glazed eyes told her she'd encouraged him too far. "We can't do this, Radford. It's wrong. What we're doing is wrong," she said, fearing she wouldn't get through to his alcohol-muddled brain.

He hovered above her, breathing raggedly, his gaze fierce, before he finally closed his eyes and leaned his head back against the chair.

She straightened her gown and cursed herself. She must be insane! How could she have done this, especially with Radford, a man who carried a full-blown war inside him, who would probably never feel settled, who was the brother of the man she'd promised to marry.

Drowning in shame, Evelyn pushed herself to a sitting position, her palm resting on Radford's chest for support. Though his heart pounded, the steady rise and fall beneath her hand told her he'd passed out. She felt more awake than she'd ever been in her life.

"Radford?" she called quietly. He didn't respond. She lifted her gaze to his handsome, sleeping face, knowing she'd taken advantage of his condition to appease her curiosity. "I'm sorry," she whispered. "You didn't deserve this."

Neither did Kyle. He'd always treated her with respect and was the only person she'd ever been able to depend on. How could she have been such a slave to her curiosity that she would betray her lifelong friend?

She slipped from Radford's arms, anxious to run from the truth of what she'd done. Her hair caught and she turned to tug it free. The sight of Radford's fist closed around a mass of her black curls sent a rush of sympathy straight to her heart.

She knelt before him and unwound her hair then brushed her lips across his knuckles. "I should never have kissed you," she whispered with deep remorse. Because now she knew there was an ocean of difference between kissing Kyle and kissing Radford.

Chapter Eleven

The instant Radford saw daylight, he slammed his eyes shut and pressed his fists to his temples. Slowly, he sat forward, shaking, sweating, reeling; pierced by the hurtful morning light, the crashing headache, the rebelling stomach.

Fragments of the past evening flashed through his mind. He saw the bottom of a glass, over and over, his brothers laughing and ordering drinks, heard a woman's voice pleading... Then he remembered.

He'd betrayed Kyle.

Convulsed with nausea, Radford hunched over, elbows to knees, face in hands, peering blearily through his splayed fingers as he fought back the urge to vomit. A small, pearlescent type object glowed up at him from beside the chair leg, but he was forced to wait until his stomach settled before reaching down to pick it up. It was a button from Evelyn's gown.

He'd only wanted to kiss her then put it behind him. Instead he'd nearly made love to her on the porch.

If only he hadn't started that idiotic playacting. After all the alcohol he'd consumed last night, he'd been in no condition to think rationally. The alcohol had removed the filter between his brain and his mouth and he'd said things to Evelyn that should never have left his lips. Radford pinched the bridge of his nose. He'd talked about her eyes, and said he loved her hair. What a fool. The instant Evelyn stepped onto the porch, he should have gone to the livery instead of acting like an inebriated ass.

He should have never let Kyle talk him into getting corned to his eyebrows.

At least Radford had had the sense to let Evelyn think he'd passed out last night. Though she'd been a willing participant in the beginning, she was mortified by her actions and shocked by his. The only compassionate way he could now handle the incident would be to let Evelyn think he didn't remember it.

Radford tucked the button into his pocket and scooted to the edge of the chair. With a hard push, he reached a standing position out of dire necessity and sheer determination. Though his legs were uncooperative, they were functional enough to carry him to the outhouse, which seemed an ungodly distance away. A long, long time later, he entered the livery where Evelyn was forking hay to Gus. "If there is a gun out here, please shoot me."

Evelyn started at the sound of Radford's voice, dreading the accusation she knew she'd see in his eyes. When she dared to turn around, Radford gave her a wobbly smile and braced himself against a stall while guarding his stomach with his free hand.

"I'd wager your brothers are in the same condition," she commented, not knowing how to begin to apologize for her unforgivable behavior.

Radford sagged against the stall. "I hope so."

He was so pathetic it deepened her shame. By his condition this morning, Radford had definitely been too inebriated last night to know what he'd been doing. Evelyn was to blame. "I'm sorry about last night," she said, having no idea how else to begin to apologize, but knowing she must. "I accept the blame for everything." And she did. Never had she thought to have such an encounter with him. Or any man for that matter. She hadn't even allowed Kyle such liberties. The fact that Radford had touched her breast and thighs made her blush to her undergarments. At least Radford had the excuse of being intoxicated. She had none, other than her blasted maidenly curiosity.

Radford's expression changed from pained to confused. "I don't know what you're talking about, and frankly, I feel too wretched to care about anything. You could shoot me and I wouldn't hold it against you."

He was serious! Evelyn could see it in his eyes. He really didn't remember. Joy filled her. Radford wouldn't be plagued with guilt and, well, she would just have to find a way to live with her shame. After all, it would never, ever happen again. If he didn't remember then she was certainly not going to divulge their sinful interlude and put the weight of guilt on his shoulders.

"I was apologizing for leaving you on the porch all night," she said, scrambling for any excuse suitable to an apology. "I should have helped you to bed."

"Well, you might have to help me now." He leaned his head against a post. "I think I need to sit down."

Evelyn put the hay fork aside and went to him. When she would have taken his arm, Radford lifted his hand and brushed his knuckles across her cheek. "I was kidding, Evelyn, but thank you just the same. I'll be back in a few minutes." He turned and slogged out of the livery, boot heels dragging.

The instant he was gone, Evelyn rushed to Gus and stroked his forelock. Radford had no idea what his casual touches did to her, especially after that amazing kiss. Amidst profuse blushing, a slow smile started in the corners of Evelyn's mouth and blossomed to fullness. Despite the awful thing she had allowed to happen, she suddenly realized that Radford had done her an enormous favor.

He had taught her how to kiss.

Now that she knew how, she would be able to do it the right way with Kyle and perhaps they would find their missing bond. What a wonderful, uplifting thought! If she could please Kyle, maybe he would become a little less driven and a little more romantic. If they could kiss with that passion, surely they would be intimate enough to share their feelings like they used to do. Then she was certain they would fall in love.

Her burden lifting, Evelyn giggled and kissed the stallion on the nose. He snorted and shifted back in his stall. "You wait, Gus. I'm going to surprise that fiancé of mine, just see if I don't."

Later that morning, Evelyn entered the stuffy church and followed Kyle and Radford down the aisle. They were going to bring Helen home to play with Rebecca after church.

Everything was quiet except for an occasional cough and the rustle of dresses and books opening as Pastor Ainslie began service. Evelyn sat on the overcrowded bench, her shoulders wedged between Kyle's and Radford's. Their lolling legs were hard and warm as they pressed against hers, but Evelyn kept her face averted, unable to look at either man without feeling guilty. Drawing her knees and elbows toward her body, she tried to avoid their touch, but to her dismay, both men adjusted themselves more comfortably against her.

Being enveloped in the warmth of wide, solid shoulders, hard legs, and the scent of aftershave set her pulse racing.

Suddenly, both Radford and Kyle clasped her hands. Evelyn jumped then ducked her head as she struggled to remember the words to the first prayer her mother ever taught her. Kyle's wide, rough, lumberman's hand contrasted with Radford's callused palm and long fingers. Evelyn knew she'd feel those hands linked with hers for the rest of the day, but it was the urge to curl her fingers around Radford's hand that made her face burn with shame.

The instant the service ended, she rushed from the church and bumped into Amelia Drake.

"Did you find the sermon that bad?" Amelia asked.

Evelyn pressed a hand to her chest and whispered to her friend. "I had to get out of there. I couldn't breathe."

Amelia's eyes twinkled. "Pastor Ainslie does go on, doesn't he?"

Evelyn laughed and nodded her agreement, keeping one eye on her father while he approached with a limping gait.

He stopped beside them, hooked his arm around Evelyn's waist, and winked at Amelia. "You two are lovely this morning."

Knowing she looked frazzled, Evelyn glanced at Amelia's warm smile and prim but attractive dress, and agreed with her father. Amelia always looked lovely. Suddenly, Evelyn felt as if she had returned to her school days when she used to hide in her baggy dresses like a turtle in its shell, shying away from attention, watching how the boys responded to Amelia's beauty.

"I didn't see your pa this morning," Kyle said to Amelia as he and Radford joined their group. "Is he out of town again?"

"He's right over there with Mama and Agatha Brown." Amelia gestured across the yard to where Tom Drake stood talking in the middle of a small cluster of people. "He'd love to see all of you," she said, issuing a warm invitation for them to join her family.

"Thanks, Amelia, but I have to go to the mill with Duke. Give your pa my regards, though," Kyle said then turned to Evelyn. "I've got to go. I'll see you at supper."

Radford caught Evelyn's eye. "It looks like Tom and Martha are leaving, too. We'd better go get Helen."

William offered Amelia his arm. "That means I get you all to myself for a few minutes."

"We'll try to come rescue you before Papa proposes," Evelyn said, sharing a smile with Amelia before she turned and crossed the yard with Radford and Rebecca.

Throughout the morning, Evelyn watched the girls while she cut vegetables for stew. Rebecca studied Helen with a mixture of curiosity and wonder, but she didn't shy away.

Knowing the girls wouldn't take time for more than a bite of lunch, Evelyn sliced bread and spread it with jam, but before she could set their plates on the table, Rebecca followed Helen outside. Curious, Evelyn moved to the window and saw them spread Rebecca's blanket in the backyard. It was obviously Helen's suggestion by the way Rebecca kept to her small corner, but it gave Evelyn an idea.

She placed their bread and two small glasses of milk on a tray and carried it out to them. "How about a picnic today?" She bent over and set the tray between them.

Evelyn would have left them alone then, but she saw Rebecca move so far back that only her knees remained on the blanket. That small, voiceless gesture changed her mind.

Evelyn knelt on one corner. "Mind if I have a taste?"

Helen picked up a slice of the strawberry-covered bread. She tore a piece and handed it to Evelyn then did the same for Rebecca. Helen gobbled the rest of her bread in one bite, looking like a little frog while she chomped away. When she finished, she stuck sticky fingers in her mouth and sucked them, flopping her head from side to side. Her braids flew wildly around her head and made Rebecca giggle. "It's good!"

Rebecca smiled then dropped her chin and rounded her shoulders as if to draw away from the attention.

Evelyn reached over with two fingers and tickled Rebecca's side. "What's a matter. Don't you like my jam?"

Rebecca squeaked and squirmed away.

"I do," Helen piped in with her mouth full.

"I can see that." Evelyn swiped a blob of jam off Helen's cheek. "You're a mess, Missy Fisk."

The silly name made Rebecca giggle and she clapped her hands over her mouth, completely forgetting the jellied bread she held. The entire hunk stuck to her lips and nose, sending Helen into peals of laughter. After the initial surprise Rebecca began to giggle. Suddenly, it seemed she couldn't contain the laughter that burbled from her throat. To Evelyn's surprise, Rebecca mimicked Helen, flopping her head and sending a riot of curls springing wildly around her shoulders.

And that is how Radford found them. A beautiful young woman sharing a torn blanket with two silly, noisy little girls on a warm Sunday afternoon. His own daughter was almost unrecognizable in her unreserved playfulness. Evelyn with her long hair shining in the sun, her laughter floating joyfully across the lawn, wiped the jam off Rebecca's smiling face.

This is how it should be, he thought. Sunday picnics in the backyard, his daughter playing with other children, himself eagerly awaiting the evening when he could relax with people he cared about instead of bunking with grumbling coworkers.

"We're having a picnic," Rebecca yelled when she spotted him. She ran across the yard and grabbed his hand, dragging him toward the blanket while he followed along in astonishment.

Rebecca never ran!

They reached the others and she pulled on his hand, begging him to sit. Radford dutifully knelt on the blanket, his arm resting on his bent knee. His gaze collided with Evelyn's pleasure-filled eyes. She was amazing. She had given Rebecca something that he thought forever impossible.

Though his stomach was still averse to the thought of food, Rebecca was already handing him a sorry-looking slice of bread that he didn't have the heart to refuse. He captured her hand. "Maybe I'll have a nibble." He dipped his head and nipped the tip of her finger. Her eyes widened and she squeaked, yanking her hand to her belly. Radford laughed at her reaction. "Do you think I'm a monster who's going to gobble you up?"

"Are you a monster?" Helen asked in awe.

He fought back a laugh and made his scariest monster face. "Maybe I am," he said in a horribly scratchy voice.

Helen screamed and scrambled from the blanket. Rebecca giggled and raced after her friend. They hid behind the nearest tree, taking turns peeking around the trunk, Rebecca's laughing face appearing every few seconds.

Radford stared after her, realizing he was seeing the real essence of his daughter for the first time. Rebecca was not the fragile child he'd believed her to be. She was a curious, healthy little girl. Evelyn had seen that from the beginning.

Something in the way Evelyn sat there, her face bathed in sunshine, so charming in her laughter, so naturally generous, made him achingly aware of her as a woman. One glance at her slender body clothed in a blue cotton dress reminded him of where he'd had his hands last night and he wished she would change back into her baggy britches. He was infinitely more comfortable with the Evelyn who shoveled stalls and ended up as dirty as he at day's end.

Getting to his feet, he watched the girls wander off toward the swing and decided it would be a good idea to see if Kyle wanted to work on his house. "I guess monsters aren't welcome at picnics. Sorry if I ruined it."

A soft smile crept across her lips and the green in her eyes seemed to darken. "You didn't, Radford," she said quietly. "The girls loved your teasing, and I like having you around."

An indescribable warmth radiated from her. He saw it in the way she treated Rebecca and tended her horses, and in her eyes when she smiled, her voice when she laughed. It drew him like cold hands are drawn to a warm fire.

She shook the crumbs from Rebecca's blanket then stood and gathered everything in her arms. "I need to check my stew."

Radford watched her walk to the house, back straight, striding confidently, no excessive swaying of her skirts. She was as individual in her walk as she was in her manner. No posturing, no overt displays of womanly charms, no aversion to dirt and hard work. There was nothing fancy about her, yet she was utterly attractive. And Radford wished she wasn't promised to his brother.

Chapter Twelve

Evelyn rushed through dinner then pulled a chair beside the sink so Rebecca could rinse the dishes. It would slow her down, but she didn't have the heart to ignore Rebecca's hope-filled eyes. It was as if Rebecca saw each little chore that Evelyn let her help with as a special privilege.

But Evelyn wanted to get Kyle outside so she could kiss him! She'd been building her courage for two days and was finally ready to test her kissing skills. Excitement mixed with apprehension when she looked at Kyle, but he was oblivious to her nerves as he talked with her father.

"Look at you, sprite," Radford said, joining Evelyn and Rebecca at the sink. "Your belly's all wet. You look like you've been swimming in that tub instead of rinsing dishes." He leaned over her and swished his hand through the water. "Any fish in here?"

Rebecca laughed and grabbed his arm. He shook it around as though he'd caught one. "Look out. Here he comes!" He raised his hand and flicked his fingers at her, sprinkling her cheeks with fat droplets of water that made her squeal. He put a hand to her back to steady her. "Careful. You'll fall on your head."

Evelyn couldn't help but watch. Their horseplay reminded her of times with her own father and she looked to the table where he sat wearing a contented smile on his face. Her gaze drifted to Kyle and her breath caught. His eyes held such a wistful, pained look, Evelyn would have given her new stallion to know what he was thinking.

When Radford picked up the dishtowel and dried a bowl, Evelyn gaped in surprise. "What are you doing?"

"Helping. It's been a long day for all of us."

It had, but never would she expect his help in the kitchen and it shocked her that he would do it in front of Kyle and her father. She glanced at them, but they seemed amused and not about to comment. Radford dried and Rebecca babbled, splashing in the water and piling plates right side up so Radford had to dump the water off before he could towel them dry.

"Hey, sprite, where'd you hide all the forks?" Radford asked. He went to the table and peeked beneath it as if he'd find them there.

Rebecca laughed and pointed to the stove. "Over there."

He went to the stove and checked in the oven. "Can't see any forks in here."

"Right there," she said, again pointing at the stove, but Radford pointed toward the door and widened his eyes in mock horror.

"Don't tell me you took them out to the horses!"

Rebecca burst into a fit of giggles and teetered on the chair. Evelyn grabbed her as Radford shot across the kitchen. He scooped Rebecca into his arms and trapped Evelyn's hand between Rebecca and his chest. The unexpected contact jolted Evelyn and their gazes collided.

"Good catch," he said, his smile fading.

The fierce pounding of his chest warned her to pull her arm free and she stepped away from him.

Kyle shoved his chair back from the table and stood. "I've got to get over to the house. You coming, Radford?"

"Of course," he said, setting Rebecca on her feet.

"Good, because I'd like to hear if you have a plan to increase the livery business."

Evelyn caught Radford's startled expression before he followed Kyle outside. Of course Radford had a plan. Where did Kyle think their new business was coming from?

Annoyed by Kyle's arrogance and his need to rush off before she could test her new kissing abilities, Evelyn finished the dishes in an agitated state of mind. Afterward, she tried to help her father to the porch, but he argued and fussed at her until she let him manage it himself. He'd even snapped at her before dinner, claiming he could make his own way to the table. With a sigh of resignation, Evelyn sat on the porch with him, letting her eyes drift closed while her father spent the evening spinning silly tales that made Rebecca giggle.

As night settled in, Evelyn's disappointment mounted. Despite the late hour, she still hoped Kyle would stop on his way home, but she waited on the porch long after her father and Rebecca were in bed, and he still didn't come. Depressed, she sat in the dark wondering if this is what marriage to Kyle would be like, the constant waiting, the nagging feeling that they were missing something important between them, the worry that a freely given promise might grow into a sentence of imprisonment and regret.

She was so lost in thought and alone in her solitude, that the sudden flaring of a match startled her. Radford's eyes glowed momentarily in the firelight as he touched the flame to the end of his cigar. He took the chair opposite her, but minutes passed in silence while they listened to crickets and drifted in the mellow-sweet aroma of his cheroot. The breeze moved a strand of hair against her neck and she brushed it away.

He started to say something then stopped and blew out a breath.

"What?" she asked.

He shook his head as if it was nothing important.

"You were going to say something."

He took the cheroot out of his mouth and stared at the tip until it turned dark then he met her eyes. "You need to stop coddling your father."

"What?" she asked, dumbfounded.

"He's used to being in control of himself and it hurts his pride when you won't let him manage on his own. Trust me, when a man loses his physical strength, he feels he's lost everything."

"I'm just trying to keep Papa healthy."

"I know, but try not to help when you feel the urge. Remember the suggestions you made about Rebecca needing to laugh, to have a friend? Well, I wanted to think I knew what was best for her, but you were right. She's much happier now because of you. I've learned how to make her laugh by your example. You could see her needs more clearly than I. I know very little about girls, but I know what pride means to a man like your father. Let him make his own way to the table if he can. If he wants to help me in the livery then let him decide what he can handle."

"All right, Radford, but under one condition," Evelyn said. "You have to stay out of my kitchen."

"What?"

"Stay out of my kitchen." There was absolutely no way she could remain unaffected by Radford if he continued to touch her. Not after the wild kiss they had shared.

"Why?"

"Because you might confuse Rebecca," Evelyn said, giving Radford the first answer that popped into her head. She knew it was a terrible answer. If anyone was going to confuse Rebecca about the duties of womanhood, it would be Evelyn and her men's clothing.

"If it's that important to you, I won't touch another dishtowel." He leaned back in his chair and crossed an ankle over his knee. The tip of his cigar glowed then dimmed before he spoke again. "So do you have any suggestions to increase our livery business?"

"We could sell Gus if we need money."

"We don't," he said. "I've recorded all my entries in your journal. It's there for Kyle to see anytime he wants to look."

"Kyle can be crass sometimes, but I'm sure he meant well."

"How well do you know him these days?"

The question spurred Evelyn to her feet and she leaned against the corner post, thinking of their lost connection.

"He confuses me," Radford said, apparently taking her silence as a refusal to answer. "One minute I see a familiar glimpse of my kid brother then a second later, I don't even recognize him."

"Kyle's had a lot of responsibility since your dad died. I think he's just too preoccupied to be himself."

"Then why—"

His unfinished sentence hung silently between them and echoed in Evelyn's heart. Why... Why... Why was she going to marry a man who couldn't seem to share himself with her? Because Evelyn had given her word, and she wouldn't let a vague sense of unfulfillment ruin a lifelong relationship she deeply valued. Kyle would never break his promise. Neither would she.

"I didn't mean to pry," Radford said.

"I'll answer you, if you'll answer a question for me."

His expression grew guarded, but he nodded.

"Why did you keep leaving home when you knew you belonged here with your family?"

A heavy sigh escaped Radford and he looked past her into the darkness. "I was restless."

"Because of your nightmares?"

His glance flicked back to her. "Partially."

"They're about the war, aren't they?"

He didn't answer.

"My father told me war is something a man doesn't want to talk about. He said he tries to remember the good times. Do you have any good memories?"

"I suppose, although they escape me at the moment."

"Well, maybe it would help to think about the good times when you feel restless. I'd like you to stay this time."

Momentary surprise flashed in his eyes then softened to wonder as he stared at her. "Why?"

Evelyn bit her lip and looked away as a hot flush stole up her neck. Even if she dared to elaborate, she couldn't find the right words to describe the wild, thrilling emotions Radford evoked in her, or how good it felt to share her days with him. Knowing she needed to answer, Evelyn forced herself to look at him without letting her gaze dance away from his. "You make me feel less alone in the livery, and you make me laugh. You're a good partner," she said, trying to make light of her blunder. "But you were asking about Kyle, weren't you? I'm marrying your brother because I can depend on him, and because he's my best friend."

Radford arched a brow. "And?"

"That's it."

"Well, that's not—" Radford clipped his words off, met her eyes, and shook his head. "Forget it."

"What?"

"Nothing. Just be happy."

Despite her own misgivings about her relationship with Kyle, it pleased Evelyn that Radford would wish her well. She could tell he meant it by the sincerity of his voice, as though they were friends who wanted the best for each other. That's when Evelyn realized that they had somehow become friends. And they were talking. They were sharing ideas and opinions and personal feelings. It was what she used to do with Kyle. That she was sharing this with Radford on a warm September night flayed her conscience. The darkness offered too much privacy for her to be alone with a man who made her long for private evenings and intimate conversations.

She pushed away from the railing and crossed the porch in front of Radford, but he caught her sleeve. "Where are you going?"

"To bed. It's late."

He pulled a watch from his pocket, angled it toward the moonlight then looked up in surprise. "It's after midnight already. It feels like we just came outside." He smiled. "My nights have a tendency to drag. Thanks for the company."

Evelyn's heartbeat accelerated as she walked away. "Sleep well, Radford." One of us should.

Radford knew he wouldn't sleep with all the clamoring in his head. He'd wanted to talk to her about the kiss. After thinking it through, he knew he couldn't let Evelyn go on thinking it was her fault. She deserved the truth and an apology. He'd planned to confess, to admit that he'd known what he was doing that night, but the minute he looked at Evelyn brushed with shadows and moon-dust, he couldn't mention the kiss without wanting to repeat it. So he'd talked about William and asked about Kyle and caught glimpses of things he didn't want to know.

Why did Evelyn say she wanted him to stay? Was it their growing friendship? Was it because she was so attached to his daughter? Radford dragged a palm down his face and leaned against the wall of the house. Why hadn't she said she loved Kyle?

Chapter Thirteen

E velyn flexed her stiff hands as she pulled out of the livery, glad that Duke would take care of their customers for a few hours. To her delight, and Radford's shock, Rebecca had agreed to play at Helen's house for the rest of the afternoon while Evelyn and Radford went to the creek to get stones for the fence her mother had taken such pride in.

They cut across the deep field of goldenrod and tall grass then descended a narrow path that wound down into the gorge. Beauty embraced them on all sides. The sound of splattering waterfalls drew them onward until a flat sheet of water broke over a shale ledge and fell several feet into a pool.

"It's been a lifetime since I've seen a place like this," Radford said as she halted the wagon. Evelyn jumped onto the rocky earth and Radford followed. "Listen to that."

Birds twittered, water splashed, and Evelyn's heart pulsed in her ears, but she couldn't hear anything unusual. "I don't hear anything."

"That's what I mean. Peace has its own sound. If you listen closely, you can hear a rhythm in the silence."

"It sounds like home to me."

Radford closed his eyes and breathed deeply, seeming to savor the air. "Sometimes when the guns were silent I would listen to the wind rustle the grass and make the tree limbs creak. I preferred the burbling sound of the creeks, though. The plunk of a stone tumbling downstream didn't sound so lonely." He opened his eyes and met Evelyn's. "We ruined so many places like this. Twenty thousand pairs of boots could trample a field of grass and bury it in the stench of death in five minutes. Destroying the fields was as bad as killing the men."

This was the most open about his past Radford had been since coming home. Evelyn prayed that he was beginning to heal, that he would someday be able to share his grief with his brothers and move on with his life. She could see shadows of his past etched in his eyes, but knew he shouldn't be confiding in her. "Did you know I used to hide here?" she asked, trying to draw him away from his memories. The day was too beautiful, held too much promise to let his past cast a shadow.

He turned to her. "From what?"

"You and your brothers." She propped her fists on her hips. "Hiding here saved me several bruises, if I remember correctly."

"I never threatened you. From what I recall you stayed clear of me because you didn't like me."

She arched an eyebrow. "You were too old to be bothered with a tagalong, knob-kneed girl, remember?"

A slow smile tipped his lips and Evelyn knew she'd succeeded in pulling him back to the present. "Then I'm disappointed I avoided you. I think I like having a knob-kneed girl for a friend."

The sweetness of his comment warmed her heart, but Evelyn dutifully pushed it away. She would find that sweetness with Kyle. Tonight. Kyle was leaving for Buffalo with Duke tomorrow and he'd be gone for three days. She wanted to show Kyle that she could kiss before he left. If she had to track him down and sit on him to keep him stationary, she was getting her kiss this evening.

"Come on, Radford. We need to load the wagon."

With a grimace, Radford went to the edge of the creek and stacked several flat stones on top of each other then carried them to the wagon and dumped them in with a crash. "So much for peace," he said, returning for another armload.

They spent an hour gathering stones from various areas of the creek bed. After several trips they were both sweating. Evelyn eyed the water like a landed fish. If Radford hadn't been there, she'd be smack in the middle of the deep, sparkling pool. She dropped the last stone into the wagon and leaned against it. Her braid had fallen out long ago and her hair hung in a disheveled mess, its weight hot and unbearable.

"Tell me we're finished," she said with a groan.

"That depends on how high you want the stone fence."

"I don't care," she panted, "I don't need a fence."

Radford laughed, his teeth and face shining in the sun. "I seem to recall that someone wanted to repair the fence in front of the house so she could get her pretty morning glory vines off the ground."

"You've obviously misunderstood. I wanted the fence fixed, but I never said anything about helping."

"Is that so? Well, we're in this together, remember?"

Of course she remembered. He promised they'd work together and he was keeping his promise. Blast him!

She sighed with great exaggeration. "You are one cruel man, Radford."

An instant later Evelyn's screech filled the small glade and startled the birds into flight. Radford had scooped her up and held her suspended over the water, one arm supporting her shoulders, the other beneath her knees.

"Take it back," he said, grinning down at her.

She smiled, unable to resist the devilment in his eyes. "Can't. It's true."

"Take it back, knob-knees, or I'll show you how mean I really am."

"You wouldn't dare," she said with a laugh.

His smile widened and he lowered his head until they were nose to nose. "I would dare anything if it suited me."

He smelled of cigar and hay and hardworking man, but Evelyn didn't have time to appreciate the thrill racing through her body because she was suddenly airborne. She hit the water with arms flailing then came up sputtering in a tangle of sopping hair.

"You... you big... ouch!" Her foot slipped from beneath her and she went under. When she surfaced again Radford's smile had disappeared.

"Are you all right?"

He looked prepared to jump in to rescue her and Evelyn immediately saw her revenge. Ever so ladylike, she raised her hand to her forehead and whispered, "I... I think so." Just before she swooned.

She felt the thrust of the water as Radford landed beside her. Then two strong hands pulled her to the surface. His hair was streaming, water dripped off his nose, and his eyelashes were thick, black spikes. He was beautiful. Too beautiful, she decided. Slowly, she raised her hand and smacked him across the cheek with a gray blob of clay that she'd purposely gouged from the bottom of the pool.

His head jerked slightly with the impact of the mud, his eyes registering surprise, but Evelyn knew she hadn't hurt him. She hadn't intended to hurt him. She just wanted to play on even terms.

Odd how quickly a person's intentions could change, Evelyn thought, as Radford pulled her toward him. He didn't say a word, just stared at her with clay running down his cheek and dripping off his chin in clumps. He slipped his arms around her and drew her against him. She braced her hands on his chest as her body met his and she instantly regretted the action. His muscles flexed under her palms and his heart pounded beneath his wet shirt. The length of his body brushed against Evelyn's and sent a wild thrill crashing through her.

When he closed his eyes and lowered his mouth, Evelyn thought she'd faint. He was going to kiss her again. And God help her, she wanted him to.

Her eyes fluttered closed and she waited a long, breathless moment before she felt his cool, muddy cheek brush across hers. Her eyes flew open and she saw his wicked grin. The realization that Radford hadn't intended to kiss her sent a jolt of heat to her cheeks and she shrieked in embarrassment. She tried to struggle from his grip, but he clamped his arms around her.

Laughter burst from him in a melody of sound. Hearty, playful, and forgiving laughter that sent her off in another fit of thrashing. "Settle down. It's only clay."

She tried to give him a well-deserved kick in the shins, but the water slowed her thrust and she did little damage. "That was cruel, Radford."

He laughed and released her.

Evelyn struggled with the prospect of giving him just one good shove, but common sense won out and she cupped a handful of water to wash her face.

"You might want to let that dry first. It's supposed to be good for the complexion."

She fought the grin that threatened. Where had this sense of humor come from? She arched a brow at Radford. "Then I'd suggest you gather what you can carry for your own use."

Radford's laughter filled the glade and sent birds swooping. Grasping at sanity, Evelyn waded toward shore and away from temptation, not looking back as she climbed onto the wagon. Her wet bottom smacked the seat and she sat there dripping all over herself, trying to ignore his hoots of laughter. But there was no ignoring this man.

<hr />

Radford stayed in the cooling waters, unable to shake the feel of Evelyn in his arms. Her wet clothes had clung to her body, emphasizing the curves they usually hid, curves that had felt too good. A vision swept through his mind and Radford wrestled his hand into his pocket, closing his fingers around the pearl button he'd kept there since his drinking binge. No matter how hard he tried, he'd never forget how gorgeous Evelyn had looked that night lying in his lap, dazed and breathless.

He'd promised himself he'd never touch her again. It had been an honest, natural reaction to her teasing that made him sweep her into his arms with playful intentions, but looking into her sparkling eyes had fired his blood so quickly, he'd thrown her into the water to save himself. She shouldn't have tricked him into diving in to rescue her.

During that one reckless moment Radford had lost his mind and forgotten where they were, who they were, why he couldn't have her. For those few seconds he'd seen the woman who rescued his daughter, who was reaching inside him to a place no one had ever touched.

What was happening to him? He dove beneath the surface and stroked toward the cooler depths, trying to swim away from the truth. Fanning his arms, he kept himself near the bottom, his mind grappling for answers that wouldn't materialize. As his chest began to tighten with the need for oxygen, his body slowly calmed. Maybe he just needed sex. Maybe he needed to release the tension that had been building for the last five years of abstinence. No wonder his thinking was crazy. What man wouldn't be insane with lust by now?

That was it. His body was controlling his mind. All he needed to do was find an outlet for his male needs.

Radford burst from the surface in a shower of spray and a gusty release of breath. Sex was definitely the answer. Even if it didn't kill his attraction to Evelyn, it would ease the tension in his body and dull his senses.

"Do you need help?" Evelyn called from where she was poised at the edge of the pool, her frantic expression telling Radford she was ready to dive in after him.

"No!" Radford blinked the water from his eyes and put up a hand to stop her from jumping in. The last thing he needed was to have her sweet body against him again. He'd sooner drown than feel her in his arms and have to push her away. Drowning would be more merciful.

Chapter Fourteen

Though it was late when Kyle came to see her, Evelyn dragged him right back outside and into the yard. She could tell he was tired by his dark eyes and strained expression so she didn't ask him to walk in the orchard with her, though she thought it would be a more romantic setting for their passionate kiss. Instead, they stood in the middle of the yard beside his horse while his pocket watch ticked away the last ten minutes he was willing to linger before going home to bed.

Evelyn placed her hand on Kyle's warm chest and sidled close. Should she just grab him and kiss him? Or was it better to work up to it?

"What are you doing, Ev?"

Her cheeks warmed, but she didn't draw back despite her natural inclination to do so. "Why are you irritable tonight, Kyle? Is something wrong at the house?"

"Not at all. Boyd and Radford finished the walls tonight so we're ahead of schedule."

"Are you behind at the mill then? Is that why Radford has been spending so much time with you this past week?"

Kyle didn't move away, but he hooked his hand over the pommel of his saddle. "I couldn't tell you. Has it been slow in the livery?"

"We've been swamped. Radford just pushes hard to get through the chores then makes sure I'll keep Rebecca before he heads to the mill. I thought you needed the help."

Kyle didn't comment, which was fine with Evelyn. She didn't want to talk about the house or the mill or the man who had her emotions in a coil. She wanted her kiss. Now.

She smiled up at her handsome fiancé, enjoying the surprise she saw in his eyes. Maybe she needed to act bolder with him, to make him realize she was more than the girl he grew up with. "What do you say we forget about work and try one of those monkey kisses tonight?"

Kyle studied her as though she'd asked a trick question he didn't know how to answer.

"Are you afraid I'll take advantage of you?"

Kyle grinned. "I'm all yours."

"Good." She eagerly raised her mouth to his as he pulled her against him. She slipped her fingers into his hair and sank into the kiss, letting herself melt into him like she had with Radford. He was warm and comfortable, hard muscled and smelled of fresh pine, but it didn't stir her senses like the fragrant smell of hay and fresh air—or sweet cigar.

She squeezed her eyes closed, trying to block thoughts of Radford as she snuggled into Kyle. She stroked his broad shoulders, her fingers searching for hair tangled in his collar, but finding it straight and short. Irritated with her inability to stop comparing him to Radford, she broke the kiss and stared into Kyle's eyes, desperate to find a connection with the man she was going to spend the rest of her life with.

Kyle bracketed her face between his palms and kissed her again with mounting urgency then pulled her body against his. Evelyn tilted her head back and exposed her neck to his searching mouth. Now she would feel it! Now her mind would soar and her body would tighten with tension until she thought she'd die if Kyle stopped touching her.

Nothing moved or lifted within her.

Oh, please. Anything at all.

She tried kissing Kyle again, nearly clawing her way up his chest, but the result was the same. The explosion of feeling she'd experienced in Radford's arms remained absent.

Disheartened, she lowered her head to Kyle's shoulder and curled her fingers into a fist. What had Radford done to her? Why couldn't she feel the same wicked thrill in Kyle's arms?

Kyle's hands shook as he set her away from him. "If you don't wish an early visit to our marital bed, you'd better not do that again. I'm tired, but I'm not dead."

Her palm rested on Kyle's racing heart and Evelyn knew she owed him more than an apology. "I just... I wanted to... kiss you," she said on a deflating sigh, knowing it wasn't the whole truth. She wanted to compare Kyle's kiss to Radford's, to experience that rush of passion that had washed over her in Radford's arms. She'd wanted to shake Kyle out of his rigid business demeanor and show him the woman he was going to marry.

But she'd only shown herself a heartbreaking lack in their relationship.

⊷⊶

As soon as Kyle left, Evelyn hurried upstairs to the balcony off her bedroom. She hid in the shadows with her back pressed against the wall, wondering if there was still a chance she could strike a vein of passion in her relationship with Kyle.

An easy breeze fluttered across her cheeks. She leaned her head back and closed her eyes. Maybe if she kept trying she'd grow accustomed to Kyle's kiss and the feel of his wide shoulders—and forget the feel of Radford's mouth. Maybe she needed to touch Kyle more slowly, take time to build a fire between them.

The scent of cigar wafted past, and her eyes snapped open. She glanced toward Radford's bedroom door. It was open and he was sitting on the balcony. She could see the smoldering orange tip of Radford's cheroot and his booted feet resting on the railing.

Never had she felt more forlorn and vulnerable than she did at this moment, but she pressed her shoulders to the wooden slats and willed herself to stay away from him. The urge to run to him and assure herself that those glorious feelings truly existed, that she was capable of responding passionately to a man, was painfully strong.

But Radford was sober tonight.

Suddenly, she wondered how long he had been sitting on the balcony. Her gaze swung to the driveway below where moments before she had made a fool of herself with Kyle. Knowing Radford had witnessed her pathetic behavior sent a flood of burning heat through her. Mortified, she whirled toward the door of her bedroom.

"Evelyn?"

She halted with her hand on the door handle.

"What do you suppose attracts people to each other?" he asked lazily, as if the answer was no more important than whether Evelyn thought it might rain tomorrow.

It was laughable that he would even ask her such a question. Evelyn would have given in to the urge had she not felt so embarrassed and disheartened.

"I think it's deeper than physical attraction, don't you?"

She didn't answer.

"It's the resonance of a laugh that can belong to only one person, the emotion they show when they touch something, the things a person says with their body and eyes. That's what I think attraction is made of."

"I wouldn't know, Radford," she said, just wanting to hide in her bedroom.

"Of course you do. What draws you to Kyle?"

"You want me to tell you?" she asked, in amazement, turning to face him.

"I didn't think you'd mind the question."

She did, but if she didn't answer, he would know she was embarrassed that he saw her kissing Kyle. "I admire Kyle. He's strong and dependable and has made himself into a respected businessman."

"I'm talking about wanting someone, Evelyn." Radford's feet hit the floor and his knees swung in her direction. "You know that feeling deep in your gut that nags and pushes you to do things you shouldn't do?"

Evelyn's gaze flew to his gray silhouette and her heart hammered her ribs.

"Come here, Tomboy," he said quietly. "Over here where I can see your face."

Her body reacted to the deep caress in Radford's voice and her traitorous legs moved forward, trembling with each step.

"Closer. I want to see your eyes." When she neared him, Radford stood up and faced her. "I know what happened the night I came home after drinking too much with Kyle. I should have never done that to you. No matter how much I'd had to drink, or what I felt that evening, I had no right to kiss you."

The breath left her body in such a rush that she thought she might fall. She flattened a palm against her stomach. "You remember?"

"I couldn't forget something that beautiful unless I was dead. And you were beautiful, Evelyn." He trailed the backs of his fingers across her cheek. "If things were different..."

⊷ ⊷

Expelling a sigh of resignation, he lowered his hand and went to the railing, leaning on his palms so he wasn't tempted to reach out to her.

His gaze settled on the livery where he and Evelyn had been building a future together, albeit for different purposes. Somehow it made sense to combine their intentions toward one common goal.

He turned back. "I was a cad to take advantage of you like that."

"It was my fault," she said, dropping her gaze to her clasped hands. She kept her face lowered, remaining silent in her obvious embarrassment.

Deeply regretful to be the cause of her discomfort, he stepped forward and took her hands in his. "Look at me." She raised her face and he saw the anguish in her eyes. "You did nothing wrong. I forced that situation the other night."

"No you didn't. My curiosity caused the problem. I wanted to kiss you to see if it was the same as kissing Kyle."

Radford felt his hands tremble as he battled the urge to prove to Evelyn that there was definitely a difference.

She pulled from his grasp and backed away, an expression of hopelessness marring her face. "You did something to me."

"I know what I did." Just remembering where his hands and mouth had been made Radford's blood surge and his heart pound. Oh, yes, he remembered every detail of her sweet body and it was going to kill him to keep his hands to himself.

Still, it was the deeper current of emotion that drew him to Evelyn, and for the first time in his life, Radford discovered he wanted more than a woman's body. Evelyn had resurrected a part of him that had been dead for many years. She gave his daughter happiness, and him a reason to look forward to his future rather than flounder in his past. She gave him friendship and the strength to face himself.

"I wanted to know," she said, her tormented gaze locked with his. "Now, I wish to God I didn't." She spun away and raced to her room, closing the door quietly behind her as Radford stared in confusion.

What did that mean? What did she finally know? That he was attracted to her? That he had to grip the railing and battle the beast inside himself when he saw her kissing Kyle?

Chapter Fifteen

Radford approached the partially walled-in frame of Kyle's house with mounting anxiety, hoping Kyle was alone. They needed to talk. Radford couldn't continue to battle his attraction to Evelyn while sharing the same house and working beside her each day. He needed to get away from her, to get back to the mill where he should have been all along. The livery was doing well enough now that Kyle could hire someone else to help out.

Propping his saw against the wall, Radford dropped his sack of nails beside it. Voices from the other side were raised in argument and Radford sighed in frustration. The fact that Kyle's defenses were already up didn't bode well, but Radford wasn't going to back down this time. He couldn't afford it.

Neither could Kyle.

"How can you say that, Kyle?" The anger in Boyd's voice echoed clear outside and made Radford pause, his senses alert.

"Because it's true. He's at the mill every time I turn around. Just because he's home doesn't give him the right to something we've busted our backs over."

"The fact that he's our brother gives him the right." Duke's voice sent a cold sense of dread down Radford's spine. This wasn't just another bickering match between Kyle and Boyd.

"Where was Radford when Dad died and the three of us lived at the mill just to keep it going? He was off rubbing elbows with railroad barons and bedding some ballerina chit while we were stuck here sweating blood. I can't believe you two can just forget that."

"Well, I can't believe you would forget it was his money that bought the new mill," Boyd argued.

Radford sagged against the building.

"It was Mother's money."

"That Radford sent to her every month," Boyd finished.

Radford heard the enormous sigh clear outside before Duke spoke. "Kyle, you've got to get the chip off your shoulder. Radford did what he had to do."

"So did I. We've all had problems, but we didn't run off."

"Kyle!" Boyd's booming voice bounced off the wall. "The man went through a wretched war and he's experienced things I can't even imagine surviving! Do you have any understanding in that thick head of yours how he suffered, what it did to him?"

"Did he care what we went through when he left!" Kyle shouted back. "Dad said we could depend on him, but we found out otherwise, didn't we?"

Radford stood outside alone, hearing firsthand the pain he'd caused his family by running away.

"We were here for him, but he wouldn't even talk to us."

"He couldn't, Kyle," Duke said.

"Why not?" Something hard struck the wall. "Why the hell not?"

Unwilling to let Duke and Boyd fight his battles for him, Radford stepped into the doorway. "Because I couldn't stand myself."

Three shocked men swung guilty looks in his direction. Only the drone of the wind broke the silence as they faced each other. Radford had considered taking the cowardly way out and leaving before they knew he'd overheard them, but he'd made promises to Rebecca as well as himself and he was through running.

Boyd glared at Kyle. "I ought to choke you."

It didn't surprise Radford that Duke automatically stepped between them. He had always been the peacekeeper, but Radford waved him back. "No, Duke. Let it alone." He turned to Kyle. "From what I've heard, you're the one who's upset with my being home."

Kyle's jaw stiffened and he didn't answer.

Radford ignored the silent challenge, determined to set the record straight here and now. "I'll say this as clearly as possible to all of you. I didn't come home to disrupt what you've accomplished, or to take control of the mill."

"Then why have you insisted on working with us when I told you we didn't need the help?" Kyle asked.

"Because I felt I owed you something. I didn't think a strong back and another set of hands would be a problem."

"It wouldn't if I knew your purpose for lending them."

"My purpose?" Radford gave a disbelieving laugh. "My purpose was to spend some time with my brothers. I have no other motives."

"You don't need any when you're the oldest son," Kyle said. "Dad left the business to all of us, but he made sure we knew who was in charge if you ever came home. The whole time you were gone we busted our backs so we could eat, yet it was always with the knowledge that you could just sashay in and grab the reins any time you wished. You have no idea how hard we've worked for this."

"Your efforts are obvious. I'm proud of what you've accomplished. I wish I could claim as much."

Kyle snorted. "You can. You can claim anything you want when it comes to the mill."

In that moment, Radford finally understood. He would lose Kyle if he pushed his way back in. The thought of giving up the only bond he had left with his father destroyed Radford, but there was no other choice. The mill had offered him the chance to be with his brothers and work toward a secure future. But too much time had passed to resurrect an old dream. His father was dead, and Radford wasn't willing to lose what he had left of his family.

His knees weakened and he placed a hand against a door stud to steady himself. "I can't blame a man for looking out for his own interest, Kyle. I'm sorry I caused problems between you three. I think it's best if I forfeit my share of the mill."

Boyd threw up his hands and glared at Kyle. "You are one rotten son of a bitch." His feet thundered across the floor as he approached Radford. "Whether you've been here or not, you're entitled to this business. Dad left it to the four of us. Not just Kyle."

"I don't want it," Radford said quietly, the lie wrenching his gut. He felt as if someone had just stolen his boyhood—that one time in his life when he had been truly happy.

"Kyle's an ass, but that's no reason for you to give up the mill. Duke and I were just trying to get that through his fat head before you came."

Radford stuffed his hands into his tool apron. "Kyle's right. I admire him for having the guts to speak his mind. I didn't earn my place. I foolishly thought I could make up for the times I wasn't here, but it's too late for that." Radford met the eyes of each of his brothers as he struggled to speak through an overwhelming wave of regret. "I'm sorry for that," he said hoarsely.

Kyle folded his arms across his chest. "We've worked hard for that mill, Radford. Now that we're finally able to breathe without a noose around our necks, I want to protect our interest."

"I'd feel the same way in your place."

"You would," Kyle said with certainty. "But Boyd has a valid point. I shouldn't have spoken so hastily."

"You had your reasons." Radford slipped the hammer from his belt and slapped the handle against his palm. "As far as I'm concerned, I'm out." His misery was reflected in the faces that stared back at him and he wished he could run somewhere and bleed in private. "For now, I plan to concentrate on the livery and help finish this house." Swallowing the pain of his past and the fear of his future, Radford nudged Boyd with his hammer. "Are you going to stand there all night or pound some nails?"

Boyd shook his head in disbelief. "You're serious, aren't you? You're really going to do this!"

Radford tried to grin, but failed pathetically. "For a ribbon chaser you're pretty astute." He grabbed the sack of nails and tossed it at Boyd. "Let's get this house up."

The sooner Kyle's house was finished, the sooner Evelyn would be in it—and away from Radford.

━━◈ ◈━━

Evelyn pushed the wheelbarrow outside, bumping over the rutted ground in the paddock where Radford was tearing down the rotted horse shelter. He'd been quiet the past few days, but how else was he supposed to react after his brother's fiancée admitted that she'd wanted to kiss him? She couldn't even look at Radford now without a hot rush of shame scorching her face.

Avoiding eye contact, Evelyn parked the wheelbarrow under a thick branch in the birch tree. She wove a length of rope through a swatch of netting containing a small bundle of hay for Gus then scooted it aside and stepped into the wheelbarrow. Steadying herself, she reached up and crossed the two ends of the twine over the tree limb.

"Need some help?" Radford hollered.

She shook her head. "I've almost got it." Giving a firm tug, she hoisted the net of hay out of its resting place. Her makeshift platform teetered and she spread her feet to balance it. She leaned forward, wobbling as she struggled to tighten the knot, but the wheelbarrow tipped precariously to the side. Blast it! If she got down to move it, she would lose the net entirely and have to begin again. She had too many chores to waste time on this one. She inched forward, heedless of the tilting cart.

Suddenly, two strong hands circled her waist and Evelyn nearly leapt into the tree. With arms suspended above her, she dropped her chin and looked down into Radford's upturned face. From this angle, and only inches away, she noticed everything, the dampness on his forehead, the sunburn where his skin was tightest over his cheekbones, the shadow of whiskers that darkened his jawline and contrasted with his white teeth.

"Go ahead, I've got you," he said, but he didn't look happy about it.

His fingers spanned her ribs and sent ripples of sensation up her back. Desperate to escape Radford's grasp and her own guilty yearnings, Evelyn tugged frantically at the rope. Radford's hands were giving her that monkeyshine feeling again. Evelyn tried to knot the rope, but her trembling fingers couldn't accomplish the task. Something bit her beneath the chin and she jerked her hand to the injured area. "That hurt," she said, rubbing her hand over a small bump. "I already feel a welt there."

"It was a black fly, and the welt you're feeling is a mole."

She looked down. "What?"

"You have a mole under your chin. Right there," Radford said, lifting one hand to touch it.

Her stomach flipped. She was melting all over herself and Radford was talking about moles? "I have moles everywhere. You have one, too," she said. "It's on your right arm just below your elbow."

Radford glanced down and angled his elbow, revealing the dark spot she'd noticed the day they were painting the porch.

"Right there," Evelyn said, satisfied that she wasn't the only one with those ugly marks.

Radford's eyes met hers. "That's a shrapnel fragment I couldn't get out."

"You have a bullet in you?"

He grinned. "Just a speck of metal. It doesn't hurt."

"I thought it was a mole. I hate mine."

"Why? Some women used to put patches on their faces to get those beauty marks. You should consider yourself fortunate. The little one above your lip adds character to your face."

Evelyn laughed and snugged the knot. "Those women must have been out of their minds. I'd remove mine, if I could." Evelyn gave the knot a hard cinch and dropped her hands. "I'm done," she said, desperate to get away from Radford.

She jumped as Radford swung her out of the wheelbarrow. Her oversized shirt shimmied her body, and his hands slid up her ribs, his thumbs cupping the bottom of her breasts. Her gaze flew to his as an unexpected thrill shot through her. She clutched his shoulders to keep from falling, but Radford's eyes grew so dark, so intense, it reminded Evelyn of the night she woke him from a nightmare. The night he had warned her he was dangerous.

Panicked, she pushed away and stumbled backward into the cart. Radford caught her arm and tried to steady her, but she yanked away. Heat flushed through her body. Without a word, she grasped the handles of the wheelbarrow and rushed to the barn, trying to excuse Radford's hands on her breasts. It was just an accident, she told herself. They'd done nothing wrong. Her reaction was simply a mixture of surprise and embarrassment, that's all. He hadn't done it on purpose.

Watching Evelyn hurry away, Radford tightened his fists against the tingling in his hands. A couple of inches higher and his palms would have been cupping her breasts.

"Damnation!" He hadn't known it would happen.

But the look on her face said she thought he did.

Unwilling to let her think the worst, he stalked after her. They would settle this ridiculous attraction to each other once and for all. No more pretending they didn't feel it. They'd admit it, decide how best to bury it then get on with their lives—separately.

Preoccupied with what he'd say, Radford barreled in the back door of the livery and nearly flattened Evelyn. Her eyes flashed surprise as she backpedaled. Radford caught her arms then stumbled forward, tripping over the wheelbarrow and sending them both sprawling upon the straw-littered floor.

Jolted by the fall, neither of them had the sense to let go of the other. Like two people who hadn't seen each other in years then unexpectedly bumped shoulders at a train station, they stared in stunned surprise.

"Are you all right?" he asked, unsure if it was Evelyn or the fall that left him short of breath.

She blinked and released her death grip on his shirt. "What the devil are you after?"

Her bewildered expression reminded him of what he'd come to do. "I was coming to apologize."

"For what?" She tried to wiggle from beneath him.

Radford eased to her side and helped her sit up. "For what happened in the paddock."

She stood and brushed herself off while Radford gained his feet. "It was an accident."

He touched her elbow and turned her toward him. "I wanted to be sure you knew that."

Her face flushed and she lowered her lashes. "Of course I did. But since you plowed me over, the least you can do is brush the straw off my back."

In the awkward silence, Radford turned her away and caught her braid in his palm. "Are you sure you're all right?" he asked. She nodded, causing the thick, silken braid to slip across his palm. Radford let out a slow breath to calm himself. Being near her was making him crazy. He had to get out of here.

What had begun as a simple gesture to rid her hair of debris was now playing havoc with his senses. Her hair was thick and incredibly soft and the memory of seeing that disheveled, ebony mass unbound made his hands shake. He should have followed his own advice and let Boyd introduce him to one of his friendly female friends, but the idea was too calculated and contemptible to execute.

Unconsciously, he wrapped the skein around his wrist and ran his free hand over the strands, feeling as bound by the silk as he would by the clasp of an iron chain.

A sprinkling of hay fragments trickled down from the loft, sparkling like gold dust as it crossed the thick shaft of sunlight slanting in the open door. The stillness of the livery should have calmed him, but within him raged feelings he couldn't control.

"This has to stop, Evelyn."

She turned to face him, her expression confused.

"Don't look at me like that. You know what I'm talking about," he said. "I'm attracted to you. After the kiss we shared on the porch that night, I suspect you feel something similar for me." He watched a deep red hue spread across her face and was sorry his bold statement had embarrassed her. "We need to squelch these feelings."

"I know," she said, her gaze sliding away.

Radford tipped her chin until she met his eyes. "If the situation were different, I'd pursue this."

She nodded, but didn't speak.

"My allegiance is to Kyle."

"So is mine," she said, her head jerking up, her expression offended. She straightened her shirt and stepped away from him. "You should go back to the mill, Radford."

"I can't," he said softly, unable to keep the pain of his loss out of his voice.

"Yes you can. You've got to make Kyle stop playing this game. Just tell him you're coming back then do it."

Realizing Evelyn didn't know about his confrontation with Kyle, Radford could only shake his head. "It's not an option," he said then walked out the back door before he punched his fist through the wall.

⸻

Several hours later, Radford flopped upon his mattress searching for sleep, begging for it, wishing with all his soul that he could find peace in that black oblivion. But his eyes refused to stay closed and his mind continued to torment him with conversations that made his heart race.

The memory of his brothers' guilty faces staring back at him made him ache. He hadn't been prepared for Kyle's hurtful accusations. Radford could understand Kyle's need to protect what he'd sweated over. No one knew better than Radford the fierce urge to protect, whether it be an inconsequential possession or his very life. Radford had learned survival during the war and that instinct had perched on his shoulders, sinking its long claws in too deeply to be removed.

But he was so weary of battling and fighting and running. All he wanted was to share his life with his family, to give Rebecca the happiness a little girl deserved, and to work at something he could take pride in. The profits at the mill didn't entice him. His years with the railroad had left him financially comfortable and he would have mentioned that to Kyle, but it dawned on him that the issue wasn't money, it was control. Kyle was more concerned with losing his position than sharing profits. Now, it was a moot point and didn't matter anymore.

Radford flipped his pillow and folded his arms behind his head. He concentrated on keeping his breathing even and encouraged his mind to turn away from the painful confrontation with his brothers. Think of good things, he told himself. Like the sound of Rebecca's giggle and the way her nose wrinkles when she's confused. Those thoughts made him smile and the knowledge that she was happy here comforted him.

It was because of Evelyn. Rebecca felt safe with her. But Radford didn't. Not by a mile.

He mulled over their problem, turning it in every possible direction, but the answer eluded him throughout the long hours of the night. By morning he was exhausted and thoroughly sick of agonizing over the emotions that were draining him. On the way into the kitchen, he stubbed his toe on Evelyn's chair and gave her a growl for a greeting.

"You look tired," she said.

"I am." He poured a cup of coffee and took a gulp. The liquid scorched his throat and his eyes watered. "Dammit!"

"Did you have another nightmare?"

After the incident with his brothers, Radford had heard enough references to his past. And though he despised the need to do it, he was resolved to end his personal bond with Evelyn. Today. He placed his cup in the sink and turned to face her. "I believe that's my business." He forced himself to ignore her wounded expression, and he left the house.

Throughout the morning, despite his increasing shame, Radford treated Evelyn harshly. Shutting her out was the only way he was going to keep from betraying Kyle, and Radford couldn't do that when she was all sweetness and honey. He needed her to be angry enough to want to avoid him because he'd never manage it alone.

Though she'd followed him to the livery that morning without complaint, he could see the hurt in her eyes each time she glanced at him. He wiped the sweat off his forehead. It was cool outside, but he felt hot and sweaty. Watching Evelyn's bottom pointing in his direction half the morning hadn't helped.

Evelyn stood up, brushed her hands against her thighs then approached him. "This isn't the way to do it," she said softly. Her eyes darkened and she reached for his arm. The minute she touched him, Radford knew he was in trouble. "We're spending too much time together. If you'd go back to the mill, I'm sure the tension would ease and we'd both feel differently in a few days."

"Do you really believe that?" he asked, stung that she assumed the depth of his feelings were that shallow then wondering how deep hers ran.

"I don't know." She shrugged. "It can't hurt."

He shook his head, knowing that distance wouldn't kill his attraction to her.

"Please," she pleaded, giving his arm a squeeze. "Before we do something stupid again, go back to the mill and tell Kyle to send someone else to help me in the livery."

"I can't!" He jerked his arm free and stepped away from her. "I have Rebecca's welfare to think about. I can't uproot her again. And I can't step on Kyle to get what I want." He shoved his hair back, knowing he was going to drag Evelyn into his arms if he didn't get her away from him. "Why don't you go?" he said suddenly, determined to drive her out of the livery. "Marry Kyle now. Go live in his house. Have his children. Do whatever you need to do, but stay away from me."

Evelyn gasped and stared at him with pain-filled eyes that sliced him to the marrow, but he bit his tongue. He needed to get her away from him. Without a word, she bolted out the back door and he watched her run across the pasture. She mounted her white Thoroughbred bareback then raced across the orchard toward the house she would soon share with Kyle. Radford should have felt glad that she was going to his brother, but he wasn't glad at all. He felt nauseous and heartsick.

⟶⟨⟩⟵

Evelyn slowed Gabrielle to a trot as they skirted Kyle's mill then slowly descended into the gorge where she and Radford had gone to gather rocks only days earlier. The waterfalls rippled the surface of the pool as Evelyn slid from Gabrielle's back. She yanked off her boots, eager to submerse her hot body. As she pulled off her clothes a soft breeze touched her bare skin. With arms stretched toward the sky, she lunged, diving into the crystal pool, reveling in the silky coolness against her flushed skin.

She cut the water with clean, quick strokes and swam to the falls where she perched on a shelf of shale rock that rested beneath them. Head back, eyes closed, she opened her mouth and held her breath. The cool, cleansing water rushed across her teeth and tongue, forming a much smaller version of the falls.

Wrapped in her cocoon of thunder and splatter, she lifted her hands, palms up, fingers bent, letting the liquid rush under her nails. She leaned forward, enjoying the massage on her sore muscles until the pounding falls became too much and she moved to where it dropped more softly. Through the falling water, the sun created an illusion of glittering gold reminiscent of Radford's eyes. Evelyn closed her own eyes, wanting to savor the memory of the tender man she'd known before Radford had become so hurtful. She knew what he was trying to do, but his words still cut.

Lifting her face to the water, she let it pulse across her lips as if they were being gently nibbled by Radford's teeth. She drifted in memories of the last time she was here, when Radford's smoldering gaze mesmerized her and she thought he was going to kiss her. Her breasts formed high peaks as the turbulent water bubbled over them, and to her shame she remembered what it was like when he touched her there.

Heart pounding, she shot from beneath the falls and crossed the pool. She drove herself from one side to the other, seeking to exhaust the pressure that had spread through her body. Her arms tired and her legs cramped, but she continued until she dragged herself out of the water and stood trembling near her discarded clothing.

Exhaustion relieved the desire, but it didn't assuage the guilt she felt for thinking about Radford when she should be thinking about Kyle, because Evelyn had done the unforgivable.

She had fallen in love with Radford Grayson.

Chapter Sixteen

"I'll carry you over the threshold on our wedding night," Kyle explained to Evelyn as he opened the door of their half-finished home. Though she'd peeked inside the house when she last visited the mill, this was the first time Kyle was willing to show it to her.

Evelyn followed him inside feeling as if she shouldn't be here. Not after she had considered breaking their engagement. It had seemed the honest thing to do when she realized she loved Radford, but Radford didn't want her. He had pointedly avoided her the past week, forcing Evelyn to ignore her aching heart.

"We have a lot to do yet," Kyle said, closing the door behind them.

She tried to smile as she surveyed the house. It still had bare walls and partially finished ceilings, but Kyle and his brothers had accomplished an amazing amount since she'd seen it a month earlier.

Kyle guided her to the kitchen. "This is your domain," he said then began a rapid succession of questions that boggled her mind. He asked how many cupboards she wanted and where she'd like them placed, if she wanted drawers for her vegetables or preferred cupboards. Would she like a maple table or did she prefer oak? Would the Acme six-plate stove he'd ordered be big enough, or did she need a bigger one? He delivered the questions in the same brusque manner he used at the mill and she felt no excitement in choosing.

Shaking off her melancholy, Evelyn gave her opinion then returned to the parlor with Kyle where they decided on furniture. "The stove will sit near this inside wall to heat the house more efficiently," he said then pointed to a room off the parlor. "I added this other room for your father in case he changes his mind about living with us."

He was trying so hard to please her that Evelyn choked on her guilt, but it did not diminish her feelings for Radford.

"The second floor is unfinished so we can add bedrooms as we need them," Kyle said. "I thought we'd see how quick our children come before putting up walls."

In that instant, their impending marriage became real, and Evelyn realized she was going to spend the rest of her life with this man and have his children. Kyle would be her confidant and lover. He would be the center of her life, like the stove in their house. But how could she fuel his fire when she felt as cold as a stone? Could she learn? Would their home resonate with warmth and laughter, or sit silent and cold like the empty stove?

Her legs quaked as she followed him down the hallway leading to the back of the house.

"This is our bedroom, Ev." Sincerity filled his voice, but Evelyn's throat was too dry to reply. A massive fireplace lined one wall, and a large window filled the other. Outside the clear glass, a huge maple tree that was starting to change color looked like a beautiful painting that had been intentionally framed by the window. The room was designed to hold several large pieces of furniture, and Evelyn knew Kyle had given this room the most attention for her.

Shamed by her unfaithful feelings in the face of his generosity, she buried her face in his chest. "I love it, Kyle. Truly, I do."

He embraced her. "Well, that's a relief. I can't tell what pleases you these days."

"I'm sorry. I just have a lot on my mind with Papa being ill, but I promise I'll be a good wife." She meant it with all her aching heart. She would honor her husband no matter what it cost her.

Kyle tensed and eased her away, his eyes questioning, his expression suspicious. "Are you leading up to a confession that I don't want to hear?"

"Of course not!" she said, as guilt and panic raced through her body. Could Kyle possibly sense that she had feelings for Radford? Or had her comment simply struck a vein of suspicion that made him ask?

Kyle's gaze canvassed her face as if searching for something she was hiding.

"Kyle! Stop looking at me like that," she said. "There's nothing to confess."

"Good, because I'd kill the man and don't you doubt it." All humor had fled his eyes and Evelyn's heart lurched sickeningly in her chest. "I'm sensing something's going on with you, Ev." She shook her head. "All right then, we'll leave it for now. I've got a mess with Radford that I need to handle." He shoved his hair off his forehead, his expression pained as he told Evelyn how Radford had overheard them arguing over the mill and the extent to which the conversation had escalated, ending with Radford relinquishing his part ownership.

No wonder Radford couldn't go back to the mill. "You should have given Radford time to prove himself before assuming he wanted the mill."

Kyle stuffed his hands in his pockets and hunched his shoulders. "I know, but when he started showing up at the mill a couple of weeks ago, I thought he would eventually want his position back."

"If he'd wanted the mill, I can't help thinking he would have come home long before this."

"I realize that now," he said wretchedly.

"What happened to you, Kyle? You used to be so good-natured and fun. Now you only care about the mill. You seem almost greedy at times."

"Greedy?" Kyle bristled. "I'm building you a house and filling it with new furniture and you consider me greedy?"

"You're offering what you think I want, but I would prefer to have the man I used to laugh with, the boy who could dream. Not this person who would choose a business over his own brother."

Kyle's chin came up, pain flashing in his eyes. "I didn't choose the mill over Radford. I made a stupid mistake." Kyle shook his head. "Radford should have told me to go to hell, but he apologized. He gave up the mill and hasn't said a word about it since, and he's helped on our house every night." Kyle rubbed his temples. "Maybe he really doesn't care about the mill and I'm worrying about all this for nothing."

Seeing that Kyle was genuinely regretful over what had happened made Evelyn feel sympathy for both men. "I think you can assume that Radford is hurt by this and that he wants to be a partner in the mill."

With a deflating sigh, Kyle leaned against the wall. "How do I fix this mess?"

"I don't know." She had her own emotional mess to worry about fixing. "Let Radford know that you want him here, but don't push him, Kyle. I don't think Radford is someone who can be pushed."

***

Evelyn waited until the next day before approaching Radford. She heard his hammer ringing in the small stone room off the back of the livery. She listened until it was silent before she knocked on the heavy wooden door.

A moment later Radford peered out at her. "Need something?" he asked.

Dirt and sweat streaked his face, his damp hair curling against his neck. "May I come in?" she asked, wondering why men were irresistible when they were filthy.

Reluctantly, Radford stepped aside and let her enter. The door closed behind her and Evelyn was thrust into inky blackness. Radford's boots crunched across the cinders then the bellows huffed and the forge filled the small area with peachy light. It glowed warmly upon his face and Evelyn was thankful she could see his eyes. It allowed her to see the things he wouldn't admit.

"I don't assume you want to take up blacksmithing?"

"No," she answered quietly. "I saw Kyle last night and I thought you might like to talk."

"No, thanks." He pulled the long metal bar from the furnace and placed the horseshoe on the anvil. He dismissed her with a glance then pounded the iron shoe until her ears ached. Radford stuck the tongs in the fire and she waited. He turned the hot piece of iron and his jaw clenched. He pumped the bellows until she wanted to wring his neck.

"Radford!"

He glanced up and Evelyn could only guess at the fierce emotions roiling within him. Anger? Pain? Resentment? His chest and head were illuminated by the fire, but the rest of him remained shadowed. She approached him and touched his arm, knowing it was more than the heat of the forge that warmed her.

"I want to talk with you. Please."

His shoulders slumped and he stepped away from the forge. "You're not going to leave it alone, are you?"

Evelyn shook her head. "You've given me a gift that I'd like to repay."

"A gift?" he asked in surprise. "I've intruded in your livery and burdened you with a four-year-old who won't give you a moment's peace. I wouldn't call that a gift."

Evelyn smiled and released his arm. "I love Rebecca, and despite our personal problem, you're not in the way. My back aches considerably less since you've been here and, though I never thought I'd say this, it's nice having someone to work with again."

Radford turned toward the forge, but she caught his hand to keep him from returning to work. "I'm dirty," he said, trying to pull free.

"I don't care." She held tight, refusing to leave him alone with his pain. She knew how it felt when there was no one to turn to. "I know that Kyle said some awful things that he's sorry for, but that doesn't make it hurt any less, does it?"

Radford pulled his hand free, but he didn't move away. "It's better that we settled things. I wasn't comfortable with the situation anyhow. I should have been here when they needed me."

"Well, you're here now. That counts for something. Your brothers were incomplete without you, Radford. Kyle has said as much himself and truly regrets what he did."

Radford longed to hear those words, but standing in the dark with Evelyn, and knowing she was only inches away, was too dangerous. All he would have to do was lower his mouth and he could kiss her, could taste her lips that spoke such sweet words, could hold her in his arms. With a silent curse, he turned to the forge and furiously pumped the bellows until heat rolled from the coals and the entire room was filled with glowing orange light.

Evelyn blotted her forehead with her sleeve then moved to the door, hesitating with her hand on the latch. "I understand now why you can't go back to the mill," she said, looking at him as though she wanted to say more. He nodded and she glanced down at the flames. "Since we have to live and work together, do you think you might start talking to me again?" Her gaze lifted to his. "I miss our friendship," she said softly then opened the door and left the room.

Chapter Seventeen

As the month of September gave way to October the days turned comfortably cool and the leaves turned magnificent shades of red and gold. Kyle had finally found a way to apologize to Radford by rattling into the yard with a wagon full of lumber to rebuild the horse shelter that Radford had torn down.

Evelyn scoured her garden for the last of her vegetables and kept an eye on Rebecca and Helen who were digging in a fallow corner. Occasionally, she'd glimpse Radford and Kyle as they carried away the old planks then started building the new shelter.

For brothers, they were remarkably different. Where Kyle was thick-chested and heavily muscled, Radford was lean with long arms and narrow hips. Kyle's brown hair warmed to the color of deep auburn in the sun while Radford's appeared to darken to a deeper, richer brown. They were handsome, proud men and worthy of any woman's interest.

But Evelyn was still drawn to the wrong one. She'd tried to change that, but no matter how much time she spent with Kyle in the evenings, she'd been unable to nurture their friendship into passion. She owed it to Kyle to tell him about her lack of feelings, but couldn't bear the thought of hurting him. Long ago she'd promised to stand beside him, to always be there for him, and only a few short weeks ago, she'd promised to marry him. If she broke their engagement now, he'd surmise why she'd had a change of heart and the results would be disastrous.

She stood and stretched her back. Maybe when she was away from Radford she could think clearly again. If she tried, she could make a good home with Kyle, and perhaps in the intimacy of their bedroom they would both let down their guard and rediscover each other. She cast one last, regretful look at Radford and told herself to let him go.

Rebecca's terrified scream turned Evelyn's skin to ice. Everything moved forward in slow motion. A black snake slithered beneath the fence near Rebecca's feet. Radford and Kyle flew through the air, leaping the fence in unison; Kyle still holding his axe like a wild Indian with a tomahawk, Radford with a look on his face that froze Evelyn in her tracks.

Kyle reached for Rebecca, but Radford growled and shoved him aside.

Kyle stumbled back four steps before he caught his balance, a dumbfounded expression on his face as he looked at Radford. Helen crouched in fear near the fence, and Evelyn stared in shock at the savage look on Radford's face.

"Did the snake bite you?" he asked, his voice thick and trembling with fear as he inspected his daughter.

Rebecca shook her head then burst into tears and fell into his arms.

Radford squeezed his eyes shut and pressed his ashen face to his daughter's head.

Evelyn exchanged a concerned glance with Kyle before he jumped the fence and trotted in the direction the snake went.

Evelyn squatted beside Radford and touched his arm. When he looked at her, all Evelyn could see was his tormented eyes above Rebecca's curls. That he was embarrassed for shoving Kyle, for being unable to control his reaction, was obvious. He seemed so lost, so utterly pathetic in his shame, that she ached for him.

"It's all right, Radford." Evelyn moved her hand to Rebecca's back and Radford's fingers immediately linked with hers. He gripped them hard, hanging on as though Evelyn could save him from himself. "What happened?" William asked, his voice graveled and breathless.

Evelyn jumped to her feet and hurried toward him. Her father stood at the edge of the fence, breathing hard and leaning heavily on his cane. His face was white and his legs were visibly quaking. The shock had nearly undone her father and she was frantic that he would collapse. "You need to sit down, Papa." She took his arm, not caring in the least if Radford thought she was pampering him. Without her help he would never make it back to the house.

Radford stepped over the fence with Rebecca on one arm and stopped Evelyn with his free hand. "Take her," he said gently, passing Rebecca to her. He put a steadying arm around William's waist and led him slowly to the porch, explaining what happened as they went.

Evelyn beckoned to Helen, who was trailing at a distance then when both girls were tucked protectively at her side, she followed Radford and her father to the house.

When Kyle joined them a few minutes later, he clapped a hand on Radford's shoulder. "You all right?"

"Yeah." Radford grimaced. "I'm sorry."

Kyle nodded then squatted in front of Rebecca and wiped a tear off her cheek with his thumb. "That snake won't be bothering you again."

"Will he s-stay away?" Rebecca hiccupped and sniffed.

"Absolutely," Kyle said with a smile.

Rebecca threw her arms around his neck and hugged him hard. "Thank you, Unco Kyle."

The look of wonder that crossed Kyle's face was an expression Evelyn had never before witnessed on him. His big shoulders and solid neck looked so out of place with little arms wrapped around them that

Evelyn was transfixed. But when he closed his eyes and pressed a kiss to Rebecca's curls, it wrenched her heart and made her eyes tear.

As though he suddenly realized what he was doing, he stood up and backed away. Evelyn held out a hand, wanting to keep that tender side of him from slipping away, but he didn't reach back.

"Did I ever tell you about the snake that got after me when I was your dad's age?" William asked Rebecca. She hiccupped and shook her head. "It was an old hoop snake. Either of you girls ever heard of a hoop snake?" They both shook their heads. "Well, come over here and I'll tell you a story about a real snake. That black snake was just being friendly with you. It's those nasty hoop snakes that you gotta look out for."

Helen and Rebecca knelt on the floor in front of his chair, hands on knees, gazing up in anticipation. Evelyn leaned against the railing beside Kyle while Radford took a seat beside her father.

"Those old hoop snakes are poisonous and if they get you, well, you could swell right up until you burst."

"Really?" Rebecca asked, obviously displeased.

"Do they have teeth?" Helen asked.

"Can't say. I do know they bite their own tail and roll where they want to go. Looks just like a big ole buggy hoop, so if you ever see one you'd better hightail it out of there."

"I will," Rebecca promised, as if taking a solemn oath.

"I had to run from one myself when I was a little older than you. I was helping my pa build a new shed, but we ran out of wood so he made me dig taters for the day. While I was in the field, I heard a noise and what do you suppose I saw rolling right at me?"

"A hoop snake!" both girls supplied in unison, bouncing on their knees in suspense.

"That's right. I didn't have time to run so I tried to defend myself with the ash handle of my potato hook. That darn snake knocked it right out of my hand with its tail. I'll tell you, I never ran so fast in all my life. I stayed clear of there for the rest of the day, but my pa made me go back and get that doggone potato hook the next morning. We were expecting rain and he said it'd be ruined if it got wet. I looked all over for that blasted hook then I stopped and scratched my head. There was a huge chunk of wood laying in the middle of the garden that hadn't been there before, and after I took me a good look, I realized it was the potato hook. Must be that darn snake stuck its poison in that handle and blew it up to the size of a tree."

"It did?" Rebecca asked. "Did your daddy yell at you about the 'tato hook?"

Evelyn saw her father's lips twitch, but he managed to keep a straight face. "No, he hitched up the wagon and took that chunk of wood to the mill and had it cut up for our shed."

"Did Unco Kyle cut it up for you?" Rebecca asked, her face beaming.

This time it was Kyle who laughed and William continued with a chuckle. "No, sweetpea. Your uncle Kyle wasn't born yet, so someone else had to do it. Anyhow, we took that lumber and finished off our shed. But it got too dark for us to put the shingles on the roof so we had to wait until the next morning. But guess what happened?" he asked mysteriously, and both girls leaned closer.

"It had stormed all night and soaked everything for miles. When the water went down, I walked out back and looked at our shed. I blinked my eyes, thinkin' I was still sleepin' until my pa came out behind me and cursed up a blue streak. You see, the rain had washed the snake's poison out of the wood and all we had left of our shed by morning was tiny pieces of wood that looked just like toothpicks."

"That's a fib, Grandpa!" Rebecca said, giggling.

He hooted and held out his hand. "I know it is, but come up here and give me a kiss anyhow." To Evelyn's amazement, Rebecca climbed onto his lap and squeezed his neck.

"You tell good stories, Grandpa."

"Well, you're a good listener, sweetpea, and it makes Grandpa happy to share his silly tales with you." He tickled her side and made room for Helen who wasn't about to be left out. "I hope you're not going to let those snakes scare you anymore."

Rebecca shook her head. "Nope! I'll just get Unco Kyle to chase them away!"

Evelyn glanced at Kyle, who was wearing such a warm expression, that for a moment, she knew her old friend still existed somewhere beneath his business armor. Yet, even if she could find him again, she wondered if it would be enough now that she knew what passion felt like.

Chapter Eighteen

"Radford!" Evelyn yelled, rushing into Radford's bedroom. She grabbed his shoulder and shook him. "Wake up! Papa needs a doctor."

He shot up in bed, his gaze darting around the room as though expecting something to fly at him from a darkened corner. "Where are they?" he panted.

Evelyn yanked his hand to jar him from the dark world that made his eyes wild. "Papa's had an attack. I need you to get the doctor."

Radford stared at her for two full seconds then shook the remnants of sleep from his head. "Where is he?" he asked, his voice gruff with sleep as he leapt from bed. Oblivious to his nudity, he yanked on his trousers and stepped barefoot into his boots, tying his laces with quick jerks.

They rushed across the hall to her father's room where Radford checked her father's breathing and pulse. "I'll be back as soon as I can," he said then dashed from the room.

Evelyn turned up the lantern then held her father's cool, frail hand. "Papa?"

He rolled his head toward her. His face was sagging on one side, as though his muscles had given up their job of holding skin to his face. "Why arn' you in bed, pixie?" he asked, his speech slurred, his eyes glassy.

He used to ask Evelyn that same question years ago when he'd find her playing in her bedroom after she was supposed to have been asleep. Instead of chastising, he'd tuck her in bed with her doll and kiss them both good night.

Evelyn smoothed her hand across her father's chest. "It's my turn to tuck you in, Papa. Rest now. I'll be right here."

It seemed she sat at his bedside, holding his hand, for hours before Radford came back with Doc Finlay. The doctor greeted her briefly then examined her father in silence. When he finished, he rolled his shoulders and rubbed his neck. "He's coherent and responsive, but your father is very weak. Providing there isn't another attack, he'll recover. I'll check back tomorrow to see how he's coming along."

Radford took the doctor back to town and Evelyn sat in the chair next to her father's bed, holding his hand while he slept. Occasionally she would place her palm near his mouth to check his breathing. When fatigue finally claimed her, she rested her head against the side of the chair and laid her hand upon his chest. The steady beat of his heart reassured her and she closed her eyes.

For three days she sat with him, unwilling to leave his side. Radford spent his time between the barn and the sickroom while Kyle, Duke, and Boyd took turns helping in the livery and coming to visit in the evenings.

On the third night, Kyle poked his head into the room. "How's he doing?"

Evelyn glanced at her sleeping father. "He's sick to his stomach today."

"You don't look so well yourself." Kyle entered the room and pulled her into his arms, rubbing his palm across her back. "Can I do anything?"

Evelyn rested her cheek against his thick chest, thinking she could close her eyes and fall asleep right there. "You're doing enough in the livery. I really appreciate that, Kyle. Be sure to thank Boyd and Duke for me and tell them I owe them each a pie when I get my kitchen back from your mother."

"So she's chased you out, has she?"

Evelyn lifted her head and smiled. "She's been wonderful. Rebecca loves the games they've been playing. Without your mother, we would have all starved over the past few days."

"Well, she's downstairs right now planning our wedding meal, which is only three weeks away in case you've forgotten."

Evelyn met his eyes. "I know, but we'll have to wait if Papa's not better soon."

"Then make sure you take good care of him. Now that you've learned about monkeyshines, I'm eager for our wedding night," he said, pulling her against him.

"Are you fonnlin' my daughter?"

Embarrassed to be caught in Kyle's arms, yet pleased to hear the strength returning to her father's voice, Evelyn hurried to his side.

Kyle joined them and laid his hand over William's. "How you doing?"

"Shitty."

"Well, before you know it you'll be tipping a horn with me at your daughter's wedding."

William smiled weakly. "Soun's good. Now quit molestin' her while I've got my eyes closed."

"Yes, sir." Kyle grinned and gave him a squeeze on the shoulder. He cupped Evelyn's chin and gave her a quick kiss. "I'll see you tomorrow," he said then left the house.

Later that night, Evelyn's father grew pale and started heaving, his body wracked with tremors. Panicked, Evelyn sent Radford for Doc Finlay again. She paced the bedroom with growing anxiety until they arrived. After long minutes of silent examination the doctor shook his head and said her father was suffering with influenza and shouldn't be left alone in his already weakened condition.

Frightened by the added threat, Evelyn and Radford nursed her father for two days, covering him with extra blankets when his teeth chattered from chills, wiping his face with cool cloths when he burned with fever, holding a pan when he was sick and giving him water when he could keep it down.

On the third bone-weary night, Evelyn and Radford sat with the bed between them, the lantern casting a soft golden glow upon their shoulders and across the blankets. Radford's long fingers rested on the mattress inches from hers and Evelyn thought how natural it would be to reach over and link her fingers with his. She needed his strength. No one would know.

"What are you thinking?" Radford asked quietly, his eyes probing hers.

"I was... feeling relieved that Papa's resting."

He shook his head slowly, his shadowed cheeks alternately catching the lantern glow. "No you weren't."

Tension buzzed around them while he made a slow study of her face. His eyes darkened and her pulse quickened, but she was unable to look away from his masculine features and tired eyes. Something in his expression beckoned her closer, but the strain in his shoulders sent currents of warning racing through her body.

With slow purpose, he planted both feet on the floor then unfolded his long body until he was standing. She was spellbound by the magnitude of emotion she saw in his eyes. He moved around the bed, and her breath caught in her throat when he stopped beside her.

He lifted his hand to her cheek, but didn't touch her. Instead he stepped away and spoke hoarsely over his shoulder. "I need air."

Radford stood on the balcony trying to talk himself out of running. He was losing the battle. It wasn't just the physical wanting that tormented him. It was the deeper need to know Evelyn, to learn what she liked or loved. What was her favorite time of day for a horseback ride? Did she enjoy the rhythmic chirping of night peepers better than the bright sound of morning robins? Was there a special dream or hope that lay within that tender heart of hers? Was it something he could give her?

And what about Kyle? What did Radford owe him? Loyalty and trust for certain, but to what extent? Was Radford to forfeit his own happiness, his life, for Kyle? Or Rebecca's happiness? Perhaps not, but neither would he steal that very thing from his brother.

With a low, agonized groan, Radford turned his face to the breeze. "I can't do it!" he said to the night. "I can't."

Unwilling to torment himself further, he returned to William's room, annoyed to find Evelyn sleeping in the chair again. How many nights now had he told her to go to bed, that he would sit with William? Yet here she was, stubbornly asleep with her temple against the side of the chair, her braid falling across her shoulder and curling in her lap.

Radford shook her gently, but she didn't stir. He tried more insistently and still she slept, unaware of his struggle not to kiss her parted lips. Dark lashes fanned her cheeks and were surrounded by purple smudges of exhaustion. Pity welled inside him and he knelt down, slipped his arms beneath her legs and shoulders, and lifted her into his arms.

She nestled her face in his neck, but her arms slackened in fatigue and fell to her side as she drifted off again. Radford carried her to her room and placed her on the bed. As he pulled the sheet over her, he warned himself to get out of her room. But he stayed and studied the arch of her eyebrows, the shape of her mouth, her regal cheekbones and pretty nose. He cupped her jaw and rubbed his thumb lightly across her lips. Unable to help himself, Radford leaned over and placed a reverent kiss upon the mole above her mouth.

"I've wanted to do that so many times," he whispered. Then, while he still had an ounce of restraint, he left her room and began to pack.

The war had taught him to recognize his limits, and with Evelyn, he was crossing the line. He needed to get away for a couple of days to clear his mind and decide the true depth of his feelings for her.

Whether he owed Kyle or not, one thing was certain: brothers were for protecting, not betraying.

Evelyn could tell her father was as lost as she was without Radford and Rebecca. They had left yesterday morning for Syracuse to get a doctor Radford said he could trust to help her father. But her father was so much improved this evening that Evelyn thought Radford might end up wasting the doctor's time as well as his own.

Still, after the tense moment she and Radford had shared in her father's bedroom the other night, she sensed this was Radford's way of honoring Kyle.

She sat beside her father on the sofa and gently nudged his shoulder, seeking the security and comfort she'd always found there. "Let's snuggle," she said.

His lips tilted in a sad, crooked smile, his face still sagging slightly on one side, but he'd regained his speech.

He put his hand on her knee and Evelyn covered his knuckles with her palm. "Was Radford ever a coward, Papa?"

Her father's surprised glance gave Evelyn the answer even before he spoke. "I have yet to meet a man, myself included, with a deeper sense of integrity or a greater amount of courage than that young man."

Evelyn laced her fingers with her father's and stroked the thin parchment of his skin. "What happened to him? Why does he have that volcano inside him?"

"Fighting a war hurts a man's mind as much as his body. Radford couldn't shut away his conscience during the battles. His heart was present in every second of the war."

"What about you, Papa? Did fighting bother you?"

"Sure," he said quietly, "but I knew my duty and I was proud to serve with such a fine regiment of men. We never intentionally hurt anyone outside of battle. I could live with that."

"Then why couldn't Radford?"

"He suffered too deeply, I guess, and still does by the sound of his nightmares. That war lynched the soul from every one of us. We were not only facing the enemy, but ourselves as well. Most of us didn't like what we saw in our reflection. It was hard for any of us to destroy a human life. Radford knew what he had to do, but he never accepted the killin'. There were times when I couldn't stomach it, either, when I was ashamed of my actions."

"You did what you were ordered to do."

He put his arm around her. "Lay your head on my shoulder, pixie. It reminds me of a time when I used to take care of you. I miss that."

"I'll always need you." Evelyn snuggled against his side, loving the warmth and the familiar scent of him that made her feel protected despite his frailness. Their closeness offered a sense of security in a lonely house, and they sat in the silence for a few minutes, each taking comfort from the other. She held his crippled hand between her own and rubbed her thumb across the transparency of his skin, watching it shift over his bony knuckles and blue veins. He was only fifty-three, but after his seizures, he looked and acted seventy-three.

"There was a time when I thought I could take care of everyone," he said quietly, "but I was too ambitious and too proud. I made a mistake that cost Radford his peace of mind. That incident was the final straw for him and it never let him go. Every time I looked at him after that day, I saw the eyes of an old man looking back at me."

"What happened?"

"Something I still regret, but I have no right to tell. Radford's entitled to his privacy. If he chooses to talk about those times, it's his decision."

"All right, Papa, but could you talk to Radford about his nightmares? Kyle's convinced that he'll eventually leave again."

"He might, but I can see that he's tryin' hard not to." Her father's grizzled cheek caught in her hair as he rubbed it against the top of her head. "I'm asking you to respect his privacy. Radford's been through hell. Until he faces these things within himself, I don't think he will ever be settled."

Kyle was right then, Evelyn acknowledged silently, her heart crashing to her stomach. Radford's demons would eventually chase him away again. It was just a matter of time.

She sat for a long while with her head on her father's frail shoulder, her hand clasped in his. Random thoughts dashed in and out of her mind. She wondered what mistake her father had made, but she knew it would be unkind to ask him to betray Radford's confidence, so finally she let it go and changed the subject.

"Papa, why did Agatha Brown deliver a pie for you today?"

"I don't know. Maybe she's finally forgiven me for setting her aside for your mother."

"What?" Evelyn sat up and gawked at her father.

"Aggie and I were going to get married, but your mother came to town, and once I'd seen her, well..." His lips tilted in a soft smile of remembrance and his voice grew melancholy. "I'd never met anyone like your mother. There was a wildness about her that intrigued me. I tried to remain faithful to Aggie, but my heart decided otherwise."

"So you and Mother fell in love and you broke your engagement?" Evelyn asked, loving the romantic story.

"No. Your mother didn't want a thing to do with me."

"Well, you obviously got together."

He grinned. "I wore her down with my effusive charm."

Evelyn giggled. "Now, that I can believe. I'll bet she was just playing hard to get."

"Your mother disliked me. Aggie was her best friend and Mary was offended that I could consider anyone else when I'd already made a promise to Aggie. It was long after I broke the engagement before Mary would consider seeing me. Then of course, she fell instantly in love with my charming personality and begged me to marry her."

Evelyn grinned and tucked her feet up on the couch. "Then why is Mrs. Brown sweetening all of a sudden? Does she have her sights set on you again?"

"No. The day I went into her store with you and Radford was the first time in twenty-five years that she's spoken to me. I guess I just got tired of trying to avoid her and maybe she got tired of hating me. Perhaps she's just lonely."

"Then you're not interested in her?"

"When you love someone as much as I loved your mother there's nothing left for anyone else. In all these years I've never wanted anyone but your mother."

Evelyn's stomach dropped. What if she spent her life with Kyle and never lost her desire for Radford? She couldn't bear it. "How did you feel when you broke your engagement with Agatha?" she asked, knowing she needed to talk to Kyle.

"Rotten. She was a wonderful friend. But I didn't love her and I couldn't marry her after I knew how I felt about your mother. It wouldn't have been fair to any of us. I hated hurtin' Aggie, but I felt it was kinder to be honest about my feelings."

"How did you tell her?" Evelyn asked, wondering if her father knew about her feelings for Radford and was offering advice without revealing his suspicions.

"I couldn't think of any other way than to tell her the truth." His eyes grew distant, his expression sad. "She said she hated me and swore she'd never speak to me again. She didn't until the day I went in her store with you and Radford."

"It must have been awful to hurt each other like that." It would kill Evelyn to cause Kyle pain, yet it ate at her conscience each day knowing she was marrying him for less than noble reasons.

"It always hurts to lose a friend. But I couldn't pass up the chance of your mother's love."

"Is that what gave you the strength to end your relationship with Agatha?"

"No. It was knowin' there would always be a part of myself I couldn't give her. I decided that Aggie deserved more, and I didn't want to live without love."

A sinking feeling settled in Evelyn's stomach. She cared for Kyle, but it wasn't the kind of love her father and mother shared.

"Why so glum, pixie?" Her father asked, patting her hand.

Disconcerted that her heartache showed on her face, Evelyn wrestled a smile in place. "I was just wondering how Mama could have rejected you. You said there wasn't a woman around who could resist you in those days."

"Bahhh. Don't tell me you believe that malarkey. Your mother married me so I'd quit pesterin' her."

"I think she married you because she was a very smart lady who knew what a treasure she had." Evelyn wrapped her arms around her father and kissed his cheek, feeling deeply thankful for his love. "Personally, Papa, I think you're priceless."

Chapter Nineteen

Rebecca ran straight for the livery and burst through the door calling for Evelyn. Radford increased his stride and stepped into the barn behind his exuberant daughter.

"You're home!" Evelyn tossed aside a pitchfork and threw her arms around Rebecca. "I missed you, sprite." They clung together as if they'd been apart for years instead of the four days he and Rebecca had spent traveling to Syracuse and back.

"I missed you!" Rebecca declared, clinging to Evelyn's neck while Radford looked on with his heart aching. Rebecca had been utterly miserable from the minute they had left home. And so had Radford.

Not only had he missed Evelyn, but visiting the city where he and William had enlisted in the 149th NY volunteers had dredged up too many memories for Radford. He'd spent three endless years of fighting with that regiment before returning to Syracuse, battle-worn and forever changed, his pride hanging in shreds.

"Welcome home, Radford."

Evelyn's voice snapped him back to the present. He wanted to rush forward and sweep her into his arms, but he kept his feet planted despite the raw need coursing through him.

Kyle stepped from Gabrielle's stall. "What took so long to get a doctor?"

Radford choked out a laugh as he tried to gather his scattered senses. He nodded toward the doctor standing in the doorway. "I want you to meet an old friend of mine."

Amid introductions they wandered to the porch where William slept in a chair. When he opened his eyes and saw Rebecca hopping on one foot near Radford, he yelped in surprise. "Come here and give your grandpa a smooch, you little rascal."

Rebecca climbed onto his lap and squeezed his wrinkled neck until his cheek bunched beneath his eye. When she drew back, she touched a finger to his face. "You have water on your cheek, Grandpa."

"Got a little dust in my eye," he said, backhanding a tear from his face. He glanced up at Doc Kendall for a moment before recognition dawned. "Lawd! Is that really you, you old Salt Boiler?"

Radford laughed at William's use of their regiment's old nickname.

Doc Kendall chuckled and shook William's weak hand. "Who else would bother to come clear out here to see an ornery old cuss like you?"

Before William could respond, Rebecca scooted off his lap and tugged on Evelyn's hand. "I got a present for you, don't I, Daddy?"

Radford's smile was a balm to Evelyn's aching heart. How she'd missed seeing that face and hearing his laughter.

"Rebecca picked it out," he said.

"Yeah! All by myself," she declared importantly. She bent her elbow and tried to wiggle her hand into Radford's pocket. "Get it out, Daddy."

Radford laughed and reached in to withdraw the treasure. Evelyn would have thought it was gold the way Rebecca so proudly presented it to her. With care, she untied the pink ribbon and opened a small jewelry case, but when she saw what was inside, she gasped. It was gold! It was a pin in the shape of a miniature magnolia blossom, inlaid with mother-of-pearl. Evelyn traced a trembling finger over the delicate petals, remembering the day Radford told her that her mother claimed it was good luck to catch a falling magnolia blossom. Deeply touched by the beautiful reminder of her mother, and the fact that

Radford would give her something so special, Evelyn wished she could thank him, but she couldn't with Kyle looking on. Instead, she knelt down and hugged Rebecca. "This is beautiful," she said.

Rebecca drew back and captured Evelyn's cheeks between her hands. "Could you be my mama?" she asked, hope shining in her brown eyes.

The child's innocent plea for love shook Evelyn to the depths of her soul and she lifted her watery gaze to Radford. There was nothing she desired more than to make this precious child her own, to soothe her heartaches and share in her laughter, to watch her grow from dimples and curls into the graceful loveliness of womanhood. But when she glanced at Kyle's closed expression, Evelyn knew she needed to answer with caution. Warily, she shifted her gaze back to Radford, hoping for guidance, but he looked as though someone had just died. The air crackled with tension while they all awaited Evelyn's answer.

With deliberate tenderness, she took Rebecca's hands in her own and gave them a gentle squeeze. "You would make the most precious daughter a mother could have. I couldn't love you more if you were my very own," she answered, trying not to crush Rebecca's hopes while salving Kyle's concern.

Not knowing what else to say, Evelyn glanced at her father for help.

"Did I ever tell you about my old huntin' dog, Rebecca?"

Rebecca turned to her grandpa, her face lit with excitement. "You had a dog?" she asked, and Evelyn silently thanked her father for breaking the tension of Kyle's suspicious glance between her and Radford.

"Not just a dog. Red was the best dog ever born." He patted his knees. "Come up here and I'll tell you about the trick I played on him." When Rebecca was settled on his lap, he continued. "Old Red was the smartest dog I ever owned. If I wanted to go rabbit huntin', I'd take down my twelve-gauge shotgun and let Red get a look and a sniff then off he'd go. I never had to wait more than a few minutes before he'd chase up a fat cottontail for me. When it was duck season, I'd let him whiff my ten-gauge and what do you think he'd hunt up for me?"

"What?" Rebecca asked, her eyes bright with curiosity.

"Why, ducks, of course. That old dog knew just by sniffin' my gun what I wanted him to get for me."

"How'd he know?"

William knuckled away a grin and winked at Evelyn. Rebecca sat in his lap holding her foot, gazing up in rapt attention while he stretched his story to answer her. "... and if I let Red sniff rifle," her father was saying, "he knew we were going squirrel huntin'. But one day I tried to trick him. I brought out my fishin' pole and let Red sniff it a couple of times. He sat down and scratched behind his ear a bit then he jumped up and ran off like his tail was on fire."

"Where'd he go?" Rebecca asked excitedly.

"Well, I didn't know right away, but I was afraid I might have really confused him. I took my fishin' pole and headed toward the creek. And guess where I found that darn dog?"

"Where?" Rebecca asked, nearly leaping off his lap in suspense.

"In the garden diggin' worms to catch the fish with!"

Rebecca giggled and clapped her hands. "He knew! You didn't trick him one bit, Grandpa!"

Delighted laughter burst from her father, and joy surged through Evelyn's chest. What a glorious sound from a man who hadn't had many reasons for laughing since his wife died. It had taken this little girl, this newly proclaimed granddaughter, to make him happy again. Evelyn's gaze shifted to Radford, whose unrestrained, warm laughter made her eyes tear. To have a precious little girl to sit on her father's lap and giggle at his silly tales, and a charming husband who would take the time to listen was everything she could ever desire. But when

Evelyn looked at Kyle, she was scared to death she would never have that in her life.

Kyle caught her look and stood. "I have to check something at the house. Will you go with me?"

Surprised by his unexpected request, Evelyn nodded dumbly then went to the livery to get her mare.

"Did you see Rebecca's face when she saw you today?" Kyle asked as soon as they were away from the house.

Of course she had. Evelyn would never forget the beauty of that joy-filled expression. "Yes, why?"

"She was desperate to get her hands on you."

Evelyn smiled. "She missed me as much as I missed her."

"Do you think it's wise for her to be so dependent on you?"

"She needs a woman in her life," Evelyn answered.

"I agree, but it should be Radford's wife." Kyle reined in his stallion and dismounted in his side yard. "You can't be her mother. This situation is going to become confusing and painful for Rebecca when you move out."

"I love that little girl, just as you do," Evelyn said, understanding it wasn't Kyle's jealousy, but his love for Rebecca that prompted his concern. "Rebecca and I will just have to work through the problem of our separation if that becomes necessary."

"If?" Kyle took Evelyn's arm and helped her dismount. "You and Rebecca won't be living together once we're married."

"I'll be moving down the road, not across the country."

"Well, Radford might. Then what?"

He had a valid point. There was always the possibility that Radford would leave again, still even that risk couldn't make Evelyn pull away from the little girl who needed her.

Kyle raked his hair back. "Listen, Ev, I'm not telling you to turn away from Rebecca, but give some thought to how you're handling your relationship with her. I also want you to think about selling the livery and reinvesting in a new mill."

"What?"

"I'm sure your father will see that it makes more sense to invest in another sawmill that can earn more money with less effort."

"Don't you dare talk to Papa about this." Furious, Evelyn pressed a callused fingertip to Kyle's chest. "I'll never let you insult my father by telling him everything he's sweated for isn't good enough for you. I'd rather see him penniless and starving than to lose his pride."

Kyle captured her hand and slowly lowered it to her side, his eyes snapping with unleashed anger. "I expect to be treated with the same respect I've always given you."

"You call selling my heritage an act of respect?" She let the question rage between them as seconds ticked by in tense silence.

Slowly, with tightly held control, Kyle eased back and tipped his face heavenward. "Heritage is a set of characteristics that you receive from your parents. It's the traditions and culture they raise you in." He lowered his face and drilled her with a meaningful stare. "The livery is just a business with the sole purpose of making money."

"What would you know of heritage?" she asked, her voice iced with accusation. "You stripped your own brother of his."

Kyle reared back as though she'd delivered him a vicious blow. Never had Evelyn witnessed such a wounded look in his eyes and she immediately regretted her spiteful tongue. Wishing she could retract her words, she reached for his hand, but he stepped away.

"Don't be a hypocrite. If you're going to make allegations, don't sugarcoat them with apologies."

His naked pain exposed the vulnerable young man who used to share her heartaches, as well as his own, and it left Evelyn reeling with regret over her reckless words.

"I'm sorry, Kyle." She touched his arm. "That was cruel."

His nostrils flared and the familiar mask of control slipped back in place. "I have a ton of work left to finish on the house before our wedding so I'm going to have limited time during the next two weeks to see you." His gaze locked on hers. "I would like those few occasions to be pleasant."

"So would I." And she meant that.

"Then let's not discuss the livery until the wedding is behind us."

Evelyn bit her tongue. She had no intention of selling the livery, but Kyle needed to calm down before she tried to reason with him.

"I know I've been an ass on occasion, but I had hoped you held me in higher regard."

She flushed with shame. "I do." She slipped her arms around his hard waist. "It just seems we define things differently. You see with your head. I see with my heart."

"Look at me."

She raised her gaze. A tired softness shone in the brown depths of his eyes.

"For your own sake, learn to see with both and save yourself some heartache."

He kissed her then, and Evelyn tried with all her heart to return the kiss, but it was an act of apology rather than passion that united them.

Chapter Twenty

Radford made his way upstairs, taking care to miss the third step that creaked. At this late hour, he didn't want to wake William or the doctor, and especially not Evelyn, whom he'd purposely kept away from all evening. His arms itched to hold her, but after seeing Kyle's face when Rebecca asked Evelyn to be her mother, Radford knew he'd be encouraging a disaster.

He crossed through his room and entered the nursery, but was stopped by a vision so lovely it took his breath away.

October moonlight slanted through the nursery window and fell like gold dust upon Evelyn and Rebecca, who were sleeping in the rocking chair. Evelyn's cheek rested lightly upon Rebecca's curls, her arms circling the small bundle in her lap. Rebecca's ankles peeked from beneath her yellow blanket, her bare feet a miniature work of art against the slender length of Evelyn's silk-covered thighs.

Evelyn's hair draped her shoulders and the side of the chair in long, ebony waves. Her legs were bare to the knees and her gentle hands rested upon Rebecca's back.

Her dark lashes contrasted with the ivory of Evelyn's cheekbones. Radford moved closer, wishing he could see the emeralds they concealed, but he didn't wake her. He knelt beside the chair and gathered her hair in his palms. He rubbed the luxuriant strands between his fingers, reveling in the midnight satin. He loved her hair. He loved her callused hands. He loved... her.

He lifted his face and looked at the woman he had unwittingly fallen in love with. How could he not love her? Evelyn had drawn him from the darkness of his lonely world. She'd become his sun. For him, it was the first time in years that tomorrow seemed like a promise.

He touched her cheek and her eyes fluttered open. They were sultry with sleep and confusion as she sat forward.

"What's wrong?"

He placed a finger across her lips. "I need to ask you something. Why are you marrying my brother? I've never heard you say you love him."

"We need each other."

I need you more, he thought, and so does my little girl. "What about love, Evelyn?"

Sadness filled her eyes and she looked away. "Let it go, Radford."

Searching her face, he waited for her to explain, to make him understand how she could marry his brother when her eyes said she didn't love him. But she was silent, the anguish in her expression matching the pain in his chest when he finally understood that she was going to go through with her wedding plans.

Resolutely, he lifted his daughter from her lap, intentionally filling his arms to keep them from reaching for Evelyn. He stepped away from her. "I'll put her in bed. Goodnight."

She stood up, but hesitated as if she wanted to say something.

"Go, Evelyn. Please," he said, turning away from the need in her eyes.

⊷⊶

At five-thirty in the morning, Evelyn poured coffee for herself and the doctor. "How ill is my father?" she asked.

A flicker of discomfort crossed the doctor's face as he looked into his coffee cup. "If he rests and doesn't have another attack of apoplexy, he'll be fine."

"Is that the truth?"

The doctor glanced up. "Yes, but he needs his rest." Evelyn nodded and the doctor laid his elbow on the table. "How often does Radford have nightmares?"

The bluntness of the doctor's statement surprised Evelyn. She knew Radford's belt of anguish last night had been loud enough to wake everyone from a sound sleep, but she assumed no one would speak of it. She had desperately wanted to go to Radford last night, but after their brief meeting in the nursery, she knew she would cave in the minute she touched him.

She met the doctor's concerned gaze and thought maybe she'd finally found someone who could help Radford. Leaning against the sink, she cradled her cup in her palms. "Radford has nightmares quite often. Do you know of anything that can help him?"

"It depends on whether he wants help or not."

"He doesn't," she answered without hesitation. Radford kept his past shut up like a condemned house.

"Then he may be in for some problems."

"Like what?" Evelyn asked, a sense of dread filling her.

"Well, other than his nightmares, he could experience anything from unexpected acts of violence to complete insanity."

Evelyn gasped. "Are you saying it will happen?"

"Not at all." The doctor smiled like a patient grandfather. "Under the right circumstances, though, any one of us could be pushed beyond our limits. I've seen perfectly sane men lose their sanity over an event that seems insignificant until I discover the horrifying events preceding it. People who have suffered traumas seem to be more susceptible." The doctor drained his cup and set it aside. "Has Radford acted out of character since coming home?"

Evelyn's first thought was of the day Radford shoved Kyle away from Rebecca in the garden. He had overreacted to his own fear, but the feral look in his eyes and the animal snarl that had come from his throat were not normal. She'd had her own experience in Radford's bedroom, but she would never reveal that. "He is as sane as I am."

The doctor studied her, his white brows perplexed. "You've had conversations about his nightmares, though?"

More than that, Evelyn thought, but she merely nodded.

"Then maybe he'll talk with you when he feels safe."

"Shouldn't he be talking with his brothers, or his mother?"

The doctor shrugged. "Maybe Radford can't bare his soul to his family." He looked at Evelyn. "I think he needs a friend to talk to. You are friends, aren't you?"

"Yes," she said without hesitation, but in her heart, they were much more than that.

"Then he'll open up when he feels safe, when he believes he can trust you with the truth."

"Is that the only way to keep him from leaving?"

The doctor wrinkled his forehead. "Hard to say. I think Radford needs to ease his conscience before he can settle down. In my opinion, he won't find peace until he spits out what's eating at him."

Evelyn's hope flagged. Radford would never talk about something he was trying so hard to bury. "I'm sorry to sound so doubtful, Doctor, but I know Radford. No matter what I say to him, it won't convince him to tell me about his past."

"Don't be so certain. My wife found a way to reach me." At Evelyn's look of surprise, the doctor smiled. "It was her love and understanding that encouraged me to talk. I carried grief and shame so deep that I couldn't stand to look in the mirror. She held me many times while I wept the poison from my soul, and she mended my battered heart with love, time and time again."

"Radford doesn't have a wife, Dr. Kendall."

"Then he should find one."

Chapter Twenty-one

On the last Saturday of October, Evelyn experienced an excruciating attack of nerves while getting ready to attend the neighbor's wedding. In exactly one week, she would be speaking her own vows with Kyle. She would be promising to love, honor, and obey her husband. She would be consigning herself to a lifetime of friendship rather than love.

"Are you finished yet?" Rebecca asked, squirming on the bench at Evelyn's dressing table.

"Yes, but I have a present for you." Evelyn dangled an emerald silk ribbon in front of Rebecca. It was the silk ribbon her mother had given her the day before she died, but Evelyn wanted Rebecca to have it.

Rebecca's eyes widened and she raised the ribbon to her mouth, rubbing the satin across her lips. Rather than the joy Evelyn expected to feel by giving something so sentimental, she felt a deep sadness for Rebecca. How could this child's mother have given her up? The idea that any woman could abandon her own daughter was simply beyond Evelyn's comprehension.

While she tied the ribbon in Rebecca's hair, her heart strained toward the little girl who sat, ankles out, on a ratty old dressing stool with her tattered yellow blanket resting in her lap.

"There you go," Evelyn said, swallowing the lump in her throat as Rebecca climbed off the bench.

Rebecca grinned as she admired herself in the looking glass, patting her curls with tiny palms and twirling in a circle to fluff her new dress. "I want to show Grandpa how pretty I am!" she said then wheeled from the room and barreled downstairs.

Evelyn sat on her bed and pressed her fingers to her eyes to stop the sting behind her lids. How was she going to live without the daily presence of that little girl? How was she going to bear seeing Radford and Rebecca turn to another woman?

More importantly, how was she going to live with her conscience if she married Kyle knowing she could never give him the love he deserved? Despite the promises they'd given each other, it was wrong to mislead Kyle about her feelings. Somehow she would tell him the truth tonight. Though she and her father could use the security Kyle would provide, they would all ultimately suffer if Evelyn took her vows with Kyle. He'd be furious at her for breaking their engagement at the last minute, but she knew Kyle's anger would stem from a deep sense of hurt that she had broken a promise he'd invested his heart in. Still, it would be kinder than letting him find out five years from now that she couldn't love him. Maybe someday he'd forgive her. If not, at least Evelyn's honesty would allow her to reclaim the integrity she'd lost the night she gave her heart to Radford.

Radford hadn't spoken privately to her since the night in the nursery, and despite the ache in her heart, Evelyn respected his decision to honor his brother. She'd never wanted to come between him and Kyle. She'd never meant to make a promise to one and fall in love with the other.

With resolve, she drew herself up and turned toward the wardrobe. Kyle would be arriving soon to take her to the wedding and she wouldn't keep him waiting.

She took out the green silk dress that her father had purchased for her three years ago. The fabric slipped luxuriously beneath her rough fingers, but when Evelyn saw her plain face reflected in the mirror above the shimmering beauty of the gown, she understood why she'd never worn it. She would look ridiculous in anything fancier than britches and work boots. Taking a last, hopeful look at her dismal wardrobe, Evelyn realized nothing else would do for this occasion.

Resolutely, she opened the drawer and removed a package wrapped in tissue that her father had given her with the dress. She shrugged off her wrapper then withdrew the beautiful undergarments. Slipping the chemise over her bare skin, she marveled at the heavenly texture of it against her ribs. The nainsook corset was decorated with Valenciennes lace and a green interwoven ribbon that tied up the front. The matching tie-top drawers were also nainsook and trimmed with a three-inch embroidered ruffle that rested prettily above her knees. Gathering her nerve, she stepped into the gown and attempted the column of tiny pearl buttons, but her nervous fingers kept slipping. She was used to handling shovels and harnesses, not buttons the size of nail heads.

She smoothed the dress across her hips and cringed when it snagged on her rough hands. Slowly, she turned in a circle and raised her eyes to the dressing table mirror. The silky richness swirled outward then settled around her ankles like a limpid green pool. The afternoon light reflected in warm waves along the material and upward to the tailored bodice where her hair lay like a black sash across the rich fabric. Her hair... her awful hair.

Trancelike, she drew her hand over her thick braid. She loosened the crisscrossed skeins and finger-combed it into tumbled disarray. One look at her disheveled reflection reminded Evelyn she was a woman who didn't know the first thing about dancing and flirting. Her skin had grown used to woolen shirts and rough denim britches and her feet were accustomed to the height of boot heels, not pretty sandals.

Turning, she eyed the pair of matching green kid sandals with hand-turned soles and fancy ribbon laces that lay on the bed. Bought to match the dress, they beckoned until Evelyn perched on the mattress beside them. With unsure fingers she drew on her hose, careful not to snag them then slowly slipped her feet into the shoes and tied them closed with the silk ribbon. The feeling of the sleek, cool interior sent shivers up her neck.

She stood and wiggled her toes then took a couple of steps. Her hips became fluid, swaying of their own volition. Her legs felt longer, sleeker. The narrowness of the shoes offered less solidity than her boots and shortened her stride. The bows crossing her arched feet looked so feminine that Evelyn covered her mouth. She couldn't possibly wear anything so rich—so feminine. She'd look ridiculous.

It was all she had, she reminded herself, privately coveting the sleek material snugging her skin. Her back became straighter, her chin a bit higher, her hips swaying gracefully as she walked. Disconcerted, she tightened her buttocks and stiffened her legs. Four more steps and still the sway.

Ignoring her inner doubts, she brushed out her hair while her curling tongs were heating on her lamp. She had no idea how long to heat the iron and her first attempt singed her hair. After they cooled some, she tried again and managed a tight curl. It took several minutes to curl her thick hair and keep the tongs heated, but when she finished and looked in the mirror at what she'd accomplished, her hands flew to her mouth in horror. "Oh no," she whispered to her wild reflection.

Her hair flew in umpteen different directions and spiraled around her like a bushel of wood shavings. In a state of panic, she brushed through the unruly mass until she could gather it on top of her head and secure it with a tightly tied ribbon. Despairing that it could ever be contained with pins, she wrapped, tucked, twisted, and pinned, until finally the thick mass was resting on top of her head—and tumbling down the back of her neck—and spiraling around her pink-stained cheeks.

It was not the artfully coiffed hairstyle that Nancy had shown her how to arrange, but it would have to do. Kyle would be arriving any moment. She clipped on her mother's pearl earrings and took one last look in the mirror. It felt divine to be wrapped in silk so shimmering and alive it seemed to breathe. Her reflection lifted her heart, her feminine cascade of curls appealing to her woman's ego. But reality weighed her hopes, taunting her for wistful thoughts, reminding her that she was plain Evelyn Tucker who knew more about the workings of a livery than that of a woman.

Defiantly, she fastened the matching pearl necklace around her neck, pausing to smell the jasmine on her wrists. Mrs. Brown had given Evelyn the soap last week when she made her first payment on Rebecca's doll. Evelyn had used the scented cake on every inch of her body this morning, and for the second time in her life, she felt feminine. The first time was in Radford's strong arms.

⸻◊─ ─◊⸻

Radford heard Evelyn's bedroom door close and purposefully stepped into the hall in front of her, halting in stunned appreciation when his eyes met hers. The emerald vision before him left him speechless. He could see the breathless rise and fall of her chest, but his own breathing seemed to have stopped. His gaze traveled the length of her gown and returned slowly to her face that had flushed to the color of spring roses. Her eyes were the exact green of her dress and that hair... that glorious abundance of shining black ringlets that he loved unbound and swirling around her hips, surprised him that it could be so magnificent styled any other way. A single strand dangled seductively over her ear and trailed between her collarbones.

Unconsciously, he moved forward and cupped her arms in his palms, letting his hands slide down her silk sleeves until they rested at her wrists. "You're magnificent."

"Thank you." Her voice shook and she lowered her lashes.

He gently squeezed her wrists, regaining her attention. "I need to talk to you."

"Evelyn!" William called up the stairs. "There's an overdressed young man down here that says he's willing to give you a ride to the wedding if you're ready to go. You are ready, aren't you?" William hollered from below.

"Yes, Papa," Evelyn said over the railing.

"Tell him you forgot something in your room," Radford urged, desperate to steal a few minutes alone with her.

"I can't." Evelyn ducked her face. "I have to go." He tightened his hold around her wrists, but she stepped around him and gently, but firmly, pulled free. "You don't have to explain about honoring Kyle," she said quietly. "I understand. And I admire you for it."

⚓

Kyle stood by the door, as spit-shined as his Sunday shoes, and incredibly handsome. Evelyn flushed as his eyes raked her from her tumbled curls to her green-encased toes, staring until her father cuffed his shoulder.

"Come here, pixie, before this boy drools on himself," he said. He put his thin arms around her and hugged her. "Sometimes you remind me so much of your mother it tears my heart out." He kissed her cheek then steered her toward Kyle. "Go on before I start rainin' all over myself. I'll follow with Radford."

Kyle didn't move and Evelyn squirmed beneath his intense regard. "Will you quit staring like you've never seen me in a dress before?" She whisked her palms down the front of her gown. "I'm the same girl you chased through the apple orchard."

"Sorry," he said with a sheepish grin. He stepped aside and opened the door for her, but the instant it banged closed behind them, he reached out and caught her elbow. "You'd better stay away from that orchard tonight," he said, his voice alarmingly seductive. "I wouldn't let you get away this time." In a moment he would be trying to kiss her and she just couldn't let him. She cared too deeply for him to let him pursue a relationship with no future. Instead of commenting, she tugged him toward the carriage, let him assist her inside then talked about her horses all the way to the wedding.

The church was packed when they arrived and she heard the murmur begin when they entered. She huddled beneath her shawl, blushing from the surprised stares of all the guests. When the ceremony began and the bride and groom gazed at each other with adoration, Evelyn knew she'd made the right decision about Kyle.

Her legs quaked as he escorted her from the church and took her to the reception. Radford stood just inside Colter Hall beside Duke and Boyd, holding Rebecca's hand in his long, bronzed fingers. His hair was brushed back into thick, deep-brown waves that fell over his white collar. Even next to Boyd's extraordinary good looks, Radford was more attractive, more compelling in his cheviot suit of charcoal gray that complemented his lean height and dark features.

All eyes turned toward Evelyn and Kyle as though they were unknown guests. The men gawked at her the same way Kyle had earlier and she had never felt more conspicuous in her life.

Kyle touched her back and she looked up into his beaming face. "I believe you're creating a scene. The girls are green and the older ladies are breaking their necks to get a look at you. Not to mention the men."

She stared at him for a second before she laughed. "Oh, bosh. They're probably trying to see if I'm wearing my work boots beneath my dress."

He laughed and gestured toward the crowd. "Look."

She did then clasped his arm for dear life. "Get me out of this doorway and find our table." She heard his deep chuckle and silently cursed him as he winked at his brothers on the way by. The strutting cock was enjoying this while she was dodging the stares of men like Greg Hopper who was having trouble finding his mouth with his beer mug.

Kyle took her to the table their families were sharing then brought her a glass of punch. "Don't drink that too fast. I heard that Perry Morton laced it with corn liquor."

Evelyn gulped it down, hoping to calm her quaking limbs. Her father raised a gray eyebrow and she shrugged.

He laughed and shook his head.

She glanced at Kyle's mother, but she was playing with Rebecca and Helen who were ducking behind Doc Kendall's chair.

Evelyn drew a deep breath and tried to clear her mind. She watched the dancers twirl by, swirling scents of lavender powder and cologne, their laughter cheerful as they clung to each other. As her gaze traveled the room, she smelled the musty old wood, tobacco, yeasty beer, and beeswax, smells unlike her livery or Brown and Shepherd's store.

Radford stood a few feet away, laughing with his brothers and their competitor, Tom Drake, but when he spotted Evelyn, his smile disappeared. His eyes grew dark, searching hers as if asking her a silent question.

Tom's daughter, Amelia, joined their party and Radford turned away to greet Evelyn's friend. Amelia's chestnut-colored, long hair was pulled up in an elegant twist and secured with a pearl clasp that matched the buttons on her dress of mocha brown. Evelyn admired Amelia's simple elegance, but she envied her Radford's attention. When Amelia smiled and waved, Evelyn returned the greeting with sincerity. Still, she was relieved when Boyd swept Amelia into a dance and away from Radford.

"My dear, you are simply lovely tonight."

Startled, Evelyn turned to see Agatha Brown seating herself in the empty chair beside her.

"How did you get all that hair on top of your head in such a becoming style?" the store owner asked with a smile in her eyes.

"I used every pin in the house then I stole Radford's horseshoe nails. They hurt a little, but they kept it in place."

Mrs. Brown laughed delightedly. "Well, that's just the answer I deserve for being nosy."

Evelyn sobered immediately. "I didn't mean that at all, Mrs. Brown. I was jesting."

"I know that, dear. I'm just discovering how fun it is to play again. Your father tells me I used to have quite a sense of humor, that I used to make him laugh. We were just talking about the day when..."

As Mrs. Brown rattled on, Evelyn sat in a state of amazement, for she'd never really seen this side of the woman.

"... but my Frank took me to our favorite picnic area at Point Graitiot where we could watch the ships sail in and out of Dunkirk. We'd share fresh bread and cheese and"—Agatha paused, casting a conspiratorial look at Evelyn—"and a few sips of wine. It was quite romantic, really."

To think that Mrs. Brown went on picnics and drank wine was shocking. But Evelyn hung on every word, blocking Radford from her thoughts and the fact that the Grayson men were openly admiring Amelia Drake, whom Evelyn could see out of the corner of her envious eye.

"Picnics by Lake Erie were twice as romantic at night, but Frank and I were married then," Mrs. Brown said with a wink. "Do you and that young man of yours go for picnics?"

"No, he's too busy with the mill."

"No one should be too busy to spend time with their sweetheart. That's very important," she warned, waving a finger. "You need a man that would put everything aside if you asked him to. That's how you know if he really loves you."

Evelyn was certain Kyle would not take a day away from his work simply because she asked him to do so. Perhaps it didn't signify a lack of love, but it reaffirmed her decision to end their engagement.

They sat in silence for a moment then Mrs. Brown chuckled. "You're a very patient girl."

Evelyn's brows lifted. "I am?"

"I waited until you were sitting alone so we could talk. But I've been blathering like an idiot, giving you every opportunity to question me about your father, and you haven't asked a thing."

"Why, I would never... It would be—"

"Improper," Mrs. Brown finished for her. "Well, I can tell you all about being proper. You may as well be dead." At Evelyn's in-drawn breath, Mrs. Brown continued. "That's how I've felt since Frank died. I was expected to act the mourning widow, and I did because I was devastated. But after a while I forgot what it was like to be happy." She turned to Evelyn, her face pained. "I spent twelve lonely years that way and it was awful. I started to remember how special life is the day you came in the store with that beautiful little girl. I saw the wonder on her face when she spotted the doll, and I could tell by your eyes that you would have sacrificed anything in that moment to be able to give it to her. I thought, this is the spirit of love. To have someone who needs you as much as you need them. I knew that I could learn something from you."

"What could I possibly teach you?"

"Compassion. Strength. Both traits remind me of your mother."

"They do?" Evelyn asked.

Mrs. Brown leaned back in her chair, holding a glass of punch in her lap. "Your mother made up her own mind about things and had the daring to follow through with her decisions. At one time, she was my dearest friend, Evelyn. I miss her deeply."

Evelyn glanced down the table at her father to make sure he was occupied with the girls. "Mrs. Brown, would tell me about my parents? Until recently I had no idea about your engagement to my father, and sometimes I feel like I never knew my mother."

"I came over here so we could talk. I need to know my best friend's daughter. It's rather selfish of me, wouldn't you say?"

Evelyn smiled. "I wouldn't. I'm flattered."

Mrs. Brown set her empty glass on the table and folded her hands. "When your father broke our engagement, I was hurt and wrongly blamed your mother. I met Frank two years later and was shocked to find I could care so deeply for him. That's when I realized your father did me a favor. If I had married him, I would never have met Frank. I would never have known the joy I had with my husband for fourteen years. You see, your father gave me the opportunity to find true love and be happy. It was a gift. He tried to explain it to me then, but I was angry and felt sorry for myself. And I was jealous. Frank taught me to be true to myself and that is why we were so happy."

"It must be unbearable without your husband."

Agatha squeezed Evelyn's hand. "It is awful, but believe me, Evelyn, love is a gift worth any sacrifice.

Evelyn thought in that moment that she could not like Agatha Brown more. "Mrs. Brown, would you consider befriending my father again? I'm sure the two of you would make very good friends, even if you're not suited for marriage."

Agatha's eyes softened to warm brown and her lips trembled. "Your father and I renewed our friendship the day I dropped off the apple pie for him. He's even promised me a dance tonight."

Evelyn smiled. "No wonder my parents loved you."

Agatha's eyes welled up. "All these years I've kept a handkerchief up my sleeve and now I can't find the dratted thing when I need it most!"

They were still laughing when Kyle came to claim Evelyn for a dance. She pressed her elbows to her side and ducked her head. "I'd rather not, Kyle," she said, not wanting to encourage him knowing how their evening would end.

Kyle leaned down and spoke near her ear. "My arms have been empty long enough." He caught Evelyn's waist and lifted her from the chair, guiding her directly onto the dance floor without giving her a moment to argue.

She clutched his arm. "I don't know how to dance."

"You're with friends and family," he said, gesturing to Radford and Amelia who were their immediate neighbors.

She bit her lip and turned away from the sight of Radford holding another woman. "Can't we please sit and enjoy the music?"

"Not tonight." Kyle drew her into his arms. "We'll be dancing at our wedding, Ev. Tonight's a fine night to learn how to waltz."

She accepted Kyle's trembling hand, a feeling of dread pulsing through her. She focused on Kyle's broad chest, blocking out everything except the movement of their feet and the sound of the music. Undoubtedly, Kyle's sure steps and guiding hand made her ignorance of the function less obvious, still Evelyn tried to leave as soon as the song ended.

"Not yet," he said, keeping her on the floor for the full set of four songs. By the time he escorted her back to their table, Evelyn was feeling somewhat more comfortable with the dancing, but was heartsick and just wanted to go home.

The musicians played several more sets before Kyle danced with Amelia.

"Don't worry about them," Boyd said, grabbing Evelyn's hand and pulling her up from the table. "I'm going to sweep Amelia out of Kyle's arms and you're going to help me do it."

Duke and Radford caught Boyd's elbows and hauled him back. "I'm next," they said in unison.

Duke raised an eyebrow, but Radford didn't bat a lash. "I'm pulling rank, Duke. Oldest first, remember?" Without giving Evelyn a chance to decline, Radford caught her hand and led her onto the dance floor.

"Don't do this," she said, afraid everyone would see the truth in her eyes.

"You're too tense." He smiled and drew her into his arms.

"I don't know how to dance."

His eyes smiled, but he didn't. "Neither do I, but let's not tell anyone. They'll make us stop." He gave her waist a gentle squeeze. "Hang on, Tomboy. You'll do fine."

"I don't want to dance with you."

"I know." He sighed and drew her closer. "But I need to do this."

The soft strains of music filled the room with long, warm cords that drifted around them, enfolding them in a bouquet of whispers and soft caresses. Evelyn felt him drawing her closer to his chest and was helpless to fight her desire to be there. Of their own volition, her eyes lifted to his and she drank in the angles and contours of his face, the dark contrast of his brows against his tan skin.

"If you don't quit looking at me like that, I am going to kiss you right here on this dance floor. On the lips."

She pushed away. "I need to sit down."

"You're drawing attention," he said, swinging her back into his arms as though clowning with her.

Evelyn tried to steady her knees and keep from clinging to him, though she desperately wanted to bury her face in his chest and pretend the rest of the world didn't exist. "You're tearing me apart, Radford."

He leaned back and met her eyes, but she ducked her head to hide the tremble in her lip. The rush of emotion stuck in her throat and made it ache. Radford's fingers tightened on her waist. "Hey," he said quietly, but Evelyn kept her head down, not wanting him to see the moisture in her eyes. "I just wanted a minute alone with you. It wasn't supposed to be like this."

"Like what?" Kyle asked, stopping beside them, the suspicion in his voice causing Evelyn to jerk away from Radford.

"So warm in here," Radford answered, though his voice was strained. "It's nearly November. When is it going to cool off?"

Kyle slipped a possessive arm around Evelyn's waist and glared at Radford. "Maybe when you release my fiancée. Get your own partner, Radford. The last dance is mine."

"I want to leave, Kyle. Let's follow Radford and Papa home," she pleaded, suddenly afraid to be alone with him.

Kyle refused to forfeit his dance and held her prisoner in his strong arms as Radford escorted her father and Rebecca outside.

"Let's go to our house tonight," Kyle said in her ear.

Panicked, yet unable to meet his eyes while she lied, Evelyn hung her head. "I drank too much of Perry's punch and I'm sick to my stomach," she said, but the truth was, she was sick of lying and sick at heart.

Kyle pulled into her driveway silent and scowling. "What's Radford doing in the livery at this time of night?" he asked, nodding toward the small window of the tack room illuminated by soft lantern light.

"I don't know." After Kyle's scowl on the dance floor, Radford was probably staying clear of the house to avoid antagonizing him further. Kyle slowed the carriage near the porch, but Evelyn touched his shoulder. "Pull around to the far side of the driveway," she said, indicating a shadowed area away from the house and barn that would give them some privacy.

The carriage wheels crunched through dry leaves then rolled to a stop. Kyle turned to her with a smile blooming on his face. "Are you going to give me one of those monkey kisses again?"

Evelyn's chest grew tense and she met Kyle's eyes. "No," she said softly. "I want to talk to you."

His expression turned wary. "Why?"

"I know I promised I'd always be your friend, and I will," she said sincerely. "I'll always care for you, Kyle, but I... I can't keep my promise to never leave you."

His shoulders stiffened, but he remained silent, his eyes piercing hers.

"Do you remember how old we were when we made those promises?" she asked.

"Old enough to know what we were committing to," he said, his voice hard-edged.

"But too young to know that we'd be different people now."

"We haven't changed."

Evelyn curled her fingers into a fist, her chipped nails digging into her palm. Even though she sat beside him in a silk dress with her hair in curls, Kyle couldn't see that she'd changed from his childhood friend into a woman who needed love. They'd even kissed each other and he couldn't see a difference!

She lowered her gaze to the fingernail she was destroying with her nervous picking. "I want a marriage based on more than friendship and promises," she said.

"What else would you base a marriage on?" Kyle rammed his fingers through his hair. "You aren't making any sense, Ev. Something has been going on with you and I have no idea how to talk to you anymore."

"That's because we don't talk to each other. We have business meetings. We argue over the livery. You haven't spoken from your heart about your dreams since you were nineteen years old."

"I don't care about dreams," he said in exasperation. "I have too many people depending on me to let my mind wander off on a tangent."

The rising irritation in his voice unnerved Evelyn, but she forced herself to continue. "We live our lives too differently, Kyle. I want picnics and to spend time with my husband who will share a cup of tea with me late at night while we talk about our life together. I want tickling matches with our children and a man who knows how to laugh. I haven't heard an honest laugh from you in years. I'm afraid I never will." She held his gaze, her own growing misty. "I'm afraid I'll never hear you say you love me."

He closed his eyes and released a long, tired sigh. "Ev, love usually comes after marriage."

Though she was relieved Kyle didn't suddenly proclaim his love and make it more difficult for her to break their engagement, it still hurt knowing he couldn't say he loved her. "I don't want to spend the rest of my life searching for something that isn't possible between us," she said quietly.

"How do you know what's possible? We haven't spent more than a few minutes together since we got engaged. You'll see the possibilities after we've spent some private time together."

She shook her head. "No, I won't because I'm not going to marry you."

His eyebrows plunged downward. "What are you talking about?"

"I want more than a partnership," she whispered, clenching her hands in front of her.

He stared as if she'd lost her mind. "I'm not calling off this wedding, Evelyn. I've invested too much time to start over. You'll just have to settle for a man who knows about honoring his promises and being loyal. It may not be a picnic or a cup of tea, but it's my best offer."

Evelyn had never regretted anything more than the anguish she saw in his face, but she forced herself to finish making the break. "I can't accept your offer."

Kyle's fists clenched around the reins and he glared at her for several long seconds. "Get out. I can't talk to you right now."

She touched his arm. "I can explain this better if you'd just calm down and listen a minute."

He jerked away from her. "I'm not interested in talking tonight. I'm going to find Perry Morton and kill him for spiking that punch you were drinking all evening."

"It's not the punch influencing my decision."

He jumped out of the carriage, caught her around the waist, and swung her out, planting her feet on the ground. "We'll settle this tomorrow when you're thinking straight," he said then climbed aboard, snapped the reins, and bolted out of her driveway.

Confused and hurting, Evelyn turned toward the quiet sanctuary of her livery. Even if she couldn't communicate with Kyle anymore, she didn't want to lose his friendship. Tomorrow she'd go talk to him and try to make him understand that breaking their engagement had been the right thing to do.

She wandered across the lawn, seeking a place to calm her mind and find a way to reach through Kyle's anger.

When Radford stepped from the darkened doorway of the livery, she gasped and stumbled back a step. She'd forgotten about the light in the window.

Chapter Twenty-two

Radford moved into the moonlight and Evelyn's breath caught. She should go to the house, but she couldn't force herself to turn away from the appeal in his eyes.

"Remember the night in my bedroom when I said I was feeling dangerous?" he asked quietly.

A tingle of warning crawled up her back, and she took a step away from him.

"I've been out of control all evening, Evelyn. Every time I saw you in Kyle's arms, I wanted to shove him aside and pull you into my own."

Her heart pounded and her gaze locked with his.

"I can't pretend anymore. I need you," he said, his gaze dark, intense.

Stunned, she could barely force herself to reply. "I need you, too," she whispered.

He held out his hand. "Then come here," he said, his voice compelling her to move toward him.

He drew her inside the barn, pushed the door closed with his shoulder then guided her to the tack room. Soft yellow light reflected in his eyes as he lowered the lighting. "Unless you tell me otherwise, I'm going to tell Kyle how I feel. I have to, Evelyn." His dark-eyed gaze moved over her like a gentle caress as he stepped forward and brushed his thumb across her lips. "I've never experienced this feeling in my life. I don't want to lose it. I want to marry you."

Wings of joy lifted her heart. She wanted to be his wife, his friend, and mother to his beautiful daughter. Overcome with emotion, she raised her face and kissed him..

The fecund smell of hay and leather mixed with the fragrance of Radford's cologne and wool suit. The lingering hint of a sweet cigar and the light taste of whiskey upon his tongue filled her senses, leaving her reeling in the intoxicating potpourri of his kiss. He wanted to marry her...

Radford retreated first, pulling back and gritting his teeth. "I'm too weak tonight," he said, his voice hoarse and shaky. "Go inside. We'll talk more in the morning then I'll go see Kyle."

She didn't want to talk. Despite her heartache over Kyle, she felt free and alive and wanted to experience every wild emotion rushing through her veins. She kissed Radford's neck and nipped his chin with her teeth.

His whole body trembled. "If I lock that door, like I'm tempted to do, it will be a long time before it opens again."

She locked the door herself. This man was going to be her husband. They were going to share a future that she wanted to begin now.

His brows shot upward. "What are you doing?"

She silenced him with another bold kiss, but he broke away.

"You have to go."

"Not yet."

"You're killing me." He fumbled with the pins in her hair until Evelyn reached up and pulled them free, one pin after another falling to the floor until her curls tumbled over her shoulders and fell to her hips. He dug his hands into the thick strands and buried his face in her neck then he groaned and grappled for the door lock. "Go!" he commanded, but Evelyn stopped his hand.

"I broke my engagement, Radford."

He reared back, his eyes wide as he stared at her.

"I couldn't promise to love and honor Kyle when I wanted to do this with you," she said, threading her fingers into his hair.

He braced his palms against the door, his arms bracketing her head. "You're serious?"

She nodded.

"Kyle must have been—"

Evelyn put her fingers over his mouth. "He was, but we'll talk about it tomorrow." She wrapped her arms around his waist and pulled him against her. "I don't want to talk tonight."

His nostrils flared and he lowered his mouth to her neck.

She kissed his jaw and worked up to his temple. "You smell so good."

He swept her hair away from her body then let it fall around her hips. "I love your hair." He linked fingers with her and brought her knuckles to his lips. "I love your callused hands and the way they treat my daughter. I love the way they care for your father. They're beautiful, honest hands." He kissed her fingers then freed the buttons on her sleeves. "Last chance to unlock the door," he whispered, brushing her eyebrow with his lips.

Unashamed of her need, Evelyn pushed his suit coat open and ran her hands up his chest.

His eyes turned darker than she'd ever seen them. He tugged open the long line of pearl buttons down the front of her dress and gently pushed it off her shoulders. It fell to her feet. With trembling hands, he released the silk ties of her corset and pushed the straps of her chemise off her shoulders. His nostrils flared when he saw her breasts, but he didn't touch them. He untied her drawers and the ties to her stockings. The lacy undergarments fell to the floor, frothing at Evelyn's feet like a small cascade of water as she stood naked above them.

Radford's eyes swept her body. She dropped her chin and let her hair fall around her like a protective cloak.

"Don't hide. You're beautiful." He pushed her hair away then reached down and lifted her into his arms. He crossed the room and lowered her to the narrow cot against the wall. "I have an unfair advantage at the moment," he said, reaching for the buttons on his trousers.

As Radford undressed, Evelyn was unable to look away. The white of his shorts contrasted sharply with the black hair on his legs and his tanned, firm waist. When he reached for the waistband of his undershorts, his eyes met hers as he slid them down the length of his long, hard legs. When Evelyn's gaze traveled back up, she knew a moment of true amazement. He was splendid, with a lean waist and narrow hips, so regal in his desire, the boldness of him there for her to admire or fear.

He knelt before her, removed her shoes and hose then drew her down on the bed, the heat of his body branding her as he pulled her into his arms.

She smoothed her palms over his skin, not because she was so bold, but simply because she could not resist. A dark line of hair covered his chest and tapered to a vee as it descended his hard stomach. His muscles quivered as her hands traveled over his warm skin, coarse hair, and hard nipples.

He kissed her and brushed her private curls with his fingers. Evelyn gasped as he stroked her there, eliciting a warmth that spread through her thighs and stomach, and made her lift her hips toward his palm.

———

Radford gloried in Evelyn's response. She was beautiful with her head pressed back against the pillow, her throat arched, her hair tousled around her ivory skin as he brought her body to a climax.

Only then did he cover her with his own body, allowing only the slightest breach until she was ready and the effort of holding back was more than he could bear. He deepened their kiss then eased inside, taking her pained cry into his mouth.

"I'm sorry, sweetheart," he said, brushing her hair off her face.

He waited until he felt her relax then began a slow rolling movement with his hip, slowly lifting her back to the precipice, sending her soaring again as he found his own release.

In the aftermath, they lay quiet, letting their breathing slow as they held each other.

"This is so beautiful," she whispered.

"It's only that way when you share it with someone you love," he said. "Otherwise it's an empty act."

"You've never felt this before?"

He propped himself up on his elbow and looked down at her. "Never," he said, smoothing away the worry line between her eyes.

"But you have Rebecca. Surely you loved her mother?"

"You don't need to love someone to make a child with them."

She lowered her lashes. "I know. I just assumed you felt something for her mother."

He sighed, not wanting to talk about Olivia after loving Evelyn, but knowing it would ease Evelyn's mind. He traced the underside of her jaw. "When I met Olivia, I'd just come off the battlefields after three years of hell. I was trying to distract my mind from the war and I found that distraction with Olivia. She didn't love me, and I never loved her."

"I'm glad."

He smiled at her honesty. "So am I. Otherwise, I would have missed loving you."

He pulled her hand to his lips and kissed her palm. "We'd better dress and go inside."

They left the cot and he pulled on his trousers and his shirt then stood barefoot with his shirt hanging open as he buttoned Evelyn's gown for her. He brushed his bare foot across hers then smiled when she curled her toes.

"Are you ticklish?" When she nodded, he laughed. "I'll have to use that against you sometime."

"I'll make your life miserable if you do," she said then put her arms around his neck and kissed him.

"Radford!" Kyle's enraged shout, and the rattle of the door handle, jolted Radford and Evelyn apart. An instant later the tack room door smashed against the wall and vibrated with aftershocks as Kyle burst into the room. He stood like a steel beam, his fists clenched at his sides, face and neck red with anger as he took in their state of undress. "I knew you were trying to hide something from me," he said to Evelyn. He swung his accusing gaze back to Radford, his teeth bared as he moved forward. "You sneaking son of a bitch!"

"Evelyn, go in the house," Radford said, his voice deadly serious.

Kyle glared at her as if daring her to move.

"There's more involved here than you think," Radford said.

"You can't know what I think," Kyle said, crossing the floor and jerking Radford away from Evelyn by his shirt.

"Don't, Kyle. We'll both regret it." Radford tried to dislodge Kyle's hands, but they were locked on his shirt like a vise.

Kyle's fist blasted into his jaw, followed by a hard punch to the stomach that slammed him into the wall. Radford curled forward from the loss of breath, trying to reason with Kyle as darkness hummed around his head.

"Don't you dare pass out, you bastard," Kyle said from the distance. "I'm nowhere near finished."

Evelyn's voice sounded a mile away, but as Radford's head cleared he could see her standing in the doorway with her hand over her mouth, her eyes filled with horror. "Kyle, stop this!"

"Get out, Evelyn," both men said in unison.

"Not until you two regain your sanity!"

Kyle gave a derisive bark of laughter. "That's right. I am crazy. I must have been to ever trust you, or this lying bastard." He swung his fist, but Radford deflected the blow.

"Kyle!" Evelyn shrieked. She ran to him, pulling hard on his bulging arm. "Stop!"

He yanked his arm free. The loss of support propelled her backward and sent her careening into the wall. Harnesses tangled in her flailing arms and a saddle spun sideways, falling to the floor and taking her with it.

"Stay away from me!" Kyle yelled. "Don't you dare beg for him. You are as much to blame as he is."

Radford hadn't seen Kyle this out of control in all the years he'd known him. Not even during their fights as kids. But he'd heard and seen enough. He shoved past him and helped Evelyn to stand. "Get out of here," he said gently.

Kyle grabbed Radford's arm and spun him around. "Keep your filthy hands off her!" he warned. Then he threw another punch that caught Radford below the eye.

Kyle had a right to be angry and hurt, but he was going to pound Radford into fragments if he didn't stop. Still, Radford couldn't raise his fist to Kyle. Not now. Not after what he'd done.

"You're hurting him!" Evelyn cried.

"Are you afraid I'll mess up his pretty face?" Kyle asked. "Did he speak of dreams and faraway places? Did he promise you picnics and tea parties?"

"Kyle, I'm sorry. You don't understand."

"You're damn right I don't!" he said, taking a shot at Radford's exposed jaw.

Evelyn screamed and raced from the tack room.

Radford gripped Kyle's shirtfront and hauled him toward the wall. If he could just keep him pinned he could avoid Kyle's fist and not have to hit him back. But holding a man Kyle's size stationary was like trying to stop Niagara Falls from flowing. It could not be done.

Kyle shoved hard and sent Radford stepping backward frantically as he tried to keep his feet beneath him. And he would have if not for Kyle's fist. Radford felt the sting on his cheek then the door frame smash into his ribs as he slid to the floor. Pain ripped through his side and sparked the old angry fire that had once raged within him.

He would have stayed on the floor to catch his breath and rein in his growing anger, but Kyle hauled him to his feet. It had been so much easier when they were younger and Radford was bigger than Kyle. Usually a thump on the head settled any problems. Radford fervently hoped it would work now. He ducked Kyle's flying fist then swung hard, feeling great regret even before he connected with Kyle's jaw.

Kyle's head jerked and he grinned as blood seeped from his split lip. "At least you'll act like a man and fight. I was afraid you had grown completely worthless."

Radford answered the insult with his fists and Kyle greedily took them, appearing to savor the pain as he returned a hard shot for every one received.

The black rage was growing within Radford and he pushed it back, fighting it fiercely, trying to bat away Kyle's fists, unwilling to do any more damage to his brother's flesh. But the blows from Kyle's fists burst upon Radford's body in explosions of pain that felt like flying shrapnel.

The monster within Radford crawled to its knees. Panic engulfed him. He was losing control. "Kyle, stop! You have to stop now!"

Laughter filled the room and an explosion burst in Radford's head, filling the blackness with angry red sparks...

Atlanta was burning! Its blaze roared like a red monster in the night sky. Muskets cracked in the thickets and battered Radford's shirtfront with piercing shards of metal. Shells whistled past his ears and ripped the flesh from his face.

The sinister being within him rose to its feet.

That uncontrollable, animalistic urge to kill burned deep in his gut. His fists curled into weapons of death. With every fiber of his being he swung, throwing his fists out like hammers, taking great satisfaction in each dull thud that met his enemy's flesh. He would not watch another one of his friends slaughtered by this war to be left in mutilated heaps of bloodied flesh! His torn knuckles punctuated each burden this war had forced upon his conscience. He struck out at the senseless waste of lives and the animal it was forcing him to become.

Finally, he sank to his knees in triumph and wrapped his long fingers around the enemy's neck. Fingers pried at his hands, but Radford's grip was solid. Hate-filled eyes glared up at him then shifted and became Kyle's red-faced visage.

Suddenly the screams of battle became Evelyn's scream. William and Doc Kendall yanked at his arms. Radford glanced back at the enemy beneath him, and the choking, murderous Confederate became his own brother!

Radford gasped and recoiled in horror.

He scrambled away and gaped at his shaking hands as though they belonged to a stranger. That they had choked his own brother was an offense not to be borne.

Wildly he glanced around him for signs of his bed, that this was a nightmare and he wasn't yet fully awake. Sickened, he looked to William and the doctor, but the truth was in their accusing eyes. Evelyn stood in the doorway, frozen with fear.

A gasp of denial wrenched from his throat and he buried his face in his palms. "No! Nooooo..." He rocked upon the floor, balancing on the edge of sanity. He didn't do this. He didn't. Oh, God. Oh no.

Furious, he sprang from the floor and slammed his fist against the wall. The violent crack sent everyone back a step. "Dammit!" he bellowed again with all the frustration that boiled within him. He spun on Kyle and tried to point his finger, but his hand was shaking so badly he let it fall to his side. "I warned you to stop. I warned you!" he shouted.

Kyle met his rage with a cold glare. "I was past the point of heeding your warning." He got to his feet then braced his hands on his knees and hung his head. "Why, Radford?" he asked, breathing raggedly as blood dripped from his nose. "You're my goddamned brother."

Seeing him like that, bleeding, hurting, so justified in his anger, was a pain more crippling than any of Kyle's vicious blows. It sapped every ounce of Radford's remaining strength. His teeth chattered and he sagged against the wall. He turned to William and the doctor. "Would you leave us alone? Please."

They exchanged a glance then backed from the room. Evelyn lowered her hands, tears making tracks down her face as she looked at Radford. The horrified wonder in her expression cut to his bones and he felt his own throat ache with unbearable anguish.

"You have to get help." She caught her cry behind her hand and raced from the livery.

Even after his worst battle, Radford hadn't felt this defeated. He turned to Kyle. "Do you love her?"

Kyle flashed a look of contempt. "That's none of your business!"

"I need to know," Radford said, sliding down the wall until he sat with bent knees.

"I asked her to marry me, didn't I? There's your bloody answer!"

"Then why..." Radford wanted to ask Kyle why he didn't show her or tell her that. Why did he put the mill first? Why didn't he tell

Evelyn she was beautiful when it was so obvious she needed to hear that? He wanted to ask, but he couldn't.

Kyle arched a split eyebrow emphasizing the growing goose egg. "Why what?"

"Forget it."

"If you've got balls enough to sneak around behind my back then be man enough to speak your mind."

"All right!" Radford barked. "Why did you let Evelyn *and* me think you didn't love her?"

Kyle groaned and sat wearily on the floor. "I was busy and distracted." He leaned back against the heavy oak desk. His shirtfront was covered with blood. His nose had stopped bleeding, but there was a red smudge across his cheek where he'd wiped it with his sleeve. "Evelyn should know how I feel about her. We've been friends since the day I cut her pigtail off with my new jackknife. And I was building her a house." Silence filled the air for a long moment. "She knew how I felt," Kyle said forlornly. He rolled his head toward Radford, his eyes damp and accusing. "I trusted you."

"We tried to stop it."

"Shut up! I don't want to hear your pitiful excuses." He pointed a shaking finger at Radford. "Just stay away from her!"

"I can't do that." Radford eyed his brother and realized there was more to Kyle's anger. "This isn't just about Evelyn, is it?" he asked.

Kyle didn't answer.

"You've never forgiven me for leaving."

"Bullshit."

Radford shook his head. "It all makes sense now. You felt I owed it to you to fill Dad's shoes when he died. You felt I deserted you."

"You did."

"I couldn't stay here."

Kyle pierced him with a cold stare. "You were a hero, Radford. This town worshiped you. That alone would have kept our mill running without any sweat."

"It would have been a lie."

They eyed each other for an intense moment before Kyle nodded. "I'm beginning to believe that. All I've ever seen in you is a coward and a cheat." He staggered to his feet. "Is that why you've never shown us that medal of bravery you received? Because you couldn't stand to look at it and know the truth?"

Heat surged through Radford's body and made his fists shake. He raised his eyes to Kyle who stood hunched and bleeding above him. "Get out."

Kyle looked down at Radford, his scathing gaze raking him with unconcealed disdain. "I thought so," he said then turned and limped out the door, leaving Radford broken and bleeding on the livery floor.

━━◆─◆━━

Evelyn crouched beside the barn doors and hugged her trembling knees. Never had she expected to witness something so appalling—so heartbreakingly pathetic.

She could hear the mumble of deep voices from within the livery, but the absence of thrashing bodies and crashing furniture gave her hope. She raised her gaze to her father and was consumed by shame.

His expression was drawn and he leaned heavily on his cane as he stared down at her. "I can guess what happened out here tonight and for the first time ever I'm disappointed in you."

"You should be," she said, her voice quiet and hoarse from tears.

"Damn right, I should!" he said, his voice raised for the first time in over twenty years. "There's two fine young men in there who have just beaten the hell out of each other because of you."

"I broke my engagement with Kyle tonight," she said weakly, as if it would make her wanton behavior more acceptable.

"You think that makes any difference to him?" he asked. "That boy has considered you his since he was old enough to reach out and grab hold of you. It'll take more than five minutes for him to come to terms with that." He shook his head and looked away. "Those boys had a bad enough situation to handle without this trouble comin' between them."

"I never meant for this to happen."

"'Course not," he said. "But it did, and it's a damn shame is all I can say."

Tears blurred her eyes as the doctor guided her father back into the house. Suddenly, Kyle's disheveled form stood above her and Evelyn scrambled to her feet. He was beaten and bloody with ugly red welts on his neck. "Kyle..." She reached for his hand. "I'm so sorry."

His jaw clenched and he stepped away. "You've made your choice. Live with it." With that he turned and slogged toward his mother's house. He crossed the wooden bridge where they had shared endless childhood dreams, where they had stuck worms on fish hooks, and challenged each other to stone-skipping contests. She could not bear the sight of his slumped shoulders and ripped clothing and the fact that she'd betrayed her only true friend.

With an unstoppable sob, she collapsed and buried her face in her drawn-up knees. She could not bear to be the cause of so much pain and disappointment.

"It's over, Evelyn." Radford tipped her chin up and traced a wet finger along her jawline.

She was horrified at the damage she saw. His face was lacerated and swollen beyond recognition. "Have you seen your face?"

He gave a slow shake of his head. "It was your face I wanted to see."

"After what happened in there?" she asked incredulously. "After I came between you and Kyle and ruined your lives?"

He brushed her hair off her wet cheeks. "My character came between Kyle and me long before this."

"You need help, Radford." She clutched his hand and he winced. Blood speckled his knuckles and his palms were scrubbed raw. That he'd done this to himself sickened her. "You can't wash away the past, Radford. No matter how hard you scrub it'll still be in the back of your mind." She touched her fingertips to his sore palm. "Talk to me. Doc Kendall said you need someone to help you. Tell me what you're trying to wash away."

He sighed and pressed the back of his hand to his bloody lip. "I have to sort this out on my own."

"No you don't. You can let me help you," she said. "Don't you trust me?" she asked, her voice small, hopeless.

His grief-stricken eyes met hers. "It's myself I can't trust. What happened in there—he gestured with his cut chin toward the livery— is something I can't live with. I thought I could control my past, but the truth is, it's controlling me. I can't risk hurting anyone else while I work through this."

His battered image wavered in the rush of Evelyn's tears. "What are you saying?"

He stood and she arched her neck to look up the long length of him, feeling the tears streak down her temples.

"I'm broken up inside, Tomboy. I don't trust myself anymore." He looked across the apple orchard toward his mother's house where Kyle was slowly climbing the steps. "I don't know who I am, or what I'm going to become." With a resigned sigh, he turned back to Evelyn. "I need a chance to put myself back together again. I won't risk hurting you while I try to do that."

His words sliced through her. "Are you leaving?" she asked, barely able to push the words from her thick throat.

"Until I'm human again. Until I'm worthy of you."

She jumped to her feet and grabbed his hand. "Talk to my father. Please! He knows what you've been through. He can help you."

He shook his head and pulled his hand away. "I'll stay at my mother's house tonight. I'll come get Rebecca and some clothes in the morning."

"But Kyle is there!" Evelyn stepped in front of him, afraid he was walking toward another confrontation. "Please don't fight again." Tears filled her eyes. "I couldn't stand it, Radford. It's tearing me apart knowing I caused you two to hurt each other. I never meant to turn you against one another," she cried.

Radford kissed her forehead and brushed her hair off her wet cheeks. "It's over, Evelyn. This was my fault, not yours. No matter what happens, I'll never again raise my hand to Kyle."

Chapter Twenty-three

November wind howled outside and pelted the windows with cold rain. Frigid drafts crept around the sill and turned the bare wood floor to ice beneath her feet. Curling her toes, Evelyn peered into the stormy night, thinking that nature's angry outburst was an accurate reflection of her own mood.

She'd lost Kyle. She'd given him a week to calm down, but he refused to speak to her when she went to his house that morning. He'd been living there since the fight with Radford and hadn't spoken to either of them since.

Evelyn had tried to apologize to Kyle for not telling him the complete truth when she broke their engagement, but Kyle didn't want to know about her feelings for Radford or hear her apology. He told her to go back to Radford, that he wasn't interested in a secondhand woman or her lies.

Evelyn couldn't go back to Radford, because she'd lost him, too. After giving her father an apology, the two men had talked privately then Radford had taken Rebecca to his mother's house where they had been living since the night of the fight. Though Radford still came to the livery each day, and visited in the evenings with her father and the doctor who had decided to extend his stay, Radford's eyes were dark shadows of misery, and his thin body looked gaunt.

Sensing he was on the verge of collapse, and that Rebecca was suffering, too, Evelyn had begged her father to talk to Radford, but he said Radford needed to find his own way in his own time.

Fearing Radford would never be ready to talk about his past, Evelyn stole his diary from the black chest in the corner of his bedroom, vowing she would save him, no matter how low she had to stoop to do it.

Ignoring her conscience, she went to her own room and lit the lantern. The light glowed upon the black, leather-bound journal as she opened it and traced her fingers over the slanted ink. Wishing Radford would have placed his faith in her instead of forcing her to search his trunk for his past, she began to read.

⸺✦⸺

... July 1, 1863. Arrived at Gettysburg. Artillery roared on all sides, but we were not engaged that night.

July 2: General Greene ordered us to dig breastworks, which we were later grateful to have as we took shelter behind those makeshift walls, the ring of ramrods and blast of our muskets filling the night as it became an unimaginable, unspeakable hell.

July 3: Dawn arrived cool and cloudy, but we were drowned in our own sweat and weary to our soul from long hours of fighting so fiercely. We endured one fierce volley after another from the Rebel line. The battle raged. Dead bodies began to putrefy. I gagged repeatedly on the stench and squinted at the enemy through a river of tears. The metal barrel of my gun blistered my palms. The day became an endless slaughter and ammunition grew scarce. There were desperate charges from both sides. Smoke-blackened faces were streaked with sweat and tears. Our lips bled from the saltpeter in the bullet cartridges and it was hard to recognize our own men. William raced by me in a panic only to return a moment later and roughly scrub my face with his shirtsleeve. When he determined it was me beneath the grime, he hugged me fiercely, told me to keep my head down then raised his rifle again.

Enemy fire continued until the morning of the fourth, when the Confederates finally retreated. Thousands of bloated corpses scattered the ground and rocks. The earth was riddled by grapeshot and pieces of canister. Glazed, unseeing eyes stared back at me from bloody piles where men had fallen dead upon their friends.

The sounds of whistling shells and cracking muskets still roared in my ears in the silence of that desolate morning.

A dark rage churned in my gut at the pathetic waste. I yelled and cursed all men for the destruction of our families, for robbing our lives of peace. William dragged me away, but not before I gazed one last time upon the field of dead men who would never return home to those who waited for them.

Dear God... what manner of animals are we?

Evelyn closed the book, unable to see through her tears.

To read of Radford's agony was heartbreaking. She turned up the lantern and hugged the journal to her chest, feeling utterly powerless to help a man who'd suffered so much.

She had to talk to her father, to beseech him one last time to ignore Radford's privacy and try to help him before the pressure drove him insane or something terrible happened to him.

Hoping he was still awake, she crossed the hall and knocked on her father's bedroom door. He didn't answer. Knowing he'd been weak and upset since the fight between Radford and Kyle, she eased open the door to assure herself that he was sleeping.

Her father was sprawled on the floor, his skin as pallid as paste.

"Papa!" She rushed to his side, blood pounding through her ears. She shook his shoulder, but he remained unresponsive.

"Doctor Kendall! Help!" Evelyn yelled, her panicked voice echoing through the hall. She heard a thump, imagined the doctor's feet hitting the floor then his door burst open and he hobbled down the hall into her father's room.

He gripped the footboard on the bed and lowered himself to his knees with a jerky, pain-filled movement. Using two fingers, he touched her father's neck then put his ear to his chest. "Help me get him into bed," he said.

They worked their arms beneath her father's prostrate form and poured their strength into lifting him onto the mattress.

"Is he breathing?" she asked as her voice quaked with fear.

"Yes, thank God. Get my bag from my room."

Evelyn raced to the guest room, grabbed the doctor's bag from beside the satchel he'd packed in preparation for leaving on the morning train then raced back to her father's room.

"William?" Doc Kendall called. He lightly slapped her father's cheeks, but didn't receive a response. "What happened?" he asked, lifting her father's eyelids.

"I don't know," she said, sick to her stomach with fear. "I thought he might still be awake, but when I checked on him, I found him on the floor. Is he... will Papa be all right?"

The doctor's eyes were grave. "I honestly don't know. He's extremely weak. He must have been on the floor for a while." After giving her father a more thorough physical, the doctor sighed and rubbed his neck. "There's nothing to do but wait." He glanced at Evelyn. "Will you be all right alone for a while?"

Filled with fear, she nodded.

"All right then. There's nothing else to do but keep him warm," the doctor said, covering her father with blankets. He stepped back and patted Evelyn's shoulder with a fatherly kindness that surprised her. "You sit with him a while. I'll go next door and let them know what happened."

Evelyn watched the doctor shuffle from the room and prayed that Radford would return with the old man. She needed him.

Thirty minutes passed before she heard Radford's boots on the stairs. Radford came into the room and squatted in front of her chair. "Are you all right?"

Her eyes misted and she shook her head, knowing she was far from all right.

"Your father has survived unbelievable battles. He'll fight this, too."

She bit her lip and averted her face, praying Radford was right, and wondering if he was going to survive his own battle. He looked exhausted and physically abused, his hands shaky and red. She couldn't stand to look in his haunted eyes after reading his journal and knowing the torment he was suffering.

"He'll fight to get through this," Radford said, stroking his hand down her arm.

"This is my fault," she said, picking at her fingernail. "Papa's been so upset about the break between you and Kyle, and my part in it, that he could hardly eat all week. I should have never run for Papa when you and Kyle were fighting. It was too much for him."

Radford held her trembling fingers in his hand. "Regrets won't change or improve your father's condition."

"I know, but I've been so selfish!" She closed her eyes against the sting of tears. "I hurt Kyle and caused you to betray him. Now Papa's in bed because he has worried himself sick over the three of us."

"Your father's failing health isn't your fault." Radford's shoulders slumped as though the weight of the world rested on them. "Neither is my problem with Kyle. My betrayal started long before last night."

⁓⁓

"How's he doing?" Agatha asked as she entered the bedroom where Evelyn had been sitting with her father all night. Despite being tired, she was glad to see Agatha, hoping it would keep her mind off Kyle and his visit that morning. He'd been rigid and silent as a stone to her, bristling with such animosity when he passed Radford on the stairs that Evelyn thought he would strike him again. Thankfully, they hadn't fought, but both men were so tense, her nerves were frayed by the time Kyle left the house. She'd tried to thank him for coming by, but made it painfully clear he'd come to see her father, not her.

"Has he been awake yet?" Agatha asked.

With a weary sigh, Evelyn shook her head.

"Well, you must keep your faith. It's times like this when we need it most." Agatha went to William's side and tapped him lightly on the chest. "Don't you dare leave me again, William Tucker. I've yet to have the pleasure of getting even with you."

To Evelyn's utter disbelief, her father's eyes fluttered open.

"Papa!" she cried. With profound joy, she rushed to his side and clasped his limp hand.

Agatha held his other hand. "It's about time you remembered your manners and greeted me properly."

One side of his mouth lifted. "Aggie. Would rec-nize that horrennous voice anawhere," he said, his speech badly slurred.

Agatha's smile faltered. "You'd better mend fast so I can tell you what a rotten man you are for breaking my heart all those years ago."

"Ah, Aggie... Fwank was a wucky guy."

Tears filled Agatha's eyes and she pressed her handkerchief to her quivering mouth. "William, you must get well, you hear? You must!" She choked and turned away. "I'll have to come back tomorrow," she whispered then hurried from the room.

Evelyn dug her fingernails into the palm of her hand, the pain a welcome diversion from the one shredding her heart. She touched her father's paralyzed face, but his eyes were closed. "Papa?" she called, but he'd slipped away again, leaving her alone with her fear.

Carefully, she lay down beside him and rested her cheek against his thin shoulder. The shadows of evening eventually darkened the room and she rubbed her father's chest.

"Do you remember the day you took Mama and me on a picnic in the gorge? Mama made fun of your legs and you tossed her in the water." Evelyn smiled against his shoulder. "That was one of my best days. Mama looked so pretty with her hair wet, and you spent the whole day making us laugh. Sometimes, I can still hear Mama's breathless laughter echoing through the gorge. You could always make us laugh, Papa." Evelyn propped up on an elbow and stroked her father's dry cheek, silently begging him to wake. "You were the best father a girl could have, and now you're a wonderful friend. Please don't leave me."

She pressed her lips to his shoulder, smelling the starch of the sheets and the light perspiration on his nightshirt. "I feel as helpless as I did the day Mama died." She lifted her head and gazed down at him. "I didn't know men cried like that, but when you fell apart, it was awful. Seeing you like this is worse, Papa."

Her eyes filled with tears and she buried her face against his shoulder. The sound of a door closing downstairs jolted her, but she stayed close to her father.

"Grandpa!" Rebecca's small voice sounded up the stairs.

Evelyn drew a shuddering breath beneath the weight of her leaden chest then let it sigh away and ease the constriction in her throat. "I love you, Papa." She kissed his hot, dry cheek then left the bed and lit a lantern.

"Is Grandpa better?" Rebecca asked, peeking inside the door.

"We'll have to ask him when he wakes up," Evelyn said, not wanting to frighten Rebecca with the truth of his condition.

Rebecca went to the bed and touched his cheek. "Grandpa?" she called quietly. She nudged him gently, but he didn't move. Her mouth drooped. She leaned against the bed and picked at the yarn ties on the blanket. "He can't hear me."

Evelyn patted the bed. "I'll bet Grandpa would like a hug."

Rebecca crawled onto the bed and perched on her knees beside him. She took his limp hand in hers and called his name. "Why don't he wake up?" she asked, but Evelyn couldn't answer. She compressed her lips and swallowed the tears that clogged her throat.

"What are you doing on Grandpa's bed?" Radford asked as he entered the room.

Rebecca looked up and her shoulders sagged. "He won't wake up, Daddy."

Radford leaned over and cupped her chin. "Grandpa needs his sleep, and so do you. Kiss him good night, so Grandma can take you home."

"I want to stay here with you, Daddy."

Radford shook his head, but Evelyn caught his eye. "Let her stay with us," she said. Doc Kendall had delayed leaving because of her father's collapse, which provided a suitable chaperone that had allowed Radford to stay and keep vigil with Evelyn throughout the long night hours.

"All right, sprite, you can stay," he said. "Come on."

She laid her head on William's chest and gave him a hug only children know how to give then kissed his flaccid cheek. "'Night, Grandpa."

After they left, Evelyn thought about how much she loved those two. She hadn't planned to love them. But she did.

"Evewyn?"

Her father's hoarse voice startled her and she hurried to his side. "Thank the Lord, you're awake."

"Where's your movvurr?"

"Mother?" she asked, having difficulty understanding his slurred speech. When he nodded, she was sorry she'd guessed correctly. "She's not here, Papa."

He looked confused for a moment then comprehension lit his eyes. "Thaz right." His lips compressed and he averted his face. She smoothed back his thin hair, understanding how deeply his heart ached. Slowly, he returned his misty gaze to hers. "Whaa are you doin' abouu Raforr ann Kyle."

Intense shame washed through Evelyn. More than anything in the world, she'd wanted to make her father proud. "I'm so sorry, Papa. I didn't mean to let you down." Her eyes filled and her throat convulsed as she tried to hold back her tears. "I tried not to love Radford, but I do. I can't marry Kyle."

He fumbled for her fingers, his own trembling with the effort. "I unnerstan." He gave her hand a weak pat. "Our heart chooses who we love, pixie. Just wiz I could stay arounn to see my grannchillen."

She covered his lips with her fingers. "Don't say that." She laid her head on his chest, fighting the ocean that threatened to spill from her eyes. "Please don't say that."

He turned his head until her fingers lay upon his hollow cheek. "Evewyn." With resignation she lifted her head and looked down at him. "I wannn you happy. Raaforr lovz you."

"You're right, William." Evelyn's glance flew to Radford who stood in the doorway, hands in pockets, eyes dark.

"Come here, Raaforr. Wannn talk to you, too."

Radford placed a chair beside the bed. "Glad to see you're awake. Rebecca's been waiting for a story."

A weak chuckle sounded in William's throat. "Thaz your job now. And you be'er take care of my daugh'er."

"I intend to."

His gaze locked on Radford. "We need to talk, son."

"I'll check on Rebecca," Evelyn said, respectfully leaving them alone.

"Don't have muz strength for this, but some things need sayin'."

"I've got all night, William."

"I don't, so lizzen to me for once. Your father raiz four sons to be prouu of and I love all you boys. You muss find a way to fix things with Kyle."

Shame and sorrow consumed Radford. "If it takes the rest of my life, I'll find a way. I swear it."

William nodded. "Your father was a good frienn, but you and I had a spezial frienzship, Raaforr. Our time togezzer in the war was hell, but it made us close—like father and son. It made us strong." William paused to catch his breath. "I know why you thinn you're a cowarr."

The statement shocked Radford. "You were there. My actions speak for themselves."

"Bull. You're no cowarr, Raaforr. Time you faced that."

Radford believed he had accepted the truth, but he remained mute.

"Remember the promizz you made me affer Chancellorsville?"

Radford nodded, remembering the words he had spoken to William after deserting from his first battle. He'd promised to conquer his fear and face each battle like a man, to embrace each moment of his life with passion, and to trust in the caliber of his own character.

"Truz yourself, Raaforr. You're worthy of my daugh'er's love and her belief in you. Don't let her down."

Radford clasped the hand of his best friend, his father, his mentor. "I'm sorry for this situation, William. I never meant for this to happen, but I do love her. I intend to marry her as soon as I straighten out a few things."

"You're lettin' it eat you up, Raaforr. Just turn arounn and look at it!" William said, his chest heaving from emotion. "Stop runnin'. My daugh'er needs you. So does Rebecca."

"I know."

"Then take care of it." His hand trembled. "Take care of Evewyn for me." His eyes teared and he sighed tiredly. "She's my life. An' don't wait no mournin' period to marry her. Don't believe in all that bull-malarky."

"I'm hoping there won't be any need, William. I've been looking forward to parking my rocking chair next to yours someday and seeing if I can't outdo some of those tall tales you tell Rebecca."

His eyes crinkled at the corners, pushing aside the sheen of moisture that had welled up. "Never happen," he said. "Tazes years of practice to get that full of bull."

"Then you'd better perk up. Rebecca's missing you."

Radford felt the faint squeeze of William's hand. "That li'l one gave this old man sumpin' worth living for. You tell her thaz for me when she's ole 'nough to unnerstann."

Radford nodded, too overcome by emotion to answer.

William coughed weakly, winded from his moments of talking; still, he clung to Radford's hand. "Let Evewyn help you. You have nothin' to be 'shamed of, Raaforr. You need help to unnerstann that."

"Thank you," Radford said, admiring the man who had given him so much, who had protected him like a son, and taught him by example how to become a man.

"Do it for me," William said, his eyes drifting closed. "Do it for an ole man who lovz you."

Radford clenched his fist and closed his eyes, unable to watch William's struggle to breathe. He sat up and wiped William's face with the wet cloth that had been lying in the basin. "This battle isn't over yet, William. Now fight!" he whispered fiercely, his fingers clenched in the cold cloth.

But William didn't respond to Radford's command and his breathing grew more labored despite Doc Kendall's renewed attention and Evelyn's continuous prayers. The three of them sat at William's side until Radford forced the doctor to go to bed. Eventually, exhaustion claimed Evelyn, and she dozed in her chair. William's breathing grew more labored, and though he roused occasionally, he was no longer lucid.

Late in the night, Radford was finally forced to wake Evelyn. Filled with remorse, he brushed the hair from her face and watched her eyes flutter open. "You'd better wake up, love."

A flash of understanding filled her eyes and she bolted from the chair. "Papa!" She rushed to her father's side. He lay on the mattress, his face transparent, lids closed over sunken eyes. Wisps of white hair sparsely covered his skull. She took his hand and felt the squeeze of his frail fingers.

A hint of a smile tugged one corner of his mouth as he gazed up with dazed eyes. "Mary?"

Evelyn opened trembling lips to correct him, but Radford squeezed her shoulder and shook his head. They exchanged a long, meaningful look before she nodded.

Her father's grip became more insistent. "Mary?" he called, concern strengthening his voice.

Evelyn leaned close and cupped his face. "I'm here," she said, knowing it was kinder to lie.

"Knew you'd wait." He relaxed and pressed his cheek into Evelyn's palm. "Ah, Mare..." he whispered as his eyes drifted closed.

Evelyn held his hand as he passed away. Memories of her beautiful, giving father should have given her strength to face his death, but it made the pain of her loss unbearable. The unjustness of a strong man being reduced to such a weakened state made her angry and a cry of denial burst from her lips. "No!" She clasped his hand and shook it gently. "Not yet! Papa."

Her high pitched wail cut through Radford and he pulled her into his arms. He felt the stiffening in her body, heard the long, pain-filled cry as the beginning of her first sob erupted and shredded his composure. He stroked her back, his pity choking him while he listened to her lose her battle. Deep, wretched sobs erupted from her throat and she clung to him while her tears wet his shirt and soaked his chest. Each sorrow-filled cry wracked her body and pierced him with helplessness.

Her grief rent his composure. The tears he tried to suppress clogged his throat and left him gasping. He listened to her broken cries, catching fragments of things that might have been, that she'd hoped for.

He pressed his wet cheek to her hair. His own grief consumed him and he clutched her to him while they wept, knowing that each of them had lost something invaluable in their lives.

"He wanted grandchildren... and to give me away on my wedding day, and, oh, God... I wanted him to live!"

"Me, too, love. Me, too." It was agony to hear the rending of emotions that released the pain in Evelyn's soul. She had suffered so much and asked for so little. Radford cradled her in his arms and kissed her temple. "I'm sorry."

As Evelyn clung to Radford, she felt his chest heave beneath her fist and his throat convulse against her temple. She touched his wet, unshaven chin and he kissed her palm.

She drew back and looked into gold eyes that were surrounded by wet, spiky lashes. "How will we tell Rebecca?" The thought alone made her cry again and she knew that Radford wept, too, because he couldn't answer right away.

"We'll wait until morning," he finally said. "It might be easier then."

"This will never be easy."

Doc Kendall opened the door and Radford shook his head. The doc's expression fell and he squeezed his eyes shut, pressing his forehead to the door for several seconds. He glanced over at William for a moment then gave Radford a nod of understanding. "I'll go tell your family," he said then backed from the room.

After several minutes, Evelyn quieted and Radford released her. Emotionally drained, he dragged an arm across his eyes and raked his hair off his forehead. "Where is your father's suit?" he asked. "I can manage alone if you tell me where to find his things."

Evelyn was silent while tears streamed from her eyes and her shoulders shook. When Radford would have pulled her back into his arms, she straightened her back and released a quavering breath. "His underclothes are in the chest of drawers. I'll be up in a minute with water."

"Let Doc Kendall help me when he gets back."

"He's my father. I'll do this for him," she said, before leaving the room.

When she returned, she bathed her father, talking softly to him as she drew the cloth gently over his aged skin. When she finished, she brushed away her tears that had fallen upon his chest then kissed his lips. Radford shaved her father then combed what was left of his hair. Together, they dressed him. Evelyn buttoned his shirt and Radford fixed his tie and tucked his shirt into his trousers. They tugged his socks over his swollen feet and Evelyn tied the thin laces on his Sunday shoes.

"Papa taught me how to do this," she whispered then buried her face in her hands. "He taught me everything I know."

She wept while Radford rocked her, choking back his own sorrow. For William had taught him many things, too. He'd taught him how to survive a war, and how to block the horror from his mind when he had to kill a man. But most importantly, now he had shown him how to die like a man when it was his time to go. For Radford, it was like experiencing his father's death a second time, and it was nearly unbearable.

Chapter Twenty-four

Kyle and Boyd brought the coffin late in the morning then helped Radford and Duke lift William's body into the padded box. Radford met Kyle's fierce gaze over the body of their friend and sent a silent apology with his eyes.

Kyle's look said, Go to hell.

They carried the casket downstairs and placed it on a long oak table that had been cleared of pictures and draped with a lace cloth. Evelyn straightened her father's suit, tears fringing her lashes as she smoothed his hair back with her palms.

Before Radford could step around the coffin, Kyle reached out and put his hand on Evelyn's shoulder. When she turned and saw it was Kyle offering comfort, she burst into tears and fell into his embrace.

Radford stood at the opposite end of the coffin, wanting to haul Evelyn and Kyle into his arms and weep out his apology.

Afraid he wouldn't be able to control himself, Radford went to his bedroom then opened the wooden trunk that sat in the corner. Underneath a faded blue uniform, and a badly frayed hat, lay a medallion that was given to a boy undeserving of such a medal. Now it would be placed where the honor was most merited. He found the folded flag beneath a worn Bible. The edges of the cloth were frayed and held the dusty smell of age. Radford stroked his hand over the faded colors then closed the trunk and left his room.

Evelyn and Kyle were still standing beside the casket when he came downstairs, but the instant Kyle saw him, he stalked to the kitchen, grabbed his jacket off the hook, and followed Duke and Boyd outside.

Kyle's animosity cut painfully deep. Radford sighed and pinned his medal over William's heart, knowing it's where the medal belonged.

"That's your medal." Evelyn said.

"Your father earned it." He placed the folded flag in William's withered hands. "He should be dressed in his uniform," he said, but their clothing had been hanging in shreds and their boots rotting off their feet when their regiment was mustered out after three years of endless battles.

"Papa would have been touched by this," Evelyn said quietly. She drew a shaky breath then nodded toward the foot of the stairs where Rebecca waited uncertainly. "Rebecca's awake."

Radford took Rebecca to the couch, but her gaze was riveted to the coffin where William was laid out. She leaned forward and whispered in Radford's ear. "Why's Grandpa sleeping in that box?"

Pain gripped Radford's heart as he reached for Evelyn's hand. They linked fingers and he pulled her down beside them. "We have some sad news for you this morning."

Rebecca looked at Evelyn. "Is that why you're crying?" Evelyn compressed her lips and nodded. "Did you get hurt?" Rebecca asked.

Radford knew Evelyn couldn't answer. He brushed Rebecca's curls off her cheek. "Grandpa went to heaven last night."

Rebecca frowned in confusion. "He's right there," she said, "in that big box."

Radford glanced at Evelyn and felt helpless to explain a loss that was so devastating to all of them. "Grandpa's spirit went to heaven last night. Today we are going to send his body to him."

"When will he come back?"

"He won't, honey."

Rebecca glanced at the coffin. "Wake him up and tell him to stay with us." She tugged on Radford's hand. "Go wake him up."

"I can't," Radford choked out.

"Yes!" Rebecca pushed back and slid off his lap. "I don't want him to go," she said, running across the floor. She reached up and tugged frantically at William's arm, jostling the coffin as she pleaded, "Wake up, Grandpa! Don't go up there!"

Radford sprang to his feet and swung her up into his arms. Her face crumbled and she buried her face in his neck.

"He won't wake up," Rebecca cried.

"I'm sorry, baby. I'm sorry." Radford heard Evelyn's quiet weeping beside them and he drew her into his embrace. The three of them clung together at William's side, giving and receiving strength, doing what they must to make it through the moment. Radford thought he'd never lose the ache in his throat or the weight in his chest.

It was agonizing for Radford to witness their misery. Finally, Evelyn carried Rebecca to the rocking chair and told him to join his brothers.

After helping dig William's grave, Radford returned to the house to change his clothes. When he descended the stairs, he found the parlor full of people who shot curious glances at the bruises on his and Kyle's faces, but they were tactful enough not to ask questions. Evelyn stood near her father's prone body with Kyle's arm around her slumped shoulders. She was tense and pale and looked ready to collapse in exhaustion.

Kyle's presence reminded Radford that his brother had always been Evelyn's friend, that he'd always been the one to stand by her, but Radford knew it should be his arms that offered comfort. He swallowed his irritation and kept his distance from Kyle until he saw Evelyn slip outside unattended.

Now that they were alone for the first time in hours, Radford stopped behind her and slipped his arms around her waist.

"I'm falling apart," she said quietly. "I'm lost without Papa, and each time I look at Kyle and know what we've done, I despise myself. He's your brother, and my friend. Even after what I've done to him, he's still standing beside me. He would have never done this to us."

"I know. If I could turn back time, I would have told Kyle about my feelings for you long ago. I would have faced his jealousy and anger with sincere remorse rather than a rotting conscience." Radford turned Evelyn to face him. "It's too late now. We've earned our guilt. We'll just have to pray that Kyle will remember the love and learn to forgive us someday."

"He won't. To Kyle, love and honor have the same meaning." She glanced up, her eyes dark pools of sadness. "Are you ever confused about love?"

Radford traced the dried tear tracks on Evelyn's cheeks with the pad of his thumb. "I know what love is every time I look at you. I know it each time I see you with Rebecca. I feel it each time you touch me or look at me with those green eyes. Don't you ever doubt that I love you."

"Then don't go back to your mother's tomorrow."

"I have to. Doc Kendall will be going home and we can't share a house without a chaperone." He raked back his hair. "I need some time, yet, Evelyn, and so do you. We'll make it through this," he whispered. "I promise."

But Evelyn believed otherwise as she returned to a house full of friends and acquaintances who'd arrived with food and their deepest sympathies. To her surprise, her friend Amelia had brought a very pregnant cat to Evelyn, saying she might appreciate the company.

Evelyn cuddled the cat and welcomed her. The house was already too lonely. Her emotions fluctuated from gratitude to such depths of despair it exhausted her.

Too tired to consider where her future was headed, Evelyn searched the crowd for her father to make sure he wasn't overdoing himself. Undoubtedly he'd be in the middle of the excitement and she would have to send him a warning look to be careful. The sudden realization of why they were all gathered in her house hit her with such force it knocked the breath from her. She gasped and pressed a hand to her chest as the world rocked beneath her. Oh, Papa...

Agatha grasped her arm. "Are you all right?"

Crushed by the onslaught of emotion, Evelyn was unable to answer.

Radford and Kyle were immediately at her side, their gazes clashing as they each grabbed for her arm.

"Would you get my coat, Kyle? Pastor Ainslie is ready for the funeral now," she said, nodding toward the pastor who was opening the door.

Kyle nodded and went for her coat, but his kindness was beginning to smother her as thoroughly as the people pouring into her house. Another stranger had arrived and was making his way toward Evelyn and Radford.

"George." Radford extended a hand. "Thanks for coming."

"I wish it were for other circumstances," he said.

Radford touched Evelyn's back. "This is George Collins. He was our first lieutenant and a close friend to Doc Kendall, your father, and myself."

"My deepest condolences," George said, enfolding Evelyn's hand in his. "Your father was a great man and a friend I'll dearly miss."

"Thank you," Evelyn replied, feeling as though she was going to faint from the press of bodies. She sighed with relief when Kyle returned with her cloak, but nearly swooned when Radford yanked it from his hand and draped it around her shoulders.

The four Grayson men carried the casket bearing a man who had treated them like his own sons. They placed it upon thick boards crossing the grave then Radford began the eulogy.

"I believe the best way to describe a man is through his own words," he said. "William wrote this to me after our first major battle at Chancellorsville." He retrieved a piece of paper from his pocket, his nervous fingers fumbling to open it. "'A man's actions determine his worth. Should he fail himself, he fails those who love him. There are times when he will have to dig to the very marrow of his bones to find the courage to go on. But go on he must. For any man with an ounce of pride will know his duty to his family and to himself. And if a man has one person in this world to love then each day is worth the fight.'" Radford gazed at those gathered on the hill. "William Tucker knew his duty to those who loved him. And he never let us down." Radford folded the paper with trembling fingers then went to Evelyn and laid it in her hand. "May the strength that these words lent to me in times of need, comfort you, as well."

Kyle stepped forward and handed Radford William's old Enfield rifle. The cold steel burned his shaking hands as he accepted it. He remembered his initial thrill at Camp White when he'd received his own Enfield rifle. Now, he wished to never see a rifle again.

He had vowed the day his regiment was mustered out of service that he would never fire another shot, yet once again, he was forced by duty. Memories snaked their way through his mind, and despite the cold morning, he felt sweaty and nauseous.

With dread, he lifted the gun and looked down the length of the gray steel barrel, seeing nothing but the bleak gray sky. Everything was gray. Gray uniforms and glinting gray guns and caustic smoke that seared his nostrils and clogged his throat until it suffocated him. His quaking knees gave out. He stumbled and lost his grip on the rifle. To his horror the gun clattered to the earth and lay like a viper at his feet. Radford scraped his palms down the legs of his trousers, trying to rub the feel of metal off his palms. Doc Kendall's assessing gaze and George's sympathetic one pierced him with shame.

Kyle picked up the gun and gripped Radford's shoulder. "Pull yourself together," he said quietly while the crowd looked on in confusion. "Do it for William."

Boyd stepped up, flanking Radford between them. "You're home now."

"It's the four of us," Duke said from behind him. He placed a heavy hand on Radford's shoulder. "You don't have to do it alone."

Radford felt the hands of his brothers on his shoulders, lending their strength. Slowly, he drew the gun up and sighted toward the farthest cloud. His hands shook, but Kyle steadied the gun until Radford could manage on his own.

With clenched teeth, Radford pulled the trigger and fired three lone shots to mark the passing of a great man, a hero, a father. He jerked his face away from the acrid rifle smoke and thrust the gun at Kyle. But his strength was so seriously lacking, he stumbled to the casket and could barely manage the rope when they lowered it into the cold, black earth.

Chapter Twenty-five

"I want to go home," Rebecca said, bursting into tears as Radford entered the room he slept in at his mother's house. He picked her up and she clung to his neck.

"I know, sweetheart." Their lives were empty living without Evelyn and he had no idea how to comfort Rebecca when he could promise her nothing. He hadn't spoken intimately with Evelyn since the funeral three days earlier. His pathetic attempts to examine his past had begun an onslaught of vicious nightmares that he fought his way out of with violent results. He'd protected Rebecca by putting her in his mother's room, but she was rebelling against being uprooted again. Kyle had moved into his own house the day of their fight, and other than his brief comment at William's funeral, he hadn't spoken a word to Radford since.

If he could only roll back time to when he was seventeen and start all over again. He'd fight the war like a man. He'd come home to the hero's welcome he deserved. He'd shoulder the burden of supporting his family as he should have when his father passed away. He would pledge his love to Evelyn and make her his wife long before the idea ever entered Kyle's head. But he couldn't roll back time. He couldn't undo any of his mistakes. All he could do was try and make restitution.

Rebecca couldn't wait for him to wrestle down his past and pull his life together. She needed him now. So did Evelyn.

After supper, Radford trudged across the snow-covered field toward the mill, his muscles straining beneath the heavy weight of the chain Evelyn had borrowed from Kyle last August.

His arms trembled and, despite the cold, he was covered with sweat by the time he crossed the yard. How would he apologize for what he'd done? What words could convey the depth of his regret? He could offer an explanation and honest apology. The most he could hope for was an opportunity to repair the damage. The rest would be up to Kyle.

An inch of snow offered little cushion for the fifty pounds of iron that Radford dumped behind his brother.

With a yelp, Kyle spun around, his expression startled and fierce. "What are you doing?"

"Returning your chain."

Kyle kicked it. "I didn't want it back."

"And I didn't want to fall in love with Evelyn, but I'm learning that life isn't about what we want."

They measured each other while the distant sound of a saw filled the frigid air that cut through Radford's clothing, chilling his sweat-covered body.

Kyle's expression remained hard. "Are you finished?"

Kyle's anger was justified, but Radford needed to break through it, to make Kyle understand how an innocent situation evolved into betrayal. He extended his hand, reaching for his beloved brother, willing to beg for his forgiveness if it came to that. "I'm sorry, Kyle. I need to make amends and tell you why it happened."

"So you can relieve your guilt?" Kyle glanced at Radford's waiting hand then turned his back and grabbed his axe. "Not interested."

Radford curled his cold fingers into his palm, drawing away from Kyle's painful rejection. He lowered his hand, wondering if he'd ever find the words that would open his brother's heart. "I realize I deserted you when Dad died. I deserted all of you. Now, I'm deserting Evelyn when she needs me most. I can't run anymore, Kyle. It's killing me and draining the life from my daughter."

Kyle's shoulders stiffened. "What do you want me to say? That all is forgiven? That I hope you and Evelyn are happy?" He turned back to Radford. "I had a life planned and you dumped the mill on my shoulders. My wedding was one week away and you slept with my bride. How am I supposed to forgive that?"

Kyle's words sliced through Radford and he knew he was asking too much.

"Dad built this mill for you, Radford. When he was dying, he made me promise I'd keep it going. I stayed. I tore up my train ticket and unpacked my suitcase. I know you made your sacrifices, too, Radford, but for five years, I sweated blood and kept my promise to Dad. My life is here now." He swung his arm out to encompass the mill. "I built this. My back. My hands. My life." He lowered his arm, his expression raw with pain. "I was going to be a lawyer. I became a mill owner instead. This is my life. Evelyn was supposed to share it with me. I don't know what you want from me, but I think I've sacrificed enough."

Radford nodded. How selfish he'd been. How many other lives had he ruined because he'd been too consumed by his own pain? Rebecca's? Evelyn's? It didn't matter. Even one was too many.

"I became a soldier because I had to," he said, nostalgia and regret making his voice hoarse. "I wanted to be a mill owner." He met Kyle's eyes, knowing his brother deserved the truth. "I didn't want to go. I had dreams for this place." Radford's gaze traveled the mill with longing. "A lot like this, but not as grand. I would have had more men and less saw. You did it smarter." He shrugged, knowing it no longer mattered. "The Union didn't want crippled men so I went in Dad's place. I promised him I'd come back alive. He believed I came back a hero. I left because I couldn't tell him the truth."

Kyle shoved his hands in his pockets and flicked the chain with his boot. "I was wrong to say that about hiding your medal."

"It's the truth. I didn't earn it. William was a hero in every sense of the word. It's where it belongs now."

Kyle sighed. "I don't know what happened to you all those years ago, Radford, but I can't pay the price anymore. I want to get on with my life."

"So do I."

"Then do it, but don't ask me to forgive you. I don't have it in me."

Kyle's words tore through Radford like grapeshot and he stumbled back a step. Everything inside him calcified: his heart, his hopes, his dreams of reuniting with his brother. He didn't blame Kyle. But his heart ached. "I understand," he said. "I just wish I would have never hurt you. I don't have words to express my regret." He turned away, uncaring that the icy wind stung his cheeks.

"Words won't change anything. Enough has been said."

Radford turned back. "We talked with our fists. All that accomplished was beating each other bloody. My ribs are still bruised."

"I intended to break them. I'm glad to hear I didn't."

Radford nodded. "At least you're honest."

Kyle slipped the toe of his boot beneath a section of chain, making the links jangle. "We never fought like that when we were kids. Is that something you learned in the war?"

"The only thing I learned was that I was an animal. There were no rules in those battles and I didn't make any for myself. I used whatever advantage I had to stay alive."

"Well, I wish you would have told me that before I was stupid enough to hit you. My eyebrow is still lumped up." Kyle's lip twitched and Radford wondered if he had only imagined the flicker of amusement.

A spark of hope blossomed and he stared at his brother, praying Kyle's anger was beginning to thaw. "Do you think there's any chance for us, Kyle? Ever?"

Their gazes clashed, but Kyle remained silent, unyielding.

With a sinking heart, Radford made one last appeal. "I never meant to betray you. The only thing that kept me alive during the war was believing I could come back to this, to my brothers. I'll do whatever it takes, Kyle. Anything."

Chapter Twenty-six

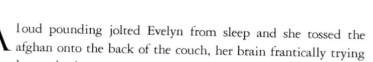

A loud pounding jolted Evelyn from sleep and she tossed the afghan onto the back of the couch, her brain frantically trying to understand why someone would be banging on her door in the middle of the night.

"Evelyn!" Nancy Grayson's voice was muffled by the door, but Evelyn could hear the panic in her call.

The instant Evelyn opened the door, Nancy pushed inside. "Is Rebecca here with you?" she asked, her eyes wild with fear.

Evelyn glanced into the dark, snowy night and her heart stopped. "No. Where's Radford?" she asked, her own panic rising.

"I don't know." Nancy burst into tears. "He left the house an hour ago. He'd had a nightmare and was thrashing around so much, Boyd went in to wake him up, but Radford was out of his mind. Both Duke and Boyd had to shake Radford awake. He was so ashamed when he realized he'd attacked his brothers that he pulled on his clothes and left the house. When I went back to my bedroom, Rebecca was gone."

"Maybe she's with Radford," Evelyn said, praying it was true.

Nancy shook her head. "He headed toward town. Rebecca's footprints went into the orchard, but they're so small, and it's so dark, the boys are having a hard time tracking them." Her eyes welled up. "She's in her nightgown. She'll freeze out there."

"Where are the boys?" Evelyn asked, grabbing her coat off the hook and tugging it on over her nightrail.

"They're still searching the orchard and the creek."

"Go to Kyle's house and tell him what's happened," she said, slipping her bare feet into a pair of her boots then grabbing the lantern off the table. "Find Radford. I'll help look for Rebecca."

The instant she and Nancy stepped outside, the frigid air took her breath away. Nancy ran back across the orchard, but Evelyn stood on the steps, feeling scared to death that Rebecca was exposed to the biting wind and snow. Her first inclination was to dash into the dark and yell for Rebecca, but she stopped in the driveway, turning a slow circle, wondering where she'd go if she were a frightened little girl.

Someplace warm. Someplace she wouldn't be alone.

Evelyn raced to the barn, but instead of yanking open the big double doors, she went to the small entrance door on the side. The livery was dark and silent. Her heart raced and her thoughts scattered as she stepped inside.

She checked the tack room, praying that Rebecca had crawled up on the cot like Evelyn used to do when she was her age, but Rebecca wasn't there. Fighting panic, Evelyn stood still and listened. The wind moaned. The rafters creaked. A sprinkling of hay slipped through the floorboards above her head and fluttered past her lantern.

Her heart leaped and she dashed toward the ladder leading up to the loft. "Rebecca!" Evelyn lifted the lantern and climbed the ladder one-handed. The instant her head cleared the upper floor and she could look into the loft, Evelyn felt her legs and arms go weak. Rebecca was sitting beside a mound of hay with a litter of two-day-old kittens in her lap. "Honey, are you all right?" she asked breathlessly, barely able to believe Rebecca was safe.

Rebecca sniffed and scrubbed her wet eyes. "Daddy was fighting and they hurt him."

"Oh, honey, your uncles were only trying to wake him up."

"He cried and he ran away."

Evelyn's breath whooshed out and she sagged against the wooden rungs of the ladder.

Rebecca stroked the kitten in her lap, her tears dripping onto the fur beneath her fingers. "He said he wouldn't leave me no more."

Evelyn pressed her fingers to her mouth, her own eyes flooding.

A bang sounded from below then hurried footsteps, and Boyd's frantic voice as he yelled for Rebecca.

"Boyd! Over here!" Evelyn squatted down and ducked her head in time to see Boyd skid to a halt beside the ladder. "She's in the loft with Missy's new kittens."

He clutched his chest and fell against a stall. Panting, he stared up at Evelyn, his face white with fear. "Is she all right?"

"Yes. Just upset."

He blew out a breath and shoved his wind-snarled hair out of his eyes. "It killed me to think she might be out in that. If anything had happened to that little one.." His lips compressed and his eyes beaded with moisture.

Her own misted, and she nodded her understanding. To even think such a thing was unbearable. After a few seconds, she dragged in a breath and said, "Go let the others know we found her. I'll keep Rebecca with me tonight."

"Good idea," he said. His shoulders lowered and he pushed himself upright. "I'll find Radford."

"Do you know where he went?"

"No, but I know where I'd go." Boyd shook his head. "He's never going to forgive himself when he realizes what happened with Rebecca." With that, he bolted out the door.

Evelyn climbed into the loft and sat down beside Rebecca and the hay pile where her new cat had made its home. She kissed Rebecca's head and snuggled her close. "I was worried about you. I'm glad you found a warm place to hide."

Rebecca kept her head down, quietly petting the kitten.

Evelyn rubbed her finger over the squirming gray kitten in Rebecca's hands. "What shall we name them?"

Rebecca give the kitten serious consideration. "His name can be Mittens," she said, pointing to his white paws.

Evelyn nodded. "That's a perfect name for him."

Rebecca put him down and scooped up another kitten. He dangled from her hands and she tucked him against her chest. "I like this one. I'm gonna call him Wiggles."

Evelyn smiled and stroked Rebecca's back, enjoying their moment together.

The mother cat sauntered over and rubbed against Evelyn. "Hey, Missy, are you checking on your babies?" Evelyn asked.

"That's their mama?"

Evelyn nodded and wiped a tear off Rebecca's cheek with her thumb. "She's making sure we take care of them."

Rebecca bent over and looked into Missy's face. "Your babies got names now," she said. When she popped back up, she looked at Evelyn with a curious expression. "Where's your mama?"

The question was so totally unexpected that Evelyn was momentarily at a loss for words. How did a person explain to a four-year-old that her mother was dead. "Do you know what heaven is, Rebecca?"

"That's where my grandpa went." She looked at Evelyn with sad, lost eyes. "Now I can't see him no more."

Evelyn cupped Rebecca's chin. "Did you know that Grandpa can still see you?"

Rebecca's eyes widened. "He can?"

"Sure. Heaven is all around us. When you go there, you can see everything." She tucked Rebecca's curls behind her tiny ear. "I'll bet Grandpa is watching you right now."

"Really?" Rebecca asked, her eyes wide. She scooped up Wiggles, held him over her head, and hollered to the barn roof, "Look, Grandpa! I got a kitten!"

In that moment, Evelyn knew that loving someone was worth any sacrifice, and that she would do whatever it took to save Radford and his precious daughter.

"I have a surprise for you," Evelyn said, hoping to entice Rebecca away from the kittens and into the house. She took the babies from Rebecca's lap and put them back with their mother.

After taking the lantern downstairs and setting it on the floor, Evelyn climbed the ladder and guided Rebecca down from the loft. She lifted Rebecca onto her hip and tucked her wool coat around them. She picked up the lantern then dashed through the frigid, swirling snow to the house, wondering if Radford was still wandering in the cold night.

"Is that the surprise?" Rebecca asked, pointing at a small blanket-covered mound beside the sofa.

Evelyn nodded. "Go ahead," she said, smiling at Rebecca's eager expression.

Rebecca trotted across the floor then pulled the cover aside. With a shriek of pure joy she reached into the cradle. "My dollie!" She clutched the doll to her chest and turned her bright face to Evelyn. "It's my dollie!"

The brilliance of Rebecca's smile was a sight Evelyn knew she'd never forget and she was glad she hadn't hidden the doll away for Christmas as she'd planned to do. This gift was too special, too significant to be given for a holiday. Gifts from the heart weren't meant to be saved.

Rebecca was asleep when Kyle knocked on the door, and Evelyn's jaw dropped when she saw him. He was the last person she expected to see at two o'clock in the morning. His eyes were dark and his cheeks were red from the wind. Her eyes misted. "You didn't find him, did you?" she asked.

He shook his head and pushed the door shut with his foot. "Boyd's been gone a while though, so I think they might be together. Duke's going into town to make sure. I know it's late, but I thought you'd want to know what's happening."

"Thank you, Kyle." She caught his cold fingers and warmed them in her palm. "I don't deserve your kindness after everything I've put you through. I'm so sorry I hurt you."

He pulled his fingers free and shrugged as if her betrayal hadn't bothered him at all, but Evelyn knew better.

"I'd like to explain what happened," she said softly.

"I'd rather you didn't."

He looked so capable standing there with his wide shoulders and thick arms, but whether he loved her or not, his muscles of steel couldn't protect his heart from the pain.

"Please. I owe you so much more than an apology." She met his eyes so he could see the sincerity in hers. "I think Radford's betrayal cut the deepest and I'm sorry for that, too. We were both unintentionally selfish."

Kyle looked at the ceiling and let out a huge sigh. "Would you mind if I went home?"

"Don't go." Evelyn caught his hand. "Please give me a minute."

Reluctantly, he met her eyes then sat down at the table.

Evelyn sat beside him. "You've been my friend forever," she began quietly. "I've always shared everything with you, my troubles, my laughter, my tears, but after your father died, you changed. You didn't talk with me anymore. You were preoccupied with the business and that eventually consumed you. After a while we didn't share anything but unspoken memories. I shouldn't have agreed to marry you, Kyle. It was selfish of me. But Papa was ill and the livery was failing and I... I wanted a family. I knew you could give me that, and also the security I needed."

"Evelyn—"

She covered his lips with her fingers. "It was the wrong reason to marry you," she insisted, lowering her hand to her lap. "I found that out when Radford came home and let me care for his daughter. I fell in love with Rebecca, and in sharing her with Radford, we formed bonds that drew us closer. Radford and I were both misfits and we found something in each other that we needed. No matter how we tried to ignore those feelings, they eventually strengthened until they wouldn't let us go. You see, I had nothing else holding my heart away from all of that. I didn't know the man I was engaged to. If I'm to be completely truthful, Kyle, I still don't believe our old friendship would have been strong enough for a happy marriage."

"I thought we had something special," he said.

"We did. A wonderful friendship that became overshadowed by our responsibilities."

Kyle pulled his hand free and braced his elbows on his knees, his fingers interlocked between them. "Then tell me what happened that night you kissed me as if you wanted to pull my clothes off. Why did you do that? I've wondered for a long time."

If she were to be any friend at all, she had to answer truthfully. "I was hoping to find the spark we were missing. I was prepared to give everything I had in search of that. I just couldn't find it in the arms of my friend."

He nodded in resignation as if he'd already known the answer, but had been unwilling to admit it. "You found that spark with my brother."

"Yes. I'm sorry."

He looked at her, his expression vulnerable. "Was it impossible to love me just a little?"

Evelyn lifted her hand and stroked his jaw. "I loved you more than a little, Kyle. You were like a brother to me. That's why I couldn't love you like a woman should love her husband. I had already found a special place for you in my heart."

He closed his eyes. "God, I've missed you."

"I've missed you, too." Evelyn moved into his embrace and he stood up, pulling her against him. They held each other like family members who have been away from each other too long.

"Is it okay if I'm not your friend for a while?" he asked, his voice hoarse with emotion. "I think it's going to take some time for my heart to figure out where to put you."

Evelyn hugged him. "Just promise to find a place for me." She put her hand over his heart. "Do you think you can find room in here for Radford, too?" Their eyes met and Evelyn realized how raw Kyle was inside, how deeply he felt Radford's loss.

He sighed and stepped away.

"You hold a big part of his heart, Kyle. He needs you. With you out of his life, Radford has become a lonely, empty man."

"It's becoming a lonely winter for all of us from what I hear."

His knowing look made Evelyn blush. "Radford's having some difficulty working things out."

"We all are." A sad smile crossed his face, and he gave her a quick hug. "Get some rest. We'll find him."

Evelyn caught his hand and squeezed. "There is a woman out there who will honestly deserve you. Find her and be happy. You deserve it."

Chapter Twenty-seven

After Kyle left, Evelyn huddled in her quilt and watched the firelight flicker behind the small glass plate in the stove. The wind shook the house and pelted the windowpanes with hard-edged sleet that sounded like pebbles. Even the walls seemed to moan with her as she buried her face in her arms.

How she longed for a house filled with Radford's and Rebecca's laughter and the sound of her father's cane thumping across the floor. If she could just feel the warmth of Radford's embrace, instead of a worn afghan and an Acme wood stove, it would help her survive the emotional storm raging within her.

The wind moaned like a wounded soldier and a shutter banged in the kitchen. She prayed it wouldn't blow off before dawn, which was only an hour away. She'd been up all night waiting to hear if they'd found Radford, and her stomach was so tense, she was nauseous.

A loud bang made her leap from the couch. That was not a shutter pounding on the kitchen door! With her heart racing, she rushed to the door, expecting Boyd or Duke, but when she opened it, the gust of frigid air was not much of a shock compared to the sight of Radford standing in the pelting ice. Snow clung to his eyebrows and beads of ice stuck to his face. The wind whisked his breath away in a long, frosty funnel. It ripped at his hair, snaking it out around his hat in short, snapping strands, but he stood before her in his barn jacket, seemingly oblivious to the biting night.

"I can't tell a tale like your father," he said, "but if you have time to listen, I'm willing to try."

Stunned, Evelyn looked at Radford's outstretched, trembling hand. Was he finally reaching out? She caught Radford's cold fingers and pulled him inside, closing out the world as she shut the door behind them. "I've been worried sick, Radford!"

"Boyd told me what happened—after he slugged me." He met her eyes; his own were dark pools of pain. "As surely as you see me standing here, Evelyn, I vow I'll never put you or Rebecca through anything like this again. Is she really all right?"

"She's in bed sleeping with her new doll, but you'll need to talk to her tomorrow. She thought Boyd and Duke hurt you, and that you were leaving her again."

He shook his head and rubbed his eyes. "I had no idea. I thought she was sleeping. I just needed to get outside and clear my head for a while."

"You were gone for hours! Where'd you go?"

"To the Pemberton. I pounded on the door until Patrick let me inside." He shrugged, his self-disgust evident in his expression. "I thought a drink would calm me down." He chafed his hands and glanced longingly at the stove in the parlor. "If there's any coffee in that pot, I could use a cup."

His eyes were rimmed with shadows and old bruises that Evelyn wanted to smooth away, but she reached for his hat instead, knowing she couldn't rush him to tell her what was burdening his conscience.

Radford caught her wrist and brushed his cold palm over her knuckles. He brought it to his mouth and placed his lips against her skin, pausing as if to savor the essence of her. "I miss you." Pain rimmed his eyes. "I reach for you in my sleep. I see Rebecca's face when she's with you and I know we should be together. But you deserve so much more. I thought I could come home and start a new life, but I brought my old one with me. I needed to give Rebecca a settled home, but she's miserable. I've stolen from my brother and beat him with my own fists." He gripped the bridge of his nose with his fingers and his voice trembled. "I feel like I'm still fighting the war, Evelyn. Every action I take is destructive. I don't know what to do anymore."

"Take off your coat, and talk to me. Tell me what you can't let go of. Even if it doesn't make a difference for you, or stop your nightmares, at least I'll understand what's haunting you."

He gazed at her, his eyes raw with unspoken pain. "You deserve to know the caliber of man you fell in love with."

"Then come sit down and I'll see if there's any tea left in the pot."

Radford stepped out of his boots and hung his coat and hat on the peg beside the door. He took two kitchen chairs to the parlor and placed them close to the stove. With a weary sigh, he sank onto the chair and pulled Evelyn down beside him. "Your shutter blew off the kitchen window."

Evelyn reached for the kettle on the stove and poured Radford a cup of tea. "It'll probably blow across town by morning."

Radford took the offered cup. "I stuck it behind the wood bin. I'll put it back on tomorrow." He stretched his legs out in front of him, propping his feet on the foot rail that circled the bottom of the stove. Evelyn stood up, but he caught the belt on her wrapper. "Where you going?"

"To get another cup."

"We can share this one."

The irony of sharing a cup of tea in the late-night hours made her eyes tear. She had tried to explain this sort of closeness to Kyle, but he'd never really understood. With Radford, it was as natural as sharing a bed.

She sat down and let him drink in silence while he lost the chill of the storm. Slowly, his shoulders relaxed and the tension in his face eased. "Thank you," he said, passing her the half-full cup of tea. He extracted a cheroot from his pocket and paused, his expression questioning. "Do you mind?"

Mind? He couldn't know how desperately she'd longed for this moment. When she shook her head, he dropped his feet to the floor, opened the cast-iron door, and touched his cigar to the flames. When it was lit, he leaned back and put it to his lips. The motion was fluid, male, and oddly beautiful.

She absorbed every detail about him as she sipped her tea and inhaled the sweet aroma of his cheroot. It brought back memories of soft summer evenings and one glorious night of Radford's lovemaking. Closing her eyes, she hoped he would find his way back to her, that he would claim the strength necessary to break free of his past, that he would trust her.

His fingers grazed her jaw and her eyes opened. "I'm sorry I broke my promise." He lowered his hand and rested his wrist on his knee, his cigar forgotten between his fingers. "I wanted to marry you and protect you and be here when you needed me. All I've done is ruin your future then walk out on you when you needed me most. I'm beginning to realize that it doesn't matter what kind of man I've been. It's the man I'm becoming without you that scares me the most."

He sat quietly, staring at the stove. "There was a time when I thought I knew all about honor and keeping promises. When I went to war in my father's place, I was determined to make him proud that a Grayson was doing his part for the Union." Radford laughed, but it was hollow and self-depreciating. "I was so green, so naive."

"You were only a boy."

"Not for long. Our regiment was involved in our first major skirmish at Chancellorsville. We were up to our asses in Grays and they were blowing us apart. Literally, and I was scared to death."

Evelyn saw the shame in his eyes, but she waited for him to tell his story.

"I deserted my troop that day like a coward."

"You claimed that status once before, but I don't believe it. Papa disputed it also."

He looked at her in disbelief. "I deserted during a battle. Our regiment was trapped on a hillside and we ate dirt for hours, but the Rebs never let up. Their shells were pecking away our flesh like buzzards on a dead carcass. When the man beside me was cut in half by shrapnel, I panicked and ran. I didn't even try to help him, Evelyn. I just ran through the shelling and bolted into the trees. I kept on running until I saw the enemy flanking our regiment's backside. Your dad was back there on that hill."

"What did you do?" she asked softly.

He opened the stove, tossed the cigar inside, and latched it shut. He leaned back with a hard sigh. "I went back to warn them, but I was too late. Most of our men were caught in thickets and cut down. Your dad and I barely made it out with only a few others."

"You earned your medal for warning your troop about the attack, didn't you?"

He nodded. "I should have been shot for deserting, not honored for an act of cowardice."

"It took a brave man to risk his life and return. A coward would have thought of himself."

"I didn't earn that medal, Evelyn. I felt ashamed when I looked across the fire at your father. He had stayed in the middle of that battle because that was his duty. He knew I deserted."

Though she understood his fear and shame, Evelyn didn't agree. Most deserters would have kept on running. Radford went back. That was all she needed to know. "Who is Thorn?" she asked softly.

He glanced at her in surprise. "Who told you about him?"

"You called his name in your nightmares. Was he a friend?"

Radford's nostrils flared, his expression pained. "Thorn and I met during the war, but he was more than a friend. He was like a brother."

The idea made her smile. "How did a Billy Yank befriend a Johnny Reb during the war?"

"You wouldn't believe the crazy things that went on out there. Thorn and I met at Gettysburg. He and two other Confederate skirmishers were captured near our ranks. We had to guard them until they could be taken off with the other prisoners." Radford shook his head, a melancholy smile lifting his lips. "I'd never met anyone like him. He sat there in the middle of the whole Union army while bullets ricocheted off trees and drilled holes in the earth around us, and he wasn't a bit intimidated. We were ducking shrapnel and he asked if we Yanks had any good coffee brewing. We all stared at him like he was crazy, but he just shrugged and offered us a smoke. The craziest part was that we all took a puff and moaned with pleasure. The idiot asked if the Northern girls could make us moan like that and every danged one of us cut up laughing."

"Did you see him again?"

He nodded. "Thorn returned to the Confederate force when the government swapped prisoners. I met up with him again at Kennesaw, Georgia, and later at Stevenson, Alabama. We were there for five months without any real skirmishes. Thorn was posted across the river as a picket for the Rebs. Mostly, he spent his day yelling across the water to us; everything from ribald jokes to the best way to win a poker hand. A few of us started rowing across the river to play cards with him, but our commanders were concerned about leaking war secrets so they put a stop to it. After that, Thorn and I met late at night. I traded coffee for his sweet Southern tobacco, and we became friends. We told each other about our families and what we were going to do when the war was over. I promised Thorn that I'd come south someday and see how a Southern boy learned to tell such good jokes and grow fine tobacco. We made a lot of plans," Radford said, his voice trailing off to a whisper.

Evelyn touched his leg. "What happened to him?"

"After his troop pulled out, we didn't meet again until Collier's Mills in Georgia. My regiment was part of Sherman's plan to take Atlanta and our mission was to cross the Chattahoochee then push into the city. We had to cross Peach Tree Creek to get there. The Rebs cut us up bad and we lost over half of our regiment right there on that creek bank."

"Is that where you were wounded?"

He shook his head. "No. We retreated and waited until Hooker and Geary could re-form their troops and join us. With the added men, we were able to drive the Rebs back behind their lines, but the fighting went on for days. By dumb luck and a few messages, Thorn and I were able to meet after dark one night in the middle of the river. I think we both knew what was coming, but we didn't have time to linger over goodbyes. The next time I saw Thorn was in a cornfield at Collier's Mill." Radford compressed his lips and stopped talking.

"That was the last time you saw him, wasn't it?" she asked, knowing in her heart this was the source of Radford's nightmares.

He nodded. "We knew the odds were against us meeting on the battlefield, but somehow we did. Rebel infantry charged my regiment in a cornfield. Thorn was coming straight at me. I knew the second he spotted me because he tried to swerve, but we were both locked in position by the men flanking us. We couldn't turn. There wasn't anywhere for either of us to go."

"Oh, Radford, you didn't?"

"He did." A sheen of moisture glinted on Radford's cheeks and he placed his hands prayer fashion against his lips.

Evelyn waited while he struggled for control.

"He had no choice. I couldn't shoot him. I just couldn't. My gun fell when he stuck his bayonet in my side."

"He stabbed you?" she asked, horrified.

"I was his enemy."

"You were friends!"

"Not on the battlefield." Radford raised sorrowful eyes to hers, seemingly oblivious to the moisture that brimmed his lids. "Your father shot him."

"Oh, my God. Oh, Radford."

"Thorn fell beside me." Radford closed his eyes, his throat convulsing. He drew a ragged breath. "We lay in the crushed cornstalks, bleeding and gripping hands. Thorn handed me a bag of tobacco and said to think of him when I smoked it. He asked me to give his watch to his fiancée and tell her that he loved her, that she didn't have to wait anymore, and that he wished he... that he was sorry he wouldn't make it back to marry her."

Radford buried his face in his hands. He couldn't go on. The memory of Thorn lying beside him with blood staining his chest, running from his mouth into his blond hair, was too much. He'd never forget Thorn's crooked smile as they lay in the crushed stalks, feet scuffling near their heads mingling with shouts and gunshot, that fierce grip of hands in that last moment before Thorn passed away. Memories assailed Radford and he recalled how Thorn had made fun of his name and called him Radical. He'd been able to make Radford laugh when he felt like blowing his own head off. He'd bragged that the Southern girls were sweeter'n peach pie. He taught Radford all the best ways to cheat at cards so he'd be able to catch his opponent at dirty dealing. He told stupid jokes that were only funny because of the way Thorn animated them.

"Thorn just punctured my side," Radford whispered. "It was the only way for him to remain loyal and not risk the men flanking him, but he forfeited his life for mine." Radford pressed his fingers to his eyes, cursing the tears that wet his fingers, cursing the reason they were there.

"You don't have to do this."

"Yes I do." His voice cracked, but he fought to speak. He was going to tell Evelyn everything. There wouldn't be any more secrets to tear him down or ruin his future. He slid his fingers into his hair and clenched his fists. "I buried Thorn in that field. After the war ended, I took his watch home to his family. His brothers' showed me the tobacco fields Thorn was so proud of. I'd heard so much about his Caroline that she felt like a sister. She wanted to know what the war was like for Thorn and if he had kept his sense of humor."

Radford's confession was tearing Evelyn's heart out, but she had to ask the question burning in her heart. "Did you hate my father for killing your friend?"

He wiped his eyes with the back of his hand and leaned back in his chair. "I loved your father. I never blamed him. He didn't know Thorn. All he saw was a Rebel who had stuck his bayonet in my side. No one had time to ask questions. We lost two hundred and thirty-three men in our brigade during those few days, and almost five hundred in the division. When it was over, we buried our dead and wept like children. We just couldn't stand it any longer."

The image of a group of bedraggled men weeping beside a string of fresh graves made Evelyn cry. She lowered her forehead to Radford's shoulder and stroked his back. "I'll never know how you survived that. I can't even imagine how you felt."

"Mad," he said. "In every sense of the word. After Collier's Mills, I went crazy."

Evelyn sat back. "Who could blame you?"

"I should have pulled myself together, but I couldn't manage it." He leaned forward and chucked a piece of wood in the stove. A spray of sparks shot up the chimney and he latched the door. With a shaky sigh, he stood up and shoved his hands in his pockets. "After Thorn died, I couldn't control my reactions. I was at the edge of sanity. I had spent months at your father's side, walking the leather off my boots, fighting dysentery, hunger, killing men who had wives and children waiting for them at home. All we did was skirmish, catch a few hours of sleep then march over the next hill and assault the enemy again. I hated it. I was homesick. I missed my brothers and my parents and the sound of our sawmill. Sometimes at night, I would break off a small pine bough and lay it next to my head. I'd smell the pine and pretend I heard the whine of circular saws rather than distant gunfire. I'd lie there and wonder if my family knew how often I thought about them."

"They knew, Radford. Kyle talked about you all the time. I know he missed you."

"When I volunteered, I never believed I'd be gone over three years." Radford leaned against the edge of the table. "After General Sherman took Atlanta in early September, our regiment returned in November. We were ordered to destroy anything of military value: railroads, bridges, public buildings, anything the South might use against us. During the siege the city turned into an inferno."

Evelyn thought of her livery in flames and it sickened her. "Those people must have been devastated."

"The residents were furious and they came out to stop us. We tried to warn them off, but they were beyond reasoning. Most of them ended up crushed beneath the heels of our troops. That night became a repeat of every miserable battle we saw. The yells, the shots, the sound of flying metal and screaming men. I couldn't stand it. The smoke burned my eyes and clogged my throat and I felt sick to my soul. I was sick to death of being forced to kill men. When I saw your father go down, my mind snapped. I killed the man who shot him. I felt like I'd climbed up out of the bowels of hell. I felt confused and out of control." Radford turned tormented eyes to Evelyn. "I was going to kill myself then, but I didn't have the guts. I figured the Confederates owed me, so I ran straight into their ranks. It was supposed to be a swift end."

"Oh, Radford," Evelyn whispered, pressing her fingers to her mouth in horror. It was pitiful to think of Radford running toward his own death with welcoming arms.

"That's why I couldn't stay here after the war. I didn't deserve my father's pride. I didn't deserve a medal when it was cowardice that made me run at Chancellorsville. And I didn't deserve your father's respect."

Evelyn lowered her hands. "My father loved you like his own son. As for courage, I don't believe you recognize it. You and Papa risked your lives in serving your country."

"I served my own needs. I was never a hero."

"It takes many traits to make a hero. It took courage to face an armed enemy. It was compassion that made you rail against such a waste. That's why I love you, Radford. You care about people. You shepherd the weak. It went against your beliefs to harm anyone. You're a son worthy of his father's pride and his brother's admiration. You're the hero my father called you." She cupped his face. "And you're the love of my life."

Radford embraced her, and she returned the hug. It felt wonderful to have his arms around her again.

They held each other, taking the comfort they had been missing for so long.

"Stay with me," she said. Her fingers shook as they trailed down his sturdy neck and over his collarbone. She felt the hard beat of his heart beneath her palm. "Please don't leave me tonight."

"Now that you know the truth, do you still want to marry me?"

"Even more than before," She said then repeated her father's words. "People don't choose who they love, Radford. Our hearts do. My head would have chosen Kyle, but my heart chose you."

"I need a promise from you," he said and Evelyn's heart sank. "Don't try to save me from my nightmares. Get Rebecca and go someplace safe until my mind clears." He cupped her face, his eyes intense. "I mean it, Evelyn. I can't bear the thought of hurting anyone again."

Compassion filled her heart and she nodded. "I promise," she said, knowing she could keep it. "But Radford, you aren't going to have any more nightmares." She caught his hands in hers. "You need to stop condemning yourself over things you can't change. Be thankful for what we've found together. We've been blessed with something few people ever know. It's up to us whether we spend our lives feeling guilty for things we've done, or rejoicing that our hearts could sift through shades of honor to find this love." She cupped Radford's jaw. "We've been trying to make amends in all the wrong ways. What we need to do is to show Kyle that something this wonderful is worth waiting for. Someday he'll realize that there is a special woman out there just for him who will prove us right. And someday you'll learn to forgive yourself and find the peace you deserve."

Chapter Twenty-eight

As if the fates had intentionally brought Evelyn and Radford together, their small wedding ceremony was blessed with a pristine dusting of snow. Inside, lanterns glowed in soft yellow hues and the iron stove radiated a cozy warmth for their twenty guests. Urns of coffee and steaming trays of food were piled high on Evelyn's lace-covered table for the intimate celebration.

They stood before Pastor Ainslie and exchanged their vows. Radford's throat closed when he placed the ring that would bind them for all time on Evelyn's callused finger. Her hand trembled as she slipped the matching band onto his finger and he thought she had never looked more beautiful. She wore her emerald silk dress and had pulled her hair up in the loose cascade of curls that he remembered from the night he first made love to her.

Boyd nudged Radford in the ribs and Pastor Ainslie repeated his question. "I... I will," Radford said, and Evelyn answered with a smile, her face radiant.

"I pronounce you man and wife," the pastor said with a smile. "You may kiss your bride, Mr. Grayson."

Radford ran his hands up Evelyn's silk-encased arms eager to make love to her, yet glad he had abstained until making her his wife. With his thumb, he tilted her chin and met her eyes, knowing there was not an emerald in the world more beautiful than what he saw. "My wife," he whispered, lowering his mouth to hers.

Evelyn read the silent promise in Radford's eyes before he brushed her lips in a tender kiss. Though propriety kept them from deepening it, her heart swelled with love and passion as she looked at her handsome husband. He stood so proud and tall in his Prince Albert suit of black crepe. The white shirt collar contrasted with his dark hair and lent him an aristocratic air. Her gaze locked with his and she longed for privacy where they might give voice to the celebration in their hearts.

"Why is she crying?" Rebecca asked in a whisper that brought quiet laughter to the small group gathered around them.

Radford offered Evelyn his handkerchief and she laughed as she dabbed her eyes. Together they turned and knelt before Rebecca, who had been standing behind them with Duke, Boyd, and his mother. Radford pulled Rebecca into his arms and kissed her cheek, but it was Evelyn she struggled to reach. "Are you really my mama now?" she asked.

Evelyn's eyes watered. "Yes, sweetheart, I really am." She wrapped her arms around Rebecca, knowing this little girl would always hold a special place in her heart. They had both found someone who understood insecurity and doubt and the needs of a wounded soul. They would always be each other's strength.

"Can we eat cake now?" Rebecca asked, and Evelyn laughed through her tears.

"As much as you want, but let's say hello to our friends before we cut it," she said, turning to their waiting guests.

Radford hugged his mother while Evelyn claimed Agatha. "I'm too old to be a matron of honor," Agatha said, "but thank you for allowing me the pleasure."

"I wouldn't have had anyone else," Evelyn said, hugging the motherly woman.

"My turn," Boyd said, sweeping Evelyn into an enormous hug. "Welcome to the family, sis." He planted a loud kiss on her cheek and grinned at Agatha. "You're next."

Laughing, Evelyn turned to their other guests. When she got to Amelia Drake, she thanked her for bringing the cat. "I love Missy and her little ones. They seem to love their warm home in the livery, and Rebecca has already named the kittens. As you can see," she said, pointing to one of the kittens that was sniffing something under the sofa, "they already have full run of the house and barn."

"I hope you won't hold this against me," Amelia said with a laugh. "I'm delighted for all of you, and very pleased to share this happy day with you and Radford."

"Thank you, Amelia. And we truly love these furry little rascals."

Turning to the rest of her waiting guests, Evelyn kissed Duke on the cheek and thanked him for giving her away. When she had him blushing, she hugged her new mother-in-law and explained that Radford and Rebecca had bought her the beautiful magnolia pin on her bodice. Martha and Tom Fisk were the next to offer their wishes, and by the time Evelyn kissed and hugged her way through their clan of children she was eager to find Radford.

He was standing at the kitchen window overlooking the wide, snow-covered yard. She slipped her arm through his knowing he was missing Kyle, the same as she was. "Is it okay if I say I miss him, too?"

Radford put his arm around her and pulled her against him. "A part of me is lost without him here."

"Me, too, Radford, but it's not just Kyle. It's Papa and Mama and your father, too. I miss them all."

Radford sighed and turned to his beautiful wife, knowing he should be standing here counting his blessings, not mourning his lost brother. This was his wedding day and it should be filled with laughter and love. Summoning every ounce of his resolve, he turned his heart toward giving his wife a day to remember. They played with Rebecca and Helen and joked with their guests while trying to ignore the dull ache in their chests from those absent.

As they cut their cake, Radford felt the sudden hesitation in Evelyn's hand and saw the look of shock on her face. He followed her gaze and experienced his own jolt of disbelief.

Kyle stood in the doorway with a large package in his hands. It was obvious in the expressions of their guests that they didn't know what to expect any more than Radford did. Together they laid down the knife and went to meet Kyle.

"You came," Evelyn said softly, as she reached for his hands.

He set the package aside and leaned it against the wall. "I couldn't miss my friend's wedding day." He pulled her into his arms and embraced her, holding her for a long, tense moment while Radford and their guests looked on.

"Be happy," he said near her ear then eased her away.

Though they had invited Kyle to the wedding, they hadn't expected him to attend, and Radford was uncertain of his brother's motivation. "I'm glad you came," he said, offering Kyle a handshake.

Kyle stared at Radford's trembling hand then slapped it away. Evelyn gasped and Radford thought she'd swoon on the spot, her pain for him apparent in her stricken expression.

"What kind of greeting is that for a brother?" Kyle asked then to Radford's amazement, Kyle put his strong logger's arms around Radford's shoulders and thumped him hard on the back.

Radford clapped his brother on the back and they hugged with a fierceness that would have cracked the bones of lesser men. To have all of this— a family, a beautiful, loving wife, a precious daughter—was surely more than he deserved. Before Radford broke down in front of his guests, he bit his lip and released his brother.

Kyle cleared his throat. "I brought you something. I hope it's appropriate." He retrieved the package and handed it to Radford.

Radford glanced at Evelyn who was sagging against the table wiping her eyes. "Looks like I'll have to do the honors. Our girl is a bit pale."

He peeled away a layer of brown paper to reveal a wooden sign engraved in large, charred letters that read:

Grayson's Lumber and Timber Works
Proprietors:
Radford Grayson
Kyle Grayson
Duke Grayson
Boyd Grayson

Also burned into the sign were four small hand axes with the blades facing inward, each axe touching to form an unbroken square. Radford immediately recognized their significance. They represented the combined efforts of four brothers, the worth and strength of their brotherhood, the values their father had raised them with. And his name was listed first, in the honorary position held by the eldest.

He swung his disbelieving gaze to Kyle who now stood beside Duke and Boyd. "Don't do this," he said quietly, aware their guests were looking on, yet unable to accept so much when he'd let them all down.

"We planned to do this a while ago. We'll hang it at the mill tomorrow."

"Why, Kyle?"

"Because I'm tired of tripping over the damned thing." Their gazes held for a moment then Kyle opened the door. "Let's get some air."

Radford followed him outside, away from the questioning eyes of their friends. They stopped on the porch and he groped for the words to express his gratitude. "I've made so many mistakes, I don't even know where to begin apologizing."

"I've made some, too, Radford. We can't undo the past, but maybe we'll find a way to start over."

"Can you do that?" he asked, unable to believe Kyle could truly forgive him for what he'd done.

"I have to." Kyle hooked an arm around Radford's neck. "I'll lose too much if I don't." Their eyes locked and Kyle gave Radford a hard squeeze. "Come on. I want a piece of that cake before Rebecca eats it all," he said then pushed Radford back inside the house.

⸺⸺⸺

Rebecca had left the house at nine-thirty in a whirl of excitement, thrilled that she could take her new doll to Helen's for the night, but Boyd lounged in the parlor until midnight, a mischievous glint in his eyes.

Evelyn shook her head, knowing the rascal was delighting in keeping Radford from his wedding bed.

Finally Radford caught his brother by the shirt collar and escorted him to the door. "Good night."

Boyd winked at Evelyn on the way outside then saluted Radford through the window. They laughed at his purposeful dallying then turned toward each other.

"That boy is a pain in the hind side," Radford said, rolling up the sleeves of his dress shirt.

"He loves baiting you." Her gaze wandered to Radford's open collar where dark hair peeped through.

"I know." He smiled down at her, allowing her to see his love as his gaze moved seductively over her body. "But I was about to kill him. You are a beautiful bride, Mrs. Grayson."

"You're the only man who's ever made me feel that way."

"That's part of loving someone," he said, pulling her into his arms. "You bring out the beauty inside them that they can't find on their own." He kissed her temple. "Because of you, I'm beginning to feel free again."

He lowered his mouth and Evelyn leaned into his embrace. The slow kiss, the lazy way he held her, stoked her need more than if he was holding her against his chest. He reached down and lifted her in his arms, twirling her in a slow circle.

"I believe it is customary to carry the bride over the threshold, Mrs. Grayson. Would you mind if it's up the stairs instead?"

She twined her arms around his strong neck. "You'll break your back."

"You're worth it." He grinned down at her and crossed the room, halting at the foot of the stairs. "Can you grab my valise for me?"

Evelyn caught the handle of his bag and nearly pulled herself from his arms. Amid much flailing and laughter, they managed to hang on to each other. "Maybe I'd better walk."

"Not on your life." Radford stumbled up the stairs and bumped against the railing, groaning in great exaggeration, until finally he stood gasping on the landing. "Too much... cake... for the bride," he panted.

Evelyn's laughter bubbled forth, echoing in the empty hallway. "I love you."

"Show me our room," he whispered in her ear.

She pointed to his door and Radford pushed it open with his foot, blinking in surprise at the transformation. Evelyn's bedroom suite had replaced the bed and dresser he'd used. A long, thick mauve rug ran the length of the bed and a candle burned on the nightstand. His old trunk was still in the corner, but several pictures now rested on the surface. Pictures of his parents and brothers and Rebecca, as well as Evelyn's parents.

Lying in front of them was a single pine bough with a huge red ribbon tied around it.

"The sprig of pine is to remind you where you came from," Evelyn said quietly, "and the red ribbon is to remind you of who you are." She stroked her palm across his cheek. "You're a good man, Radford, and a wonderful father. That's what a hero is made of."

Radford looked down at her, his love threatening to burst his chest. "Thank you," he whispered, lowering his mouth to hers. He let her body slide down the length of him until she was standing flush against him. Their bodies strained toward each other after being separated for such a painfully long time. Radford gloried in the knowledge that he would have a lifetime to love this woman.

He cupped her face between his hands, his voice hoarse with emotion. "I'll show you every day that you helped a man worthy of being saved." He kissed her with slow deliberation. Every nuance of love that radiated between them was poured into that tender, heartrending kiss. It was filled with promises and dreams, with love and passion. For the first time, Radford experienced the peace of coming home. Having the love and support of his wife and family gave him the security to be himself and that was a freedom more precious than any gold.

He plucked the pins from her hair and released the fasteners and ribbons on her dress. He took the magnolia pin from her overskirt and placed it on the stand beside their bed then pushed the gown off her shoulders. Overheated and eager, he stripped off her undergarments then moved his fingers over the hardened peaks of her bare breasts. Like fingers across guitar strings, Evelyn's musical moans of pleasure were the sweetest song he'd ever heard.

He shed his clothes as they explored each other, touching, kissing, stoking the passions that raced through their bodies. "My wife," he whispered, lowering her to the mattress where his hips moved to join them as man and wife. "My beautiful wife."

The slow rolling of hips, the murmurs, the ebb and flow of two bodies straining toward each other filled his ears. The brush of starched sheets against Radford's knees contrasted with the satin of Evelyn's thighs as they soared together.

Afterward, Radford eased to her side. "I've never loved like this." He traced the delicate arch of her eyebrows, the curve of her cheek, the softness of her lips. "I don't deserve you," he whispered. "But I'm never letting you go."

As the candle burned low, it cast a pale luster upon Evelyn's magnolia pin that lay on the table beside it. Feeling truly blessed, she hugged the man in her arms, knowing her lonely soul had finally found its true mate. She slipped her fingers through Radford's hair, loving the soft texture, the rebellious wave, the reckless length of it.

"Do you ever wish for anything?" she asked quietly, believing that inside every heart there lived an unfulfilled longing, a private hope, a secret dream lost in the shadows of obligation and duty.

"Sometimes I wish you had another mole... right here," he said, his eyes twinkling as he touched a fingertip to the corner of her lip. She wrinkled her nose at his teasing and his expression grew tender, his smile fading as he gazed down at her. "I have no wishes, Tomboy. All my heart could ever hope to hold is right here in my arms."

━═╪╸ THE END ╺╪═━

Thank you for reading Shades of Honor. If you would like to be notified about future books, please visit www.wendylindstrom.com and sign up for New Book Alert!

Also, if you enjoyed reading *Shades of Honor* please consider posting an online review of this book. Every favorable review is extremely helpful and increases my ability to publish more books more quickly. I have many wonderful stories to share with you!

Connect with me at
http://twitter.com/wendylindstrom
http://www.Facebook.com/AuthorWendyLindstrom

Author's Note:

SHADES OF HONOR

While researching the Civil War, I was deeply touched by a memoir written by Capt. George K. Collins entitled *Memoirs of the 149th Regt N. Y. Vol. Inft. 3d Brig., 2dDiv., 12th and 20th A. C. War of 1861.* This was a beautiful, poignant story of young boys who fought all the major battles of the war and became men under horrific circumstances.

Though this particular regiment was formed in Syracuse, New York, many courageous volunteers came from the Fredonia area where this story is set. Situated on the brim of Lake Erie in rustic country sown with grape vineyards, Fredonia is the home of the first gas well. In the nineteenth century Fredonia was also a leader at establishing The Women's Christian Temperance Union, as well as the first Grange (a national fraternal association originally made up of farmers). During the years surrounding the Civil War, the Pemberton Inn in Fredonia was reputed to have been a station for the Underground Railroad (an overland system that helped escaped slaves to freedom).

Although I've taken some liberty with landmarks in Fredonia to suit this story, I have attempted to honor the history of this quaint village built around a beautiful Common that is decorated with twin fountains and ancient maple trees that turn glorious shades of red and gold each fall.

Peace and warmest wishes,

Wendy

Wendy Lindstrom

Wendy Lindstrom is a RITA Award-winning author of "beautifully poignant, wonderfully emotional" historical romances. Romantic Times has dubbed her "one of romance's finest writers," and readers rave about her enthralling characters and the riveting emotional power of her work. For more information about Wendy Lindstrom's other books, excerpts, and sneak previews, visit www.wendylindstrom.com.

Please remember to sign up for
New Book Alert! and post your online review!

CPSIA information can be obtained at www.ICGtesting.com
Printed in the USA
LVOW08s1713130614

389977LV00001B/118/P

[8]